Great
Stories of the
SEA

Great Stories of the SEA

Edited by Norman Ravvin

RED DEER PRESS

The Publishers
Red Deer Press
56 Avenue & 32 Street Box 5005
Red Deer Alberta Canada T4N 5H5

Credits
Front cover artwork courtesy of the Beaverbrook Art Gallery, Fredericton, NB, Canada: William Gay York (b. 1817); detail from "*Bark Mokanna* in a Gale," 1866; oil on canvas; 53.6 x 80.7 cm; purchased with funds from Mrs. A. Murray Vaughan.
Cover and text design by Boldface Technologies Inc.
Printed and bound in Canada by Friesens for Red Deer Press.

Acknowledgments
Financial support provided by the Alberta Foundation for the Arts, a beneficiary of the Lottery Fund of the Government of Alberta, and by the Canada Council and the Department of Canadian Heritage.

Canadian Cataloguing in Publication Data
Great stories of the sea
ISBN 0-88995-219-1
1. Sea stories. 2. Short stories, Canadian (English)* 3. Short stories, American. 4. Canadian fiction (English)—20th century.* 5. American fiction—20th century. I. Ravvin, Norman, 1963–
PN6120.95.S4G73   1999   808.83'10832162   C99-910343-1

5 4 3 2 1

Editor's Note

To acknowledge the historical significance of the writing styles reproduced in this collection, all originally published spellings, punctuation and grammar have been preserved.

For Dave

Contents

Acknowledgments

"Separating" by Jack Hodgins from *Spit Delaney's Island* © Macmillan, 1976. Used by permission, courtesy of Jack Hodgins c/o the Bella Pomer Agency.

"Snapshot: The Third Drunk" by Silver Donald Cameron from *East of Canada: An Atlantic Anthology*, Edited by R. Fraser © Breakwater, 1978. Used by permission, courtesy of the author.

"Luna Moths" by Joan Clark from *Swimming Toward the Light* © Macmillan, 1990. Used by permission, courtesy of the author.

"The Christmas Wreck" by Frank Stockton from *The Great Modern American Stories*. Edited by W.D. Howells © Garrett, 1969. Used by permission.

"The Dual Personality of Slick Dick Nickerson" by Frank Norris from *A Deal in Wheat and Other Stories of the New and Old West* © Books for Libraries Press, 1903. Used by permission.

"Elevation" by Audrey Thomas from *Goodbye Harold, Good Luck* © Penguin, 1986. Used by permission, courtesy of Penguin Canada.

"The Divine Right of Kings" by Bill Gaston from *Sex is Red* © Cormorant Books, 1998. Used by permission, courtesy of Bill Gaston and Cormorant Books.

The editor gratefully acknowledges the assistance of Michael Debeyer
in assembling this collection.

Introduction

Norman Ravvin

The last frontier keeps changing. Today it's cyberspace
seen on the sea-blue screen of
a hacker's laptop. Not that long ago
it was outer space, where astronauts
bobbed in the dark like babies teth-
ered to the mother ship's umbilical
cord. But before the technological
marvels of space travel and virtual
worlds, there was the unknowable
sea—the last unmarked territory. If
you sailed on it, thought some of its
first explorers, you'd fall off the edge
of the earth. The poet Charles Olson
said it best when he described the
North American continent as "a
stretch of earth—seas on both sides,
no barriers to contain as restless a
thing as Western man."

To remind us how central sea-
faring was during the early generations of European settlement on this
continent, Olson describes the whaling industry, the Silicon Valley of its
day, where high-tech ships and
rugged individuality brought home
the equivalent of gold in the blubber
of harpooned whales. In the 1850s
whale oil produced material for candles and fuel for lamps; the mouthful
of flexible baleen the whale uses to
strain food from seawater was the
nineteenth century's plastic: the
source for hair combs, hoopskirt
frames, corsets, fishing rods and

umbrella ribs. It's tempting to think of whaling crews as the nineteenth-century precursor to modern sports teams (leaving out the astronomical pay); whalers challenged the limits of physical endurance and thrived on individual strength alongside the prospect of reliable teamwork. Once Herman Melville returned from his stint aboard a whaling ship, he wrote stories of the city that portrayed landlocked men as madmen who'd turned their back on the sea.

The oldest stories collected in this volume reflect this turning point, when sea travel was no longer at the center of North American life and no longer the economic engine it had once been. The men in Frank Stockton's "The Christmas Wreck" reveal the humorous side of misfortune at sea. Frank Norris's "The Dual Personality of Slick Dick Nickerson" follows the trail of a crew of San Francisco sailors whose scheming doesn't prevent them from being conned themselves in an Alaskan port. For the darker side of life at sea, there's T.G. Roberts' "A Complete Rest" or Stephen Crane's classic "The Open Boat." And Emily Carr's "Sophie" stands as a reminder of the native life that once thrived on coastal shores.

The contemporary stories included here are portraits of people whose lives are haunted or enlivened by the shorelines they live beside. Jack Hodgins and Audrey Thomas draw wonderful portraits of island living on Canada's Pacific Coast. Silver Donald Cameron, Joan Clark and Bill Gaston do the same for the Canadian East Coast.

I first saw the sea as a kid when my parents took me to Vancouver to visit family. We stayed in a hotel down by Coal Harbour, where, in those days, there were still shipyards at the edge of the downtown, alongside a rail line that began at the harbour. From the hotel window I could hear men at work, pounding steel, calling to one another from one rusting hulk to the next, and there was a wonderful oily smell, a bit like the greased-wood scent of railroad ties, mixed with the salt air. And of course there were characters—men with jobs nobody discussed in school when we were asked what we might like to do when we grew up. For a city kid from the prairies, the shipyard life looked as unpredictable as the circus, rough-edged and fun. It looked like freedom.

A less romantic view of the sea came to me from my father, who had spent time at sea in the Canadian Navy, roaming the Atlantic in search of German subs. The most unforgettably awful thing he saw aboard ship was a man, swept overboard by what seamen called a green one, a lick of wave that made the ship seem very small. Swabbing the deck in a raging storm was his punishment for violating a rule of shipboard conduct. The man's mop went with him, clutched like an old friend, but his shoes stayed behind, useless on the deck.

The authors included in this collection are Canadians and Americans, living and dead. Together their works convey the sea's pull and its danger, its beauty and its estrangement from us. Melville set the stakes high when he wrote that in "landlessness alone resides the highest truth, shoreless, indefinite as God." Heady words, whose meaning is given weight by these stories.

People driving by don't notice
Spit Delaney. His old gas station is nearly hidden now
behind the firs he's let grow up along
the road, and he doesn't bother to
whitewash the scalloped row of half-
tires someone planted once instead
of fence. And rushing by on the
Island highway today, heading north
or south, there's little chance that
anyone will notice Spit Delaney seated on the big rock at the side of his
road-end, scratching at his narrow
chest, or hear him muttering to the
flat grey highway and to the scrubby
firs and to the useless old ears of his
neighbour's dog that he'll be damned
if he can figure out what it is that is
happening to him.

Hitch-hikers do notice, however;
they can hear his muttering. Walking
past the sheep sorrel and buttercup
on the gravel shoulder, they see him
suddenly, they turn alarmed eyes his
way. Nodding, half smiling at this
long-necked man with the striped
engineer's cap, they move on through
the shade-stripes of trees, their own
narrow shadows like knives shaving
the pavement beside them. And all
he gives back, all they can take away
with them, is a side-tilted look they
have seen a hundred times in family
snapshots, in the eyes of people out
at the edge of group photos unsure

Separating

Jack Hodgins

they belong. Deference. *Look at the camera, son, this is all being done for you, it has nothing to do with me.* He does not accept their attention, he admits only to being a figure on the edge of whatever it is they are really looking at: his gas station perhaps, or his rusty old tow truck, or his wife piling suitcases into the trunk of her car. He relocates his cap, farther back on his head; his Adam's apple slides up his long throat like a bubble in a tube, then pushes down.

Spit Delaney cannot remember a time when he was not fascinated by the hitch-hikers. His property is close to a highway junction where they are often dropped off by the first ride that picked them up back near the ferry terminal. On these late-summer days, they line up across the front of his place like a lot of shabby refugees to wait for their second ride. Some walk past to get right out beyond the others, but most space themselves along the gravel, motionless, expressionless, collapsed. In pairs or clusters they drape themselves over their canvas pack-sacks and their sleeping bags. Some stretch out level on the ground, using their gear as head-rests with only an arm and an upright thumb to show that they're awake, or alive. They are heading for the west coast of the Island, he knows, the Pacific, where they have heard it is still possible to live right down on the beach under driftwood shelters and go everywhere naked from morning until night. The clothes they are so eager to shed are patched jeans and wide braces and shirts made to look like flags and big floppy hats. There is a skinny boy with a panting St. Bernard tied to his pack with a length of clothes line; there is a young frizzy-haired couple with a whining baby they pass back and forth; there is a grizzled old man, a hunched-over man with a stained-yellow beard, who must be at least in his seventies though he is dressed the same as the others. Stupid old fool, thinks Spit Delaney, and grins. Sitting on his rock, at the foot of the old paint-peeled sign saying B/A, he isn't afraid to envy.

There are ninety miles of road, of this road and another, between the rock at his road-end and the west-coast beaches they are heading for. It runs grey-silver over hills and along bays and through villages and around mountains and along river banks, and is alive already with traffic: tourists set loose from a ferry and racing for campsites, salesmen released from motels and rushing for appointments. Beginnings are hard, and endings, but the long grey ribbon that joins them runs smooth and mindless along the surface of things. In his head Spit Delaney can follow it, can see every turn, can feel himself coming over the last hill to find the ocean laid out in the wide blue haze beneath him. The long curving line of sand that separates island from sea and man from whale is alive with the quick flashing movements of people.

Behind him the trunk lid slams shut. His wife's footsteps crunch down the gravel towards him. He can tell without looking that she is wearing the crepe-soled shoes she bought in a fire sale and tried to return the next day. Spit Delaney's heavy brows sink, as if he is straining to see something forty miles across the road, deep into brush. He dispatches a wad of throat-phlegm in a clean arc out onto a stalk of dog-daisy, and doesn't bother watching it slide to the ground.

She stops, a few feet behind. "There's enough in the fridge to last you a week," she says.

He ducks his head, to study the wild sweet-pea that twists in the grass between his boots.

She is going, now.

That is what they have agreed on.

"Sit down when you eat," she says. "Don't go standing up at the counter, the way you will."

The boy with the St. Bernard gets a ride at this moment, a green GMC pickup. They leap into the back, dog and boy, and scramble up close to the cab. Then the boy slaps his hand on the roof, signal to start, and settles back with an arm around the dog's neck, laughing. For a moment his eyes meet Spit's, the laugh dies; they watch each other until the pickup has gone on past the other hitch-hikers, on up the road out of sight behind trees.

I am a wifeless man, Spit tells the disappeared youth. This is the day of our separation. I am a wifeless man.

In his fortieth year Spit Delaney was sure he'd escaped all the pitfalls that seemed to catch everyone else in their thirties. He was a survivor.

"This here's one bugger you don't catch with his eyes shut," was his way of putting it.

And wasn't it obvious? While all his friends were getting sick of the jobs they'd worked at ever since they quit high school and were starting to hop around from one new job to another, Spit Delaney was still doing the same thing he'd been doing for twenty years, the thing he loved: operating Old Number One steam locomotive in the paper mill, shunting up and down the tracks, pushing flatcars and boxcars and tankcars off and onto barges. "Spit and Old Number One, a marriage made in heaven," people joked. "Him and that machine was made for each other, a kid and his toy. That train means more to him than any human could hope to." Only it wasn't a joke, it was true, he was glad to admit it. Who else in all that mill got out of bed at four o'clock in the morning to fire up a head of steam for the day's work? Who else hung around after the shift was over, cleaning and polishing? Roy Rogers and Trigger, that's what they were. Spit and Old Number One. He couldn't name another person whose job was so much a part of himself, who was so totally committed to what he did for a living.

In the family department, too, he was a survivor. While everyone else's kids in their teens seemed to be smashing up the old man's car or getting caught at pot parties or treating their parents like slaves or having quiet abortions on the mainland, Jon and Cora looked as if they were going to sail right through their adolescence without a hitch: Cora would rather watch television and eat chocolate cake than fool around with boys or go to parties; Jon would rather read a book than do anything else at all. The two of them looked safe enough. It was a sign that they respected their father, Spit would say, though he admitted some of the credit had to go to his wife.

Stella. That was one more thing. All through his thirties it seemed as if every time he turned around someone else was splitting up. Everybody except him and Stella. Friends broke up, divorced, couples fell apart and regrouped into new couples. The day came when Stella Delaney looked at him out of her flat, nearly colourless eyes and said, "You and me are just about the only people we know that are still married." You couldn't count on the world being the same two weekends in a row. It was a hazard of their age, boredom was doing it, Stella told him, boredom and the new morality. People suddenly realizing what they didn't have to put up with. There was no sense inviting anybody over for Saturday night, she said, they could be separated by then. But, miraculously, by the time Spit reached his fortieth year, he and Stella were still married, still together. However, if they intended to continue with their marriage, she told him, they'd have to make some new friends. Everyone else their age was newly single or newly remarried or shacking up with people half their age; what would they have in common?

The secret of his successful marriage, Spit insisted, was the way it started. Stella was a long-legged bony-faced woman of twenty-two, already engaged to some flat-assed logger from Tahsis, when Spit came into the kitchen at the back of her father's store. She was doing peach preserves for her first married winter, and admiring the logger's dinky little diamond ring up on the windowsill in front of her. Her big hands, in the orange mess of peel and juice and carved-out bruises, reminded him of the hands of a fisherman gouging out fish guts. The back of her cotton dress dipped up at the hem, to show the tiny blue veins behind her knees and the pink patches of skin where she'd pressed one leg to the other. He touched. She told him "Get lost mister, I got work to do," and he said "That logger musta been bushed and desperate is all I can say" but stayed to win her anyway, and to rush her off to a preacher's house on the day before her intended wedding. With a start like that, he said, how could anything go wrong?

It couldn't. He was sure of it. Things that were important to him, things that were real—his job, his family, his marriage—these things were surely destined to survive even the treacherous thirties.

But before he had time to congratulate himself, things began to fall apart. He insisted later that it was all because the stupidest god-damned question he ever heard just popped into his head all of a sudden. He didn't look for it, he didn't ask for it, it just came.

He was lying on his back in the sand at Wickanninish Bay, soaking up sun. He'd driven over with the family to the west coast for the weekend, had parked the camper up in the trees above the high-tide line. Stella was lying beside him on her giant towel, reading a magazine, oiled and gleaming like a beached eel. The question just popped into his head, all of a sudden: *Where is the dividing line?*

He was so surprised that he answered out loud. "Between what and what?"

Stella turned a page and folded it back. Most of the new page was taken up with a photograph of a woman who'd increased her bust measurements in a matter of days and wanted to show Stella how to do the same.

"Wha'd you say?"

"Nothing," he said, and rolled over onto his side to face away from her. Between what and what? he asked himself. Maybe he was beginning to crack up. He'd heard of the things that happened to some men at his age.

Between what is and what isn't.

Spit sat up, cursing.

Stella slid her dark glasses down her nose and peered at him. "What's the matter with you?"

"Nothing," he said. *Where is the dividing line?* When the words hit him again like that he jumped to his feet and shook his head, like a cow shaking off flies.

"Sand fleas?" she said.

"It's nothing," he said, and stomped around to shake the sand out of the hair on his legs.

"Too much sun," she said, and pushed herself up. "We better move up into shade."

But when they had settled down by a log, cool in the shade of the wind-crippled spruce, she told him it might just be this beach that was spooking him. "This Indian Lady at Lodge," she said, "told me her people get uneasy along this beach." Spit knew Sophie Jim by name, but Stella always referred to her as This Indian Lady at Lodge. It was some kind of triumph, apparently, when Sophie was finally persuaded to join the Daughters, their first native. "She said there's a story that some kind of Sea-Wolf monster used to came whanging up out of the Pacific here to gobble up people. It came up to sire wolves for the land too, but went back into the sea to live. She says they're all just a little nervous of this place."

Spit's brain itched from the slap of the sudden question. He wanted to go home, but the kids were far out on the sand at the water's edge, and he could holler at them till he was blue in the face without being heard above the roar of the waves.

"She said all up and down this coast there are stories. About monsters that come out and change people into things. To hear her tell it there must've been a whole lot of traffic back and forth between sea and land."

"A whole lot of bull," he said, and put on his shirt. It was cold up here, and what did he care about a lot of Indian stuff? He knew Indians. When he was a boy the people up the road adopted a little Indian kid, a girl, and told it around that nobody, *nobody* was to dare tell her what she was. When she was ten years old she still hadn't figured out that she wasn't the same as everybody else, so Spit sat her down on the step and told her. He had to tell her three times before she believed him and then she started to howl and cry and throw herself around. But she dried out eventually and went Indian with a vengeance, to make up for lost time. He couldn't go near her without having to listen to a whole lot of stuff she'd got soaked up into her brain from hanging around the Reserve. So he knew all about Wasgo, Stella couldn't tell him anything new about that guy. He knew about Kanikiluk too, which was worse. That son of a bitch would think nothing of stepping out of the ocean and turning a man into a fish or making a piece of seaweed think it was human. He knew all about the kind of traffic she meant.

"They say we crawled up out of there ourselves," she said. "Millions of years ago."

"Let's go home," he said. "Let's get out of here."

Within fifteen minutes they had Cora and Jon herded up off that beach and pushed into the back of the camper and had started on their way back across the island to their little house behind the gas station. It wasn't really a gas station any more, though he had never bothered to pull the pumps out; the shed was a good place to store the car parts and engine pieces he kept against the day they would be needed, and the roof out over the pumps was a good place to park the tow truck. Nor was it a real business—his job at the paper mill was enough for anyone to handle—but he'd fixed up the tow truck himself out of parts and used it to pull people out of snowbanks in winter or to help friends when they got their tractors mired in swamp.

When he got home from the coast he did not go into the gas station to brood, as he might have done, nor did he sit behind the wheel of his tow truck. This was too serious for that. He drove all the way down to the paper mill, punched himself in at the gate, and climbed up into the cab of Old Number One. He knew even then that something was starting to go wrong. *Where is the dividing line?* He sat there with his hands on the levers deep into night, all the way through to the early morning when it was time to fire up her boilers and start getting her ready for the day's work ahead. *And what does it take to see it?*

And, naturally, that was the day the company picked to tell him what they'd done with Old Number One.

Sold her to the National Museum in Ottawa.

For tourists to gawk at.

Sons of bitches. They might as well have lopped off half his brain. Why didn't they sell the government his right arm too while they were at it?

The hundred-and-thirty-ton diesel-electric they offered was no consolation. "A dummy could run that rig!" he shouted. "It takes a man to put life into Old Number One!"

He ought to be glad, they told him. That shay was long past her usefulness, the world had changed, the alternative was the junkyard. You can't expect *things* to last forever.

But this was one uncoupling that would not be soon forgiven.

First he hired a painter to come into the mill and do a four-foot oil of her, to hang over the fireplace. And unscrewed the big silver 1 from the nose to hang on the bedroom door. And bought himself a good-quality portable recorder to get the locomotive's sounds immortalized on tape. While there was some small comfort in knowing the old girl at least wasn't headed for the scrapyard, it was no easy thing when he had to bring her out on that last day, sandblasted and repainted a gleaming black, to be taken apart and shipped off in a boxcar. But at least he knew that while strangers four thousand miles away were staring at her, static and soundless as a stuffed grizzly, he would be able to sit back, close his eyes, and let the sounds of her soul shake through him full-blast just whenever he felt like it.

Stella allowed him to move her Tom Thomson print to the side wall to make room for the new painting; she permitted him to hang the big number 1 on the bedroom door; but she forbade him to play his tape when she was in the house. Enough is enough, she said. Wives who only had infidelity to worry about didn't know how lucky they were.

She was president of her Lodge, and knew more than she could ever tell of the things women had to put up with.

"Infidelity?" he said. It had never occurred to him. He rolled his eyes to show it was something he was tempted to think about, now that she'd brought it up, then kissed the top of her head to show he was joking.

"A woman my age," she said, "starts to ask what has she got and where is she headed."

"What you need is some fun out of life," he said, and gathered the family together. How did a world tour sound?

It sounded silly, they said.

It sounded like a waste of good money.

Good money or bad, he said, who'd been the one to go out and earn it? Him and Old Number One, that's who. Hadn't he got up at four o'clock every damn morning to get the old girl fired up, and probably earned more overtime that way than anybody else on this island? Well, was there a better way to spend that money than taking his family to Europe at least?

They left her mother behind to keep an eye on the house. An old woman who had gone on past movement and caring and even speech, she could spend the time primly waiting in an armchair, her face in the only expression she seemed to have left: dark brows lowered in a scowl, eyes bulging as if in behind them she was planning to push until they popped out and rolled on the floor. Watching was the one thing she did well, she looked as if she were trying with the sheer force of those eyes to make things stay put. With her in the house it was safe to leave everything behind.

If they thought he'd left Old Number One behind him, however, if they thought he'd abandoned his brooding, they were very much mistaken; but they got all the way through Spain and Italy and Greece before they found it out. They might have suspected if they'd been more observant; they might have noticed the preoccupied, desperate look in his eyes. But they were in Egypt before that desperation became intense enough to risk discovery.

They were with a group of tourists, standing in desert, looking at a pyramid. Cora whined about the heat, and the taste of dry sand in the air.

"It's supposed to be hot, stupid," Jon said. "This is Egypt." He spent most of the trip reading books about the countries they were passing through, and rarely had time for the real thing. It was obvious to Spit that his son was cut out for a university professor.

And Cora, who hated everything, would get married. "I can't see why they don't just tear it down. A lot of hot stone."

Jon sniffed his contempt. "It's a monument. It's something they can look at to remind them of their past."

"Then they ought to drag it into a museum somewhere under a roof. With air conditioning."

Stella said, "Where's Daddy?"

He wasn't anywhere amongst the tourists. No one in the family had seen him leave.

"Maybe he got caught short," Jon said, and sniggered.

Cora stretched her fat neck, to peer. "And he's not in the bus."

The other tourists, too, appeared uneasy. Clearly something was sensed, something was wrong. They shifted, frowned, looked out where there was nothing to see. Stella was the first to identify it: somewhere out there, somewhere out on that flat hot sand, that desert, a train was chugging, my God, a steam engine was chugging and hissing. People frowned at one another, craned to see. Uneasy feet shifted. Where in all that desert was there a train?

But invisible or not it got closer, louder. Slowing. *Hunph hunph hunph hunph.* Then speeding up, clattering, hissing. When it could have been on top of them all, cutting their limbs off on invisible tracks, the whistle blew like a long clarion howl summoning them to death.

Stella screamed. "Spit! Spit!" She ran across sand into the noise, forgetting to keep her arms clamped down against the circles of sweat.

She found him where in the shrill moment of the whistle she'd realized he would be, at the far side of the pyramid, leaning back against its dusty base with his eyes closed. The tape recorder was clutched with both hands against his chest. Old Number One rattled through him like a fever.

When it was over, when he'd turned the machine off, he raised his eyes to her angry face.

"Where is the line?" he said, and raised an eyebrow.

"You're crazy," she said. "Get a hold of yourself." Her eyes banged around in her bony head as if they'd gone out of control. There were witnesses all over this desert, she appeared to be saying, who knew what kind of a fool she had to put up with. He expected her to kick at him, like someone trying to rout a dog. Her mouth gulped at the hot air; her throat pumped like desperate gills. Lord, you're an ugly woman, he thought.

The children, of course, refused to speak to him through Israel, Turkey, and France. They passed messages through their mother—"We're starved, let's eat" or "I'm sick of this place"—but they kept their faces turned from him and pretended, in crowds, that they had come alone, without parents. Cora cried a great deal, out of shame. And Jon read a complete six-volume history of Europe. Stella could not waste her anxiety on grudges, for while the others brooded over the memory of his foolishness she saw the same symptoms building up again in his face. She only hoped that this time he would choose some place private.

He chose Anne Hathaway's Cottage in Stratford. They wouldn't have gone there at all if it hadn't been for Jon, who'd read a book on Shakespeare and insisted on seeing the place. "You've dragged me from one rotten dump to another," he said, "now let me see one thing I want to see. She was twenty-six and Shakespeare was only my age when he got her pregnant. That's probably the only reason he married her. Why else would a genius marry an old woman?" Spit bumped his head on the low doorway and said he'd rather stay outside. He couldn't see any point in a monument to a woman like *that*, anyway. The rest of them were upstairs in the bedroom, looking at the underside of the thatched roof, when Old Number One started chugging her way towards them from somewhere out in the garden.

By the time they got to Ireland, where they would spend the next two weeks with one of her distant cousins, Stella Delaney was beginning to suffer from what she called a case of nerves. She had had all she could take of riding in foreign trains, she said, she was sure she'd been on every crate that ran on tracks in every country of Europe and northern Africa; and now she insisted that they rent a car in Dublin for the drive down to her cousin's, who lived about as far as you get on that island, way out at the end of one of those south-western peninsulas. "For a change let's ride in style," she said, and pulled in her chin to show she meant business. She was missing an important Lodge convention for this. The least he could do, she said, was make it comfortable.

The cousin, a farmer's wife on a mountain slope above Ballinskelligs Bay, agreed. " 'Tis a mad life you've been living, sure. Is it some kind of race you're in?"

"It is," Stella said. "But I haven't the foggiest idea who or what we're racing against. Or what is chasing us."

"Ah well," said the cousin, wringing her hands. "God is good. That is the one thing you can be certain of. Put your feet up and relax so."

She knew about American men, the cousin told them. You had to watch them when they lost their playthings, or their jobs, they just shrivelled up and died.

Stella looked frightened.

Oh yes, the cousin said. She knew. She'd been to America once as a girl, to New York, and saw all she needed to see of American men.

Spit Delaney thought he would go mad. He saw soon enough that he could stare out this farmhouse window all he wanted and never find what he needed. He could look at sheep grazing in their little hedged-in patches, and donkey carts passing by, and clumps of furze moving in the wind, he could look at the sloping farms and the miles and miles of flat green bog with its brown carved-out gleaming beds and piled-up bricks of turf and at the deep curved bay of Atlantic ocean with spray standing up around the jagged rocks until he was blind from looking, but he'd never see a train of any kind. Nor find an answer. Old Number One was in Ottawa by now, being polished and dusted by some uniformed pimple-faced kid who wouldn't know a piston from a lever.

"We'd've been better off spending the money on a swimming pool," Stella told the cousin. "We might as well have flushed it down the toilet."

"That's dumb," Cora said. She buttered a piece of soda bread and scooped out a big spoonful of gooseberry jam.

"Feeding your pimples," Jon said. He had clear skin, not a single adolescent blemish, nor any sign of a whisker. Sexually he was a late developer, he explained, and left you to conclude the obvious: he was a genius. Brilliant people didn't have time for a messy adolescence. They were too busy thinking.

"Don't pick on your sister," Stella said. "And be careful or you'll get a prissy mouth. There's nothing worse on a man."

A hollow ache sat in Spit's gut. He couldn't believe these people belonged to him. This family he'd been dragging around all over the face of the earth was as foreign to him as the little old couple who lived in this house. What did that prim sneery boy have to do with him? Or that fat girl. And Stella: behind those red swollen eyes she was as much a stranger to him now as she was on the day he met her. If he walked up behind her and touched her leg, he could expect her to say Get lost mister I got work to do, just as she had then. They hadn't moved a single step closer.

I don't know what's going on, he thought, but something's happening. If we can't touch, in our minds, how can I know you are there? How can I know who you are? If two people can't overlap, just a little, how the hell can they be sure of a god-damn thing?

The next day they asked him to drive in to Cahirciveen, the nearest village, so Jon could have a look around the library and Stella could try on sweaters, which she said were bound to be cheaper since the sheep were so close at hand. Waiting for them, sitting in the little rented car, he watched the people on the narrow crooked street. Fat red-faced women chatted outside shop doors; old men in dark suits stood side by side in front of a bar window looking into space; a tall woman in a black shawl threaded her way down the sidewalk; a fish woman with a cigarette stuck in the middle of her mouth sat with her knees locked around a box of dried mackerel; beside the car a cripple sat right on the concrete with his back to the store-front wall and his head bobbing over a box for tossed coins.

The temptation was too much to resist. He leaned back and closed his eyes, pressed the button, and turned the volume up full. Old Number One came alive again, throbbed through him, swelled to become the whole world. His hands shifted levers, his foot kicked back from a back-spray of steam, his fingers itched to yank the whistle-cord. Then, when it blew, when the old steam whistle cut right through to his core, he could have died happily.

But he didn't die. Stella was at the window, screaming at him, clawing at the recorder against his chest. A finger caught at the strap and it went flying out onto the street. The whistle died abruptly, all sound stopped. Her face, horrified, glowing red, appeared to be magnified a hundred times. Other faces, creased and toothless, whiskered, stared through glass. It appeared that the whole street had come running to see him, this maniac.

Stella, blushing, tried to be pleasant, dipped apologies, smiled grimly as she went around to her side of the car.

If her Lodge should hear of this.

Or her mother.

The chin, tucked back, was ready to quiver. She would cry this time, and that would be the worst of all. Stella, crying, was unbearable.

But she didn't cry. She was furious. "You stupid stupid man," she said, as soon as she'd slammed the door. "You stupid stupid man."

He got out to rescue his recorder, which had skidded across the sidewalk almost to the feet of the bobbing cripple. When he bent to pick it up, the little man's eyes met his, dully, for just a moment, then shifted away.

Jon refused to ride home with them. He stuck his nose in the air, swung his narrow shoulders, and headed down the street with a book shoved into his armpit. He'd walk the whole way back to the cousin's, he said, before he'd ride with *them*.

She sat silent and bristling while he drove out past the last grey buildings and the Co-op dairy and the first few stony farms. She scratched scales of skin off the dry eczema patches that were spreading on her hands. Then, when they were rushing down between rows of high blooming fuchsia bushes, she asked him what he thought she was supposed to be getting out of this trip.

"Tomorrow," he said. "Tomorrow we go home."

Spit Delaney had never travelled off the Island more than twice before in his life, both those times to see a doctor on the mainland about the cast in his eye. Something told him a once-in-a-lifetime trip to Europe ought to have been more than it was. Something told him he'd been cheated. Cheated in a single summer out of Old Number One, his saved-up overtime money, the tourist's rightfully expected fun, and now out of wife as well. For the first thing she told him when the plane landed on home territory was this: "Maybe we ought to start thinking about a separation. This is no marriage at all any more."

He stopped at the house only long enough to drop them off, then fled for coast, his ears refusing the sounds of her words.

But it was a wet day, and the beach was almost deserted. A few seagulls slapped around on the sand, or hovered by tide pools. Trees, already distorted and one-sided from a lifetime of assaults, bent even farther away from the wind. A row of yellowish seaweed, rolled and tangled with pieces of bark and chunks of wood, lay like a continuous windrow along the uneven line of last night's highest tide. Far out on the sand an old couple walked, leaning on each other, bundled up in toques and Cowichan sweaters and gum boots. The ocean was first a low lacy line on sand, then sharp chopped waves like ploughed furrows, then nothing but haze and mist, a thick blending with uncertain sky.

There was no magic here. No traffic, no transformations. No Kanikiluk in sight. He'd put ninety miles on the camper for nothing. He might as well have curled up in a corner of the old gas station, amongst the car parts, or sat in behind the wheel of his tow truck to brood. The world was out to cheat him wherever he turned.

Still, he walked out, all the way out in the cold wind to the edge of the sea, and met a naked youth coming up out of waves to greet him.

"Swimming?" Spit said, and frowned. "Don't you tell me it's warm when you get used to it, boy, I can see by the way you're all shrivelled up that you're nearly froze."

The youth denied nothing. He raised both arms to the sky as if expecting to ascend, water streaming from his long hair and beard and his crotch, forming beads in the hairs, shining on goose-bumped skin. Then he tilted his head.

"Don't I know you?"

"Not me," Spit said. "I don't live here."

"Me neither," the youth said. "Me and some other guys been camping around that point over there all summer, I go swimming twice a day."

Spit put both hands in his pockets, planted his feet apart, and stretched his long neck. He kept his gaze far out to sea, attempting to bore through that mist. "I just come down for a look at this here ocean."

"Sure, man," the youth said. "I *do* know you. You let me use your can."

"What? What's that?" Why couldn't the kid just move on? You had to be alone sometimes, other people only complicated things.

"I was waiting for a ride, to come up here, and I come into your house to use the can. Hell, man, you gave me a beer and sat me down and told me your whole life story. When I came out my friend had gone on without me."

Spit looked at the youth's face. He remembered someone, he remembered the youth on that hot day, but there was nothing in this face that he recognized. It was as if when he'd stripped off his clothes he'd also stripped off whatever it was that would make his face different from a thousand others.

"You know what they found out there, don't you?" the youth said. He turned to face the ocean with Spit. "Out there they found this crack that runs all around the ocean floor. Sure, man, they say it's squeezing lava out like toothpaste all the time. Runs all the way around the outside edge of this ocean."

"What?" Spit said. "What are you talking about?"

"Squirting lava up out of the centre of the earth! Pushing the continents farther and farther apart! Don't that blow your mind?"

"Look," Spit said. But he lost the thought that had occurred.

"Pushing and pushing. Dividing the waters. Like that what-was-it right back there at the beginning of things. And there it is, right out there somewhere, a bloody big seam. Spreading and pushing."

"You can't believe them scientists," Spit said. "They like to scare you."

"I thought I recognized you. You pulled two beer out of the fridge, snapped off the caps, and put them on the table. Use the can, you said, and when you come out this'll wash the dust from your throat. You must've kept me there the whole afternoon, talking."

"Well, nobody's stopping you now. Nobody's forcing you to stay. Go on up and get dressed." If all he came up out of that ocean to tell about was a crack, he might as well go back in.

Which he did, on the run.

Straight back through ankle-foam, into breakers, out into waves. A black head, bobbing; he could be a seal, watching the shore.

Go looking for your crack, he wanted to shout. Go help push the continents apart. Help split the god-damned world in two.

"There's no reason why we can't do this in a friendly fashion," Stella said when he got home. "It's not as if we hate each other. We simply want to make a convenient arrangement. I phoned a lawyer while you were out."

She came down the staircase backwards, on her hands and knees, scrubbing, her rear end swinging to the rhythm of her arm. Stella was death on dirt, especially when she was upset.

"Don't be ridiculous," Spit said. "This isn't Hollywood, this is *us*. We survived all that crap."

She turned on the bottom step, sat back, and pushed her hair away from her eyes. "Not quite survived. It just waited until we were off our guard, until we thought we were home-safe."

He could puke.

Or hit her.

"But there isn't any home-safe, Spit. And this *is* Hollywood, the world has shrunk, it's changed, even here." She tapped the pointed wooden scrub brush on the step, to show where here was.

Spit fingered the cassette in his pocket. She'd smashed his machine. He'd have to buy a new one, or go without.

"Lady," he said, "that flat-assed logger don't know what a close call he had. If he'd've known he'd be thanking me every day of his life."

Though he didn't mean it.

Prying him loose from Stella would be like prying off his arm. He'd got used to her, and couldn't imagine how he'd live without her.

Her mother sat in her flowered armchair and scowled out over her bulging eyeballs at him as if she were trying to see straight to his centre and burn what she found. Her mouth chewed on unintelligible sounds.

"This is my bad year," he said. "First they take away Old Number One, and now this. The only things that mattered to me. Real things."

"Real!" The old woman screeched, threw up her hands, and slapped them down again on her skinny thighs. She laughed, squinted her eyes at the joke, then blinked them open again, bulged them out, and pursed her lips. Well, have we got news for you, she seemed to be saying. She could hardly wait for Stella's answer.

"The only things you can say that about," Stella said, "are the things that people can't touch, or wreck. Truth is like that, I imagine, if there is such a thing."

The old woman nodded, nodded: That'll show you, that'll put you in your place. Spit could wring her scrawny neck.

"You!" he said. "What do you know about anything?"

The old woman pulled back, alarmed. Her big eyes filled with tears, her hands dug into the folds of her dress. The lips moved, muttered, mumbled things at the window, at the door, at her own pointed knees. Then suddenly she leaned ahead again, seared a scowl into him. "All a mirage!" she shrieked, and looked frightened by her own words. She drew back, swallowed, gathered courage again. "Blink your eyes and it's gone, or moved!"

Spit and Stella looked at each other. Stella raised an eyebrow. "That's enough, Mother," she said. Gently.

"Everybody said we had a good marriage," he said. "Spit and Stella, solid as rocks."

"If you had a good marriage," the old woman accused, "it was with a train, not a woman." And looked away, pointed her chin elsewhere.

Stella leapt up, snorting, and hurried out of the room with her bucket of soapy water.

Spit felt, he said, like he'd been dragged under the house by a couple of dogs and fought over. He had to lie down. And, lying down, he had to face up to what was happening. She came into the bedroom and stood at the foot at the bed. She puffed up her cheeks like a blowfish and fixed her eyes on him.

"I told the lawyer there was no fighting involved. I told him it was a friendly separation. But he said one of us better get out of the house all the same, live in a motel or something until it's arranged. He said you."

"Not me," he said. "I'll stay put, thank you."

"Then I'll go." Her face floated back, wavered in his watery vision, then came ahead again.

"I'd call that desertion," he said.

"You wouldn't dare."

And of course he wouldn't. It was no more and no less than what he'd expect, after everything else, if he thought about it.

All he wanted to do was put his cassette tape into a machine, lie back, close his eyes, and let the sounds of Old Number One rattle through him. That was all he wanted. When she'd gone he would drive in to town and buy a new machine.

"I'll leave the place clean," she said. "I'll leave food in the fridge when I go, in a few days. Do you think you can learn how to cook?"

"I don't know," he said. "How should I know? I don't even believe this is happening. I can't even think what it's going to be like."

"You'll get used to it. You've had twenty years of one kind of life, you'll get used to another."

Spit put his head back on the pillow. There wasn't a thing he could reach out and touch and be sure of.

At the foot of his obsolete B/A sign, Spit on his rock watches the hitch-hikers spread out along the roadside like a pack of ragged refugees. Between him and them there is a ditch clogged with dry podded broom and a wild tangle of honeysuckle and blackberry vines. They perch on their packs, lean against the telephone pole, lie out flat on the gravel; every one of them indifferent to the sun, the traffic, to one another. We have all day, their postures say, we have for ever. If you won't pick us up, someone else just as good will do it, nobody needs you.

Spit can remember a time when he tried to have a pleading look on his face whenever he was out on the road. A look that said Please pick me up I may die if I don't get where I'm going on time. And made obscene gestures at every driver that passed him by. Sometimes hollered insults. These people, though, don't care enough to look hopeful. It doesn't matter to them if they get picked up or not, because they think where they're going isn't the slightest bit different from where they are now. Like bits of dry leaves, letting the wind blow them whatever way it wants.

The old bearded man notices Spit, raises a hand to his forehead in greeting. His gaze runs up the pole, flickers over the weathered sign, and runs down again. He gives Spit a grin, a slight shake of his head, turns away. Old fool, Spit thinks. At your age. And lifts his engineer cap to settle it farther back.

Spit cannot bear to think where these people are going, where their rides will take them. His mind touches, slides away from the boy with the St. Bernard, sitting up against the back of that green pickup cab. He could follow them, in his mind he could go the whole distance with them, but he refuses, slides back from it, holds onto the things that are happening here and now.

The sound of Stella's shoes shifting in gravel. The scent of the pines, leaking pitch. The hot smell of sun on the rusted pole.

"I've left my phone number on the memo pad, on the counter."

The feel of the small pebbles under his boots.

"Jon and Cora'll take turns, on the weekends. Don't be scared to make Cora do your shopping when she's here. She knows how to look for things, you'll only get yourself cheated."

He'd yell *Okay!*

He holds on. He thinks of tourists filing through the National Museum, looking at Old Number One. People he'll never see, from Ottawa and Toronto and New York and for all he knows from Africa and Russia, standing around Old Number One, talking about her, pointing, admiring the black shine of her finish. Kids wondering what it would be like to ride in her, feel the thudding of her pistons under you.

He'd stand at the edge of the water and yell *Okay you son of a bitch, okay!*

"It don't look like there's going to be any complications. My lawyer can hardly believe how friendly all this's been. It'll all go by smooth as sailing."

Spit Delaney sees himself get up into the pickup with the youth and the St. Bernard, sees himself slide his ass right up against the cab, slam his hand in a signal on the hot metal roof. Sees himself going down that silver-grey road, heading west. Sees himself laughing.

He says, "My lawyer says if it's all so god-damned friendly how come you two are splitting up."

"That's just it," she says. "Friends are one thing. You don't have to be married to be a friend."

"I don't know what you're talking about," Spit says. It occurs to him that he has come home from a trip through Europe and northern Africa and can't remember a thing. Something happened there, but what was it?

He sees himself riding in that pickup all up through the valley farmlands, over the mountains in the centre of the island, down along the lakes and rivers, snaking across towards Pacific. Singing, maybe, with that boy. Throwing his arm around the old floppy dog's ugly neck. Feeling the air change gradually to damp, and colder. Straining his neck to see.

"I got my Lodge tonight, so I better get going, it'll give me the day to get settled in, it takes time to unpack. You'll be all right?"

Sees himself hopping off the green pickup, amongst the distorted combed-back spruce, the giant salal, sees himself touching the boy goodbye, patting the dog. Sees himself go down through the logs, through the white dry sand, over the damp brown sand and the seaweed. Sees himself at the water's edge on his long bony legs like someone who's just grown them, unsteady, shouting.

Shouting into the blind heavy roar.
Okay!
Okay you son of a bitch!
I'm stripped now, okay, now where is that god–damned line?

The man on the left is Phonse. The man on the right is Wilf. The man in the center appears to be drunk.

Falling down drunk. Head lolling, hair lank. Slumping between Phonse and Wilf. His knees loosely bent. Held up by an arm over Phonse's shoulders, another over Wilf's, each of them grasping his hand to keep him from falling. The drunk wears a dark suit. Phonse and Wilf in shirt-sleeves are grinning, grinning too heartily. Even in this dog-eared, wrinkled old photograph, the well-dressed drunk looks pale.

* * *

Phonse stamps on the plank floor of the Anchor Tavern, roaring for another.

"See 'im," grunts Jud. "Says it's dear, but he's havin' another."

"Didn't make beer money today anyways," Phonse says. "Got just about enough for a chowder, that's all."

"Them scales is wrong," Jud repeats. "We had that old box full up last week and they said it was two thousand pounds. Now we get half-filled and they say fifteen hunnert."

And the smell: the pungent, malty tavern, the sour reek of the fish-meal plant, sweat and tobacco,

Snapshot: The Third Drunk

Silver Donald Cameron

and beneath all, like a bass figure in an old song, the salt nip of the beaches and kelp, and cold spray over the stones. . . .

"What the Jesus you gonna do?" Phonse shrugged. "Not like the old days. Didn't need no money in the old days." He winks at me. "You should of been here then, boy. By the Jesus, we had some right roarin' times in them days."

"Need money now," Jud said.

"You can't starve a fisherman, though," Phonse insisted. "Old Wilf Rattray used to say that all the time, ye can't starve a fisherman. D'you mind old Wilf, Jud?"

"Can't really say so. I was just a kid."

"He must have drowned in—let's think now. In the big storm in sixty-three, just before Christmas. He was on a wooden side dragger out o' North Sydney."

"I was about ten then."

"Must of been that sixty-three storm. Wilf was at Reg Munroe's wake in sixty-two, and there wasn't anyone from here drowned off a dragger for a couple of years after sixty-three, I don't believe."

"I got a sort of vague recollection of him."

"Oh Jesus, he was a great old boy. Your old dad there, he'd mind him, don't you, Alfred?"

"Great old boy?" Alfred rumbled; "He was a goddamn Jonah, was Rattray. Black Foot Rattray, we used to call him."

Phonse winked at me again. "Call 'em Black Foot when they're so goddamn unlucky their feet get dirty in the bath."

"Black Foot Rattray," muttered Alfred, shaking his head.

"Great old fellow all the same," Phonse insisted. "He wa'n't so much unlucky as stupid. Sign him on as engineer, he'd go down and tinker with the engine. A tinkerer, that's what he was. No matter how sweet she'd been runnin', Rattray'd have her bustin' head gaskets and burnin' out bearings the first day at sea."

"I shipped along of him once," Alfred declared. "Never again. That was the trip he cut off his finger in the winch, an' Jesus, he'd *already* had us back home once with engine trouble."

Phonse started to laugh. "He was a Jonah, right enough. But he was a barrel of fun at a party. We had good parties in them days."

Alfred chuckled. "We did so," he murmured. "We had some parties, all right."

* * *

No bullshit: there is no bullshit in Widow's Harbor. Drifting along the coast with a little money and no plans, all my futures behind me, I followed the back roads off the back roads and discovered Widow's Harbor at the dead end of a rocky peninsula thrusting into the Atlantic like an arthritic finger. In Toronto, someone else was editing manuscripts. Someone else was meeting the Senator for lunch at the Westbury. Someone else was agreeing to be at the television studio a little before 3:00 for makeup. Someone else.

As for me, I was sitting on a precarious lobster trap at the end of a sagging wharf, sharing a bottle of Abbey Rich Canadian port ($1.40) with Phonse and Alfred Nickerson. After that there was a dozen of Tenpenny and some talk about gill-netting and long-lining and the lobster season, and then there was some McGuinness rum, and then there must have been something resembling a decision not to drive on that night. Around noon the next day I found myself surrounded by clean flannelette sheets with the threads showing, in a small, white, slant-ceilinged room, and when I stumbled downstairs I discovered Phonse's wife Laura making lunch for the kids who would be coming home from school. Laura snickered at my headache and poured some black coffee. Phonse had gone fishing at 4:00 A.M.

"He's usually away by three," she said, "but I guess you fellows really tied one on last night. Phonse, he was some full."

There seemed no reason to leave the next day, or the next, and when I found the shack across the road was for rent, I took it. I could make enough to get by on if I were to run into Halifax every week or so with some radio talks, and I had friends in Widow's Harbor. It was a good place to read, talk, drink, and grow strong. In the scrubby woods, mushrooms erupted from the pine needles underfoot. I combed the beaches for driftwood to be converted to lamps for the shack. There were deer and rabbits to be hunted with Purvis, my landlord; nets to be mended with Phonse and Alfred; and radio talks to be written about these things and others. I found I was living comfortably on about a sixth of my Toronto salary, and at that I was making a good thousand dollars a year more than Phonse or any of the others.

Widow's Harbor can afford no bullshit: it lives too near the bedrock of health and illness, shelter and food, death and tax sales. No one can hide: the snow-filled easterlies and the neighbors' tongues scour every cranny. Toronto's bruises soon fade. They are not, after all, catastrophes: on this bare rock, along this open coast, where even death is contemptibly familiar, the loss of a salary or a lover stands revealed as a petty misfortune at most.

* * *

"Come on over for some breakfast," says Phonse, shaking my shoulder, "and get a wiggle on. Supposed to be a blow coming up tonight, but we'll make a few sets before she hits."

Two shirts, heavy sweater, pea jacket; long johns, two pairs of pants; extra socks, rubber boots. Crossing the road in the coal-black night, slithering on ice, still stupid with sleepiness. Phonse frying bacon and eggs. The kitchen clock: 2:15.

"You usually have bacon and eggs?"

"Me? Naw, just bread and molasses and away I go. Don't usually have company for breakfast, though."

"For Christ's sake, Phonse."

"Stop bitchin' and eat."

Down the snowy road to Alfred's, plastic bags of bread and molasses in our hands. Grunts of greeting, and down to the wharf. Fluffy snow on the *Harvey and Sisters,* a sweet, forty-foot Cape Islander with a high flaring bow; she set Alfred back four grand. Lines cast off, the Buick v-8 sends a throaty purr through the big hot stack spearing up through the wheelhouse. Frost on the windshield. A light chill wind ruffles the harbor.

The purr turns to a heavy burble as we clear the harbor mouth, line up the yellow leading lights, and make an hour's straight steaming to the fishing grounds on Widow's Bank. Desultory talk. Phonse pisses over the side, back in the wide cockpit among the waiting tubs of trawl.

Then overboard go the highflyers, buoys with tall flagstaffs, easy to see even in the eerie pre-dawn, and the trawl pays out, the baited hooks every fathom or so, and a highflyer at the end. Steaming back up the long lines for an hour and a half at sunrise, and hauling in fish.

"Another taxi driver, Jud."

"Why do you call pollack taxi drivers?"

"Dunno. We just do, that's all. Oho! Them big steakers is what we like to see."

Monkeyfish and dogfish to be thrown back. Cod and flounder. A day of heavy hauling, icy water everywhere, with one coffee break, bobbing around in the fo'c'sle with the engine shut off. As the short day closes in, Alfred spins the wheel, heads *Harvey and Sisters* toward shore.

And Phonse with a deft slash rips each fish from vent to gill and throws it to Jud, who scoops the guts out and overboard in one swift motion, tossing the fish into the bin in the center of the cockpit. They gut a fish every six seconds. Every forty feet, regular as dripping blood, the guts hit the ocean, and the gulls come, a few at first, then a crowd, finally a swarm, dropping like dive bombers on the livers and intestines and half-digested mackerel. Ten minutes ago there wasn't a gull in sight; now hundreds hover over *Harvey and Sisters.*

The wind is rising, the whitecaps multiply, the promised blow is coming. Numb with cold already, I hunch in the wheelhouse, watching the first flakes of snow fly over the black water. Alfred has swung a hinged bench into place, and sits high behind the windshield, holding her steady by the compass now, back to Widow's Harbor. Phonse and Jud stamp in, shaking like wet dogs.

"Son of a bitch," Jud observes.

"Yessir," Phonse agrees. "Yessir, she's all of that."

Just outside the harbor, the storm hits: the sea begins boiling, the shriek of the wind sails in above the throb of the v-8. A whitecap foams into the cockpit.

"Self-bailing," Phonse reassures me. Another whitecap froths over the stern.

"Runnin' her a little close, Alfred," says Alfred.

"Save us some scrubbin'," Jud philosophizes. And we are in, inside the harbor, with the wind down to nothing and the sea no more than a chop. The motor dies down, and *Harvey and Sisters* idles over to the fish buyers' dock. After Jud and Phonse fork the fish into the crates for weighing, we will scour the boat clean and bait the trawl for the next day, coiling it carefully in the tubs so it will pay out smoothly.

"What's the time gettin' to be, there?" Phonse asks me.

"Two-fifteen."

"Good enough," Jud nods. "Be home by seven-thirty, quarter to eight."

"Might even be time for a beer," Phonse reflects for a moment. "Do you think, Alfred?"

"Might be," says Alfred.

* * *

You can't starve a fisherman. In the old days you didn't need money.

"Why, sure," says Phonse, draining a beer glass. "Look now, everyone had his own cow, so there was your milk and butter and cheese. Everybody had a few chickens, so there was your eggs and some of your meat. Everybody had a kitchen garden, so there was your vegetables, and the women got enough in preserves—well, you seen Laura's preserves even now, ain't you? We got enough there for two years even if we never *ever* got anything out of the garden this year. And there was always deer in the woods, more 'n now, and rabbits and ducks, sometimes a moose. You didn't have to be any too fussy about the season then, either. Then you had your wild berries—blueberries and cranberries and blackberries and bakeapples—you ever see bakeapples growin' wild? They look like a little orange hat on a green spike, just one to a bush, the swamps was full of 'em. Some folks had pigs and sheep, and the sea was always full of fish and lobsters, and we wa'n't too upset about the season on them, neither."

"You still aren't," I said, remembering an evening with a dozen of the biggest, reddest, juiciest out-of-season lobsters I ever saw.

"So they say," Phonse countered, with a huge grin.

" 'Course I wouldn't know. You take a chance now, you can lose your boat and your car and pay a big fine. I wouldn't fool around with that sort of stuff."

"Christ, no," I said, shaking my head. "Wouldn't be worth it."

Alfred burst out laughing.

In the old days, the cows were put out to summer pasture on Meadow Island, in the harbor mouth. You took a rowboat and two men: one rowed, and the other held the cow's head up, and the cow swam over to the island. Horses will swim without coaxing, but you have to help a cow.

"I mind one time," said Phonse, "I had to go get the cow at the end of the summer. Well, Jesus! Spent two days on that goddamn island and do you think I could catch that old son of a whore? No sir, couldn't get near it. 'Course I always hated that Christly cow. I'm not a goddamn farmer, I'm a fisherman. But my old mom, she hadda have a cow, so of course I hadda get it out to the island in the spring and back in the fall. But I couldn't even catch the bastard.

"So I come back with six other fellows and a motor boat, and we cornered the bugger and put a rope around her neck and led her down to the beach, but when we got her there do you think she'd go in the water? Not on your Jesus life she wouldn't. We all got in the boat and sagged on the rope, and she wouldn't budge an inch. Just dug her old hooves down in the sand and that was that.

"Well, I got mad. I said to myself, I don't care if I kill that cow or break its neck or whatever the hell happens I don't care. So I cracked the old throttle full out, and I let out all the slack and went roarin' out into the harbor, and that rope come taut and 'bout jerked that cow's head right off. She drove her hooves down in the sand to the knees and then she buckled, just come a-flyin' up in the air like a cork out of a bottle and hit the water about thirty feet out. I never let up on the throttle one bit till I got to the other side, I like to *drowned* that cow, and she was comin' up and down and sideways and wallowin' around, her eyes buggin' out, you never saw anything like it. Jesus, I said to myself that's the last time I ever have anything at all to do with that cow; and it was. Vet killed her before the next spring come around."

I was laughing too hard to speak.

"It's true, honest to God. And we had some parties, too."

"We did," sighed Alfred. "Oh, I guess we did."

"Remember that time Muriel Naugler and Loretta O'Leary got loaded at the beach party?"

"Lord, Lord," said Alfred.

"Jesus, that was some funny. The two of them got lit, and Loretta, she'd been foolin' around with Harry Naugler, and Muriel started to come onto her about it. So Loretta gave *her* a scandalizin', said if she was any kind of a wife to him there wouldn't be nothin' anyone could do about it, and Muriel—well, I guess she got right savage wild then. So she starts screamin' about how she's got a dose of clap from Harry bringin' it home from Loretta, and Loretta says it was Harry give it to her in the first place, so who'd he get it from, that's what she wants to know, and before anybody can say Boo they're clawin' at each other and tearin' off each other's clothes and pullin' hair and I don't know what all, and they're practically bareass to the weather—and all the guys standin' around, you know, and cheerin' and watchin' and havin' a great old time."

"What a night," sighed Alfred.

" 'Twas the women broke it up, but it must of taken them a good half hour. Those days," Phonse explained, "used to have parties some-place or other every night, practically. Nothin' else *to* do. There wasn't no television, and you couldn't get nothin' on the radio, and the movies was a travelin' affair, used to come here once every two weeks, so what else could ye do?"

"The wakes was the best," Alfred opined. "D'ye mind Reg Munroe's wake?"

"Guess I do," declared Phonse. " 'Twas me picked up the coffin."

* * *

The cable from Halifax was very specific: TRAWLER ATLANTIC STAR RAMMED AND SUNK BY FREIGHTER HALIFAX HARBOR, it said, REGINALD MUNROE KILLED STOP REMAINS SHIPPED CNR MONKSTOWN CHARGES COLLECT STOP PLEASE ARRANGE COLLECTION REMAINS YOUR END STOP SINCEREST REGRETS DEEPEST CONDOLENCES THIS TRAGEDY STOP CORONER CITY OF HALIFAX.

Phonse had been living with Reg's sister Alice, and while Alice comforted her mother, Phonse offered to take his pickup truck the fifty miles to Monkstown and bring Reg's corpse home.

"Lord Jesus, I'll never forget it," said Phonse. "I got down there about noon, and didn't they have him standing on his head in the freight shed? They had boxes of stuff and bales and rolls of linoleum and bicycles, and tucked away right in the middle of it was old Reg, standin' on his head. I said to the agent he might at least let the fellow lie down, but he said he was stuck for space, it was just before Christmas, you know, and the shed was right jammed. It looked some strange, though, that coffin standin' on its head in all that pile of stuff." Phonse waved his glass in the air. "I b'lieve I'll have another."

"Me too," said Jud. "Phonse, I been wondering if there ain't some way we can get them scales checked."

"Dunno," said Phonse. "We could try, I guess."

* * *

I tried to imagine that trip home over the twisting road to Widow's Harbor with the corpse of your woman's brother behind you in the truck. Tried to imagine how you would secure it against the swings and bounces of that unkempt gravel road. What would the coffin look like? Plain, no doubt; would there be places to tie ropes?

The road winds through fifteen miles of forest with hardly a house to be seen, nothing but scrubby evergreens in low, folding country. Perhaps it would have been snowing, isolating Phonse and the corpse in a moving dome filled with drifting white flakes, settling a coating of fluff on the coffin so that in the truck's lights it would seem, as you looked over your shoulder through the rearview mirror, as though the coffin were becoming vague in outline, but alarmingly larger. The truck would be slipping and slithering around rock outcroppings, over little wooden bridges, past the entrances to abandoned logging roads. The coffin growing and fading.

Reg Munroe, fisherman. Alice's brother. Dead, as you could be dead yourself any day of your working life. Drowned. Lying back there in the box of the truck, cold and bloodless, chewed up by the big blade of some freighter.

The road comes down to the shore at Owl's Cove, a handful of houses clustered around a gas pump. The winter night comes down, and nothing shows but a scattered light; and after that, darkness, and surf beside the shore road, flying cloud and wind.

Phonse would have remembered, surely, all the ghost stories: the Spanish galleon in flames that enters one little cove every seventh year, the woman in white seen in the bows of a sinking windship just before a shipwreck, the tales of jealousy, torment, and murder recalled in minor-key folk songs as common as rocks along this shore. Once, fishing in a dragger on the Grand Banks, Phonse had found a human skull and a thigh bone in the nets: some poor sailor or fisherman drowned God knows how many decades or even centuries before, one of those lost at sea whose bodies were never found, nibbled clean by the codfish and sand fleas. The crew had gathered around on the afterdeck, passing the skull from hand to hand, uncertain what to do with it, and finally they had cast it back into the heaving sea whence it had come, to continue its long rest without further disturbance.

Reg Munroe, Alice's brother, fisherman, in a coffin in the back of the truck, a coffin growing larger as the snow continued to fall and the truck ground along the foaming edge of a cold sea. . . .

* * *

"Jesus, Phonse!" I said. "That must have been some spooky ride."
"What's that?"
"Down from Monkstown with that coffin."
"Nah, shit, there wasn't nothin' spooky about that. There was three of us went, and we took a bottle o' rum and got right polluted. Nah, somebody had to do it, an' I had the truck, that's all." He pulled at his beer and then wiped his lips on his checked shirt-sleeve. "But I tell you somethin' that wasn't too canny when we got here."

A mile before Widow's Harbor they nearly went off the road, swerving to avoid a snow-shrouded figure trudging along. Stopping the truck to give the fellow a proper old scandalizing. Phonse was greeted by a cheery, "Evenin', Phonse, thanks a lot," and Jack Kavanaugh climbed into the crowded cab. "What's that in the back?"

"That's Reg Munroe's corpse."

"No," said Jack, "it ain't."

"It *is*," Phonse protested. "I picked him up in Monkstown. I got signed papers and everythin'."

"You look inside?"

"Hell, no."

"Well, it ain't Reg."

"How come you're so Jesus sure?"

"Well," said Jack, "Reg's body come in by sea this afternoon. I seen it. I'm just goin' in to the wake."

"Go away."

"It's *true,* Phonse."

"Snappin' Jesus Christ," said Phonse reverently. "Then who the hell have I got in the back of the truck?"

"It ain't Reg; that I do know."

"Well, Jesus," said Phonse grimly. "Soon's we get to town I think we better have a look at you, stranger."

Under a streetlight they stopped and opened the coffin. A man's face stared out at the sky. Snowflakes fell on his eyes: they did not melt. Phonse whistled low.

"My God, it's Teddy Lundrigan."

"I didn't even know Teddy was dead," Jack marveled.

"Nor I," Phonse agreed. "But I'd say he is, all right."

* * *

"That was some wake," Phonse chuckled. "By the Jesus, I was half cut already. I went right wild that night."

"I'll never forget you runnin' down them stairs with your trousers around your ankles," said Alfred.

"Oh my God, yes. Jesus, Ma Munroe was some savage when she come up and found all four couples ridin' together in them two beds. Didn't she take the broom to us, though?"

"Didn't she?"

"And Alice, she was right owly when she found out about me being up there with Stella."

"But she wa'n't nobody to talk. She was married to Buzz when you were livin' with her, wa'n't she, and him off workin' the lake boats in Upper Canada?"

"He always wanted to get me for a divorce," Phonse said. "But he never did." He turned to me. "But that ain't the best of it, or the worst, dependin' how you look at it."

"No?"

"Hell, no. See, later on that night we was just right out of our trees, you know? I don't think I was ever so full, never ever in my life. And old Wilf Rattray, him that drowned on that dragger, him and I heard that old Reg was cut up some when that freighter run them down. So what d'ye suppose we did?"

"What'd you do, Phonse?"

"We went into the room where the two corpses was, see, 'cause it was one big wake for the two of them, and we took old Reg out of his box and stripped him down. There was nothin' on his face, but his chest and legs was cut up pretty bad, all black and blue and the chest crushed in. Funny thing to see, all them cuts and him not bleedin'."

"Jesus, Phonse!"

"Well, hell, we didn't think old Reg'd mind. I wouldn't have minded, if it had of been me instead of him in that box. I mean, shit, we was old friends. Anyways, what d'ye suppose we did then?"

"Christ, Phonse, I hate to think."

"Why, we dressed him all up again, just like he was, and then old Wilf and me, we put one of his arms around each of our necks and had our pictures took."

"That's right," said Alfred, shaking his head. "That's right. God save us, you did that."

"Sure," said Phonse. "Sure we did. I still got the picture." He drew out his wallet.

* * *

The man on the left is Phonse. The man on the right is Wilf. The man in the center appears to be drunk.

There were three of them on the beach that morning, walking past the sand dunes and train tracks, gulls wheeling and mewing overhead. Their father carried Races' pitchfork, Ardith a tin bucket. Madge, the youngest, was empty-handed, a privilege fast disappearing now that she was shooting up: already she was past her father's elbow. She skittered beside him in erratic bursts, trying to keep up. Laddie was a big, broad-shouldered man with fair, sunburnt skin. In his shadow Madge did not feel long-legged and spindly, but compact and petite.

Luna Moths

Joan Clark

Ahead of them the clam flats spread smooth and shiny as a giant platter, rimmed by a strip of river a thin molasses colour now that it had been emptied of the sea. The out going tide had left behind pewter-coloured sand, ribbed like a washboard and strewn with broken shells. Once Madge had seen a seal in the river going out with the tide. Lying on its back, the seal had been rocking gently, coasting along with the water. On the flats were six large gulls, motionless as decoys. They waited until the three people had removed their shoes and socks and were walking across the wet sand before they swung to the air.

Close to the river, Laddie plunged the fork into an airhole. Madge heard the suck of water and air. She knew the clam was digging with its foot, going deeper. She half wanted it to escape, to make the chase more exciting. But her father was quick, quicker than the clam. There was a crack of shell and the pitchfork was held up, the clam speared on a tine. The clam's foot dangled in the air, helpless and limp.

"A big bugger," Laddie said. "Pull it off."

Madge pried the clam loose. She watched the slippery foot being sucked inside the shell before she threw the clam into the bucket. Laddie brought up a coven of smaller clams, their shells clamped shut, feet locked securely inside. Ardith knelt down to retrieve them.

"Thatta girl," Laddie said. "You keep up with me now."

Madge watched the bulge of muscle above her father's elbow as he levered the fork up through the sucking sand. His arms were covered with fine hairs, red-gold against his blue shirt. There were two damp circles beneath his arms, evidence of a solid, monolithic strength, a swift, sure knowledge of how the job should be done.

The gulls coasted onto the sand farther away where the river flowed beneath a train trestle. Madge ran toward them, arms flapping, sending gulls screaming into the air. She stopped and looked back at the diggers, her father bent over the fork, Ardith huddled beside the bucket. From this distance they looked small and peaceful, joined together by the darkness of their shapes against the pale expanse of sand. Madge found a large shell, knelt down and used it to scoop out an airhole. She dug jerkily, doggishly, sand flying every which way. She brought up a medium-sized clam, its foot distended into a swollen white lip. She scooped out more airholes, brought up more clams. She slipped off her pink shorts and piled the clams in the middle so they wouldn't dig themselves back into the sand. When she had built a small mound, she carried the shorts back and emptied the clams into the bucket, which by now was nearly full.

"Your mother won't like you dirtying your shorts. She just did the wash yesterday," Laddie said. "Try and be more helpful." The disapproval was in his voice, not in his face.

Madge studied her father's face, the smooth forehead, the shaved skin shiny with sweat, the large nose and ears. Her father was a high wall she couldn't scale; there was no place to get a toehold. There was no opening, no way to get inside him to know what it was like to be him looking out through those blue windows.

"A few more and we'll have enough," he said. He held the fork upright and rested his foot on it.

"Why don't you be a good girl and get me some seaweed?" he said to Madge. "There's nothing like clams steamed in seaweed." He lowered his foot and went back to work.

Their family wouldn't be eating the clams. Clams made her mother sick. They were for sailors off the ships tied up at the docks in Liverpool. Since the war had begun, Laddie sometimes had sailors to the house for poker and beer. As soon as the clams were dug, he was going back to town. They wouldn't see him again until next weekend, because after tonight he would be working night shift at the paper mill.

"All right," Madge said. This was a clear and simple way to please her father, a way she didn't have to look for. Ardith never had to look for such ways. She seemed to know exactly what their father wanted and was able to provide it. *Your father and Ardith are like two peas in a pod.* Madge's mother had said this once when Laddie was helping Ardith build a fur-trading fort for a history project, while Madge moped around the house, restless and out of sorts. Her mother made it sound as if this sameness was something she had no control over, that she despaired of, that she would change if she could, but at the same time took pleasure and pride in.

Madge brushed the wet sand from her shorts and put them on. By the time she got back to the cottage, the shorts would be dry. Her mother wouldn't care anyway. The main reason they had moved to the beach for the summer was so her mother wouldn't need to bother with things like wrinkled clothes and snarled hair.

Madge walked to the train trestle where the river pooled deep and brown. She scrambled up the embankment to the tracks that smelled of hot tar and wild roses. She crossed quickly, carefully, anticipating a foot caught beneath an iron tie, the train hurtling toward her, the engineer blowing his whistle, gesturing that she get herself unstuck. The sand on the other side of the tracks was warm and dry. Madge heard her heels squeak against it. She splashed across the shallow, frilled river mouth. Here waves broke so softly, so continuously, they hardly seemed waves at all but unravellings, rows and rows of liquid cloth being pulled apart by the gentle tug of an invisible thread. On the far side of the sandbar the water became deeper. Madge waded toward the seaweed-covered rocks, feeling put upon, unimportant, because she had been so easily dispatched upon an errand. It occurred to her that maybe her father had been trying to get rid of her in order to get the work done more quickly. At the same time, now that she was alone, she felt she had been released, set free.

She came to a tidal pool in a hollow between rocks. She saw the sideways scuttle of a crab as it disappeared beneath a curtain of brown seaweed at the bottom of the pool. She reached into the water, groping through the curtain until her fingers ached with cold. She saw a starfish splayed on the side of a rock. It was the colour of her shorts, of the roses growing beside the tracks. Madge peeled the starfish off the rock and placed it on the palm of her hand, shivering when its tentacles tickled her skin. She heard the train whistle. Dropping the starfish into the water, she yanked fistfuls of seaweed from the rocks and ran towards the tracks. She stood in the shadow of the trestle and waited for the train.

It came, the thundering engine bearing down on her, the vibrating cars swaying and groaning, shaking the ground where she stood, turning her bones to jelly. She watched the engine clatter past, deafening her. The impassive faces stared out, painted on glass, framed like movie stars on a screen. It didn't occur to Madge that some of the passengers might be anxious or afraid: a mother going to visit a sick child in a Halifax hospital, a young woman leaving home for the first time, a sailor returning to his ship two days late. Madge imagined the faces as belonging to people who were carefree and spoiled, who sat at tables covered with white cloths and were fed dessert. Their passing intruded on her aloneness, made her feel stranded, left out.

The caboose jiggled past, leaving a gust of hot, swirling air. Once again, Madge was released. She skipped over the tracks and onto the clam flats. Gulls were squawking and pecking at the holes her father had dug, now collapsing into grey mud slides. Madge ran, arms spread wide, seaweed streaming from her hands, scattering gulls. She wandered through the dunes, looking in the coarse speargrass for nests, holding one hand over her head in case the circling gulls should swoop down to peck her. She went toward a clutch of eggs. Dropping the seaweed, she got down on her hands and knees and felt in the grass. They weren't eggs at all but smooth white stones. She looked around for more eggs before she remembered the seaweed and went back for it.

By the time she found her shoes and socks, put them on, and walked back to the cottage, Laddie had already eaten his noon dinner and left for town. "Dad got tired of waiting for you," Ardith said, "*I* had to get the seaweed for him. Mum's cross at you for being late," she went on. "We have to be quiet. She's lying down."

Madge wasn't worried about her mother's crossness. These days her mother didn't have the energy to stay cross. Most of her energy had been given to the war effort. That was what she called folding bandages for the Red Cross in the bare room over the firehall, working in the sailors' canteen on Water Street, nursing survivors torpedoed by subs. For this last job she had put on a white uniform and navy blue cape and gone to the basement of the high school, which had been converted into a hospital. Dressed in her uniform, with her hair pulled back in a bun beneath her cap, her mother had looked like the nurse in the Victory Bond poster. The woman in this picture had pale skin, dark hair, a firm chin. She had her arms around two children, a boy on one side, a girl on the other. Bombs exploded behind them, but the woman looked straight out of the picture, determined and resolute.

While their mother rested, Madge and Ardith went out to the road and into the ditch where purple vetch, black-eyed Susans, and pink lupins grew in tangled profusion. There was a numbing laziness in the heat, in the locust's dry hum, the bee's insistent buzzing. Madge didn't like being on the road in such heat. The openness, the intense sun, the insects, the length of her bare arms and legs made her feel unprotected, spied upon. It wasn't a time to be standing at all, but lying down, beneath the shade trees of Races' pasture or in the mossy spruce woods beside their cabin. Madge couldn't pass up the opportunity of catching a butterfly for Ardith, who was afraid of them. It was a demonstration of fearlessness and bravado, an easy and useful accomplishment.

Madge was hunched over a butterfly fanning its wings on a black-eyed Susan, waiting for them to close so she could quickly pinch them between her fingers, lightly, in order not to remove too much of their golden dust. It was an ordinary cabbage butterfly with yellow, brown-spotted wings. Ardith, who stood behind her with the chloroform jar, already had two other cabbage butterflies in her collection, but they had pale, silvery wings. She also had two monarchs, a red admiral, and a tiger swallowtail, all of which Madge had caught for her. These were pinned to a felt board, carefully labelled and described. Ardith had a card table set up on the porch at the cottage to hold her collections. As well as butterflies, she collected shells, which she kept in pigeonholes their father had made for her, and leaves ironed between layers of waxed paper and glued onto bristol board. At home, in his top bureau drawer, lined up in neat rows, their father had coins from different countries, match folders given him by sailors, badges he had earned when he was a King's Scout in Sydney.

The fragile wings opened, shut, opened, shut, slow, slower, the pauses longer, sleepier. There was a quivering pause stretched out like a sigh as the wings came together and stayed, becoming so thin and papery they might have been mistaken for a sliver of yellow light.

"Now!" Ardith whispered.

There was a spurt of gravel on the roadside.

Madge looked away from the butterfly just as Francis Race dropped his bike in the ditch. When she looked back, the butterfly was wobbling drunkenly over the barbed-wire fence toward the swamp.

"It's gone!" Ardith wailed. She glared at Francis Race. "It's all your fault!"

"Stupid girl," Francis said. He stood there, confident and knowing, with his bare feet and tanned chest, his pants rolled up to his knees, spears of uneven straw-coloured hair falling over his eyes. "You need a net to do it right."

"Pest," Ardith said. "Go away!"

"Can't." He grinned. "I live here."

"Boys!" Ardith huffed and crossed the road.

Francis pulled out a stalk of tender new grass and chewed on it. He stared boldly at Madge.

"Want to see inside the old boat?" he said.

He had already shown her the baby pigs in the sty, the green apples in the orchard, the black bull staked in the back pasture. Being shown the black bull was how she had got into trouble.

Madge stared at her sister's back.

Ardith turned. "You know what Mum said." She went into their driveway.

For supper that night their mother had made potato salad and devilled eggs. They sat on the screened-in verandah, plates on their knees, and looked across the road and the railway tracks, past the dunes to the sea shining smooth and blue in the sun. A fog bank hovered along the horizon; above it, white clouds piled on top of each other, huge and opalescent.

"Looks like rain," their mother said. "I hope we sleep through it."

After they had finished eating, their mother nodded toward the pitchfork standing in the corner of the verandah.

"One of you girls should return the fork to Races," she said.

"It's Madge's turn," Ardith said. "I went and got it *and* the milk."

"*I* went for the seaweed," Madge said. "Besides, Mum said *you girls.*"

Although she was trying to gain advantage from it now, *you girls* always made Madge feel angry and dissatisfied. She was disappointed that their mother couldn't take the trouble to clearly separate them into Madge and Ardith, that she lumped them together to smooth out differences.

"You were late," Ardith said. "It doesn't count."

"That's enough," their mother said sharply. "It's clear you're the one to do it, Madge."

Madge eased her thigh from the lawn chair, which had stuck to her skin, raising long, red welts.

"And make her do the dishes," Ardith said. "I did them two nights in a row."

"You wash and Madge can dry."

Ardith got up and stomped inside. The porch boards bounced beneath her weight.

"She gets away with murder around here!" she said. Their mother looked at Madge.

"You'd better take it over now, before there's any more fuss."

This was said wearily, placatingly. Madge knew that her mother was also saying *Co-operate, you know I'm not feeling well,* but she felt her mother's avoidance more strongly. Her mother's avoidance was the reason her father had given her the hairbrush last week, though it was her mother who had decided she should have it. *Fuck* was the word she'd been spanked for. *Your mother and father fuck.* That was what Francis Race had said when he was showing her the black bull. He had leaned over the pole fence and said: "The bull fucks the cows. That's how they get calves." Madge came home and told Ardith; it wasn't often she got such information first, information that was a straight forward recital of facts. Ardith told their mother.

Madge picked up the pitchfork.

She couldn't afford to hold out against Ardith. Besides, it wasn't her inclination. Her inclination was to drift like a seal with the incoming tide.

The old boat that had once belonged to Francis Race's grandfather in the days when he had been a fisherman was on the other side of the road behind the hay barn. Madge had to stand on an upturned apple box to climb inside. There was the smell of oil and stagnant water. She stood on the warped decking and looked between the broken boards at the pool of murky water below. There were grey rings of gasoline on top, yellow scum around the edges. In front of her was the cabin. It was dark and sinister-looking, with a gaping hole where the engine had been taken out. The sides of the boat came up to her chest. To Madge all this was foreign territory. She had never been in anything larger than a rowboat. What prevented her from bolting over the side was the simple fact that she had been *asked* to come aboard. That she could have huffed off like Ardith and still have had the satisfaction of being asked didn't occur to Madge. She wanted to bask in the warmth of being well-favoured, chosen, singled out.

Francis pointed to another apple box in the bow of the boat.

"You take the lookout," he said. "I'll steer."

He went into the cabin where a bicycle wheel was tied to a wooden sawhorse. He straddled the sawhorse and began turning the wheel. He made a revving noise and shouted, "Watch out for German subs!"

Madge looked through her curled-up fingers, across the dunes, scanning the shining sea.

"Where're we headed?" she asked.

"West Indies. For a load of rum."

Madge heard Ardith calling from the other side of the hay barn. She ducked down.

Ardith called again, closer this time; she had recrossed the road.

Madge crouched lower.

Francis stopped revving. He crept over the floorboards toward Madge.

"Madge?" Ardith's voice was querulous, timid. It was right there, at the corner of the barn.

Madge felt the heat rising from her cheeks, the coolness of Francis's bare arms against hers. She reached up and peeled off a large curl of black paint from the gunnel.

"Madge?"

The voice was back on the other side of the road, lingering.

Francis's mouth was against her ear.

"Lie down on the boards."

With the same stealth, the same urgency to hide and conceal from her sister, Madge stretched out, belly down, on the weathered boards.

"Not that way," Francis whispered. "On your back."

Madge rolled over.

Francis lay on top of her, his face close to hers. He had a faint barn smell.

"This is fucking," Francis said. He bobbed up and down. His face was flushed and serious.

"Madge!" Ardith was still on the road.

Francis propped himself on one elbow and fumbled inside his pants. He bobbed up and down again.

Madge felt something soft against her thigh, something pointed and tickling. She giggled.

Francis put his full weight on her.

The skin between her halter top and her shorts pinched as it was squeezed between the boards.

"You're too heavy." She gave him a shove.

Francis rolled off and onto his belly. He lay there, flat against the boards, looking red-faced and cross.

Madge jumped out of the boat onto the swampy grass. She ran to the road.

Ardith was walking into their driveway.

"Ardith! Wait up!"

Her sister kept on walking. Ardith would go inside, bring her movie magazines out to the porch, and sit on the water-stained sofa, cutting and trimming photographs for her scrapbook. She would ignore Madge for the rest of the afternoon. Madge recognized this as a trade-off for not telling their mother she had been with Francis Race. This didn't mean Madge was convinced being with Francis was wrong. Saying *fuck* outright was wrong, but she hadn't said it, Francis was the one who'd said it. What had gone on in the boat was something else. She saw Francis's red face bobbing up and down, his unsheathed, naked *thing*—she and Ardith didn't have a name for it—tickling her thigh, as a game, a game that was harmless but required secrecy and stealth in order to work. It was like watching Miss Wigglesworth undress when she forgot to pull down the blind, or Uncle Dillon take a pee in the bushes behind Grandfather Burchell's toolshed. For Madge, anything to do with naked flesh was a revelation. She felt a need to hide, to store, to cherish such revelations. Even if she could have found the words, she wouldn't have handed these tingling satisfactions over to Ardith. Madge's collections were covert, unobtrusive, easily diminished.

That night Madge and Ardith lay on the creaky metal bed under a quilt. The quilt was made of floral circlets set in squares. The petals were hexagons sewn from dimity dresses, wide satin ribbons, flannelette nightgowns faded as old wallpaper, flowers within flowers stitched together by fine threads and insulated with cotton batting. Their mother had bought this quilt from Francis's grandmother, who had made it on a wood frame set up on Races' verandah. Across the living room, in the other bedroom, Madge heard her mother cough. Madge looked at Ardith sleeping beside her. Ardith was on her back, legs spread, mouth slightly open, breathing in and out with the curtains above the bed. She looked pink, defenceless, babyish. Through the open window Madge heard the rollers thundering on the beach. The tide was coming in. It began to rain, a light freckling on the rooftop. It was like picking out random notes on an old piano. Madge waited, holding back sleep, trying to measure the size of the drops, the different sounds they made on the roof. They were coming more heavily now, large polka dots bouncing off shingles faster, thicker, faster, mounting to a pounding crescendo. Madge reached up, closed the window, then burrowed deep into the lumpy mattress, giving herself over to the rhythm of rain and surf.

In the morning she was the first one up. She tiptoed through the cool, silent rooms. A moth was clinging to the screen door that slapped shut behind her, but she didn't look at it. She was looking down at her nightgown, which she was holding above her legs so it wouldn't touch the long wet grass growing on either side of the path.

The trees around the outhouse dripped, the drops glistening on wet spruce needles. Tatters of cloud drifted over the trees, remnants of the fog that had come in with the tide. Madge hitched her nightgown higher and sat down on the outhouse seat, looking through the open doorway. It was then she saw the green moths.

They were all over the cottage, the sides, the roof, even the stone chimney. She had never seen so many moths and never this huge, luxurious kind. She was used to flimsy brown moths that beat themselves to frenzied shreds against the outdoor light. Madge pulled down her nightgown and, forgetting to hold it above the grass, walked along the path to the back door, keeping her eyes on the moths, afraid they would disappear if she looked away. The moths seemed painted on, like the faces in the train windows. Madge looked at the moth on the screen door. It had long trailing wings that flowed down from its body like a ballgown, a soft mint colour such as a beautiful woman might wear, richly draped and caught below the waist with golden clasps. These clasps were two yellow moons, one on each wing. On its head were two feathery antennae, swaying gently like fans.

Madge walked through the tall wet grass to the front of the cottage, intending to go in the porch door, but the screening was covered with moths. They went up the front of the cottage and over the top like a net. There were hundreds of them. The wonder and enchantment of it, that this green velvety net had been cast over the cottage while she had been sleeping. She went around to the back door and opened it, carefully so the moth would stay on the screen.

Ardith woke up grumpy and dishevelled, but she agreed to look. They went out to the front porch and stared at the undersides of the moths. The bodies were furry and small, so small it seemed incredible they could support such large wings. Tiny legs clung to the holes in the screen. One of the moths moved slightly, putting its legs into other holes, dragging its wings upward.

Ardith shivered and rubbed her bare arms. Ardith did not like moths any better than butterflies. There was too much potential for sudden and unexpected movement.

"They're all over the cottage," Madge said. "I'll show you."

She had to hold the screen door wide to allow Ardith safe passage. Still, the moth did not budge.

Once she was outside in the grass, looking up at the roof, Ardith forgot herself.

"Look at them!" she said. "Where did they come from?"

There was a wedge of sunlight on the roof. It shone on the wings, making them a paler, translucent green. The moths in the shade were moist and velvety.

"There's so many of them, they must be migrating," Ardith said knowledgeably, "like monarchs do."

They stood side by side in the wet grass, speaking in whispers. There was something magical about this visitation. It wasn't something to be managed or tampered with. Its magic lay in fragility and calm.

The fog vanished.

The wedge of sunlight widened, encompassed the roof.

Down by the road a locust hummed.

One by one, the moths began to lift, singly, then in groups, detaching themselves from shingles, boards, bricks, screening, rising into the air, a loose, green, fluttering cloud. The cloud rose higher, lifted over the spruce trees. At this height it began to lengthen and thin, swooping and diving like a dragon kite. The tail of the kite swung over the clearing where the sisters stood. It dipped down suddenly, one moth coming within inches of Ardith's head. She screamed and covered her nose. The scream seemed to unbalance the moth. It wobbled lower, then flew on a slant, as if its wings were unevenly weighted. It stayed close to the ground, bobbing and jerking along the wooded path toward Races' house. Madge watched it disappear in the shadows of the trees.

Ardith was on the back step.

"Look! The one on the back door is still here!" she said. "Get it. Quick!"

Madge cupped her hand over the moth. Beneath her fingers she felt the feathery antennae tickling her palm. She felt the wings quiver. Goose pimples came up on her arms.

Ardith went around to the front porch and came back with the chloroform jar.

"There!" she said triumphantly after Madge had slid the moth into the jar.

They took the moth inside. Their mother was in the kitchen putting the kettle on to heat. She looked better today, stronger, more like the woman on the poster.

Ardith showed her the bottle.

"That looks like a luna moth. They have them down south," their mother said. "I wonder what it's doing up here?"

Madge told her about them being all over the roof.

"Maybe they came north with the Gulf Stream," their mother said, "then drifted in with the fog."

"Their wings were wet," Madge said.

"They probably stopped here to dry them off. The cottage must have been the first solid spot they came to that was high enough."

Madge believed this. The moths drifting north with the Gulf Stream, just happening to land on their cottage—the randomness and chance of this impressed her.

She saw their mother as having this same randomness. There were crevices inside her, mysterious corners where she tucked away surprising bits of information like this. You would think she was miles away, not even knowing you were there when, *presto!* she would plunk some bit of information down in front of you, matter-of-factly, as if there was nothing to it at all, and walk away.

Already she had gone into the bedroom to put on her slacks.

The moth wasn't labelled until the end of the summer when they had driven back to town. After the car was unpacked and everything put away, Ardith and Laddie looked through the *Encyclopaedia Britannica* for more information. This is what Ardith printed on a square of cardboard: *Luna Moth, a species of saturniid moth. Wing spread, four inches. Light green with tail-like projections on back wings. Occurs in southern parts of North America.*

While Ardith was doing this, Madge went outside and down the driveway to the back garden which had grown luxurious and opulent during her absence. Her father didn't like gardening and had let it go. Roses had become careless and wanton, strewing their petals onto the unclipped grass. Currant bushes dripped clusters of crimson berries. Hollyhocks towered overhead as if they had sprung from magical seeds. Weeds looked unfamiliar and alien now that they had grown enormous. Madge sat in the long, lush grass, took off her shoes, and shook out the sand, not from any sense of fastidiousness or duty, but to get used to the transformation. Sitting here in the garden, surrounded by outsized plants, she felt she had shrunk. Earlier this afternoon, when they had come through the front door bringing with them their clean beach smell, their stiff towels, their suitcases and boxes, Madge felt she had grown huge. While she had been gone, the house had closed in on itself. The rooms were narrower, the ceilings lower, the air darker. Her bedroom was grey and smelt of dead flies, of being shut up. Out here in the garden the air was green with yellow openings where the sun poked through. Madge put on her shoes and stood up so she would feel tall. She walked around the garden, carefully as she would in a jungle. Round and round she walked, thinking about these transformations, about the fact that while she had been somewhere else, this fantastic and amazing growth had taken place.

The Christmas Wreck

Frank Stockton

"Well, sir," said old Silas, as he gave a preliminary puff to the pipe he had just lighted, and so satisfied himself that the draught was all right, "the wind's a-comin', an' so's Christmas. But it's no use bein' in a hurry fur either of 'em, fur sometimes they come afore you want 'em, anyway."

Silas was sitting in the stern of a small sailing-boat which he owned, and in which he sometimes took the Sandport visitors out for a sail; and at other times applied to its more legitimate, but less profitable use, that of fishing. That afternoon he had taken young Mr. Nugent for a brief excursion on that portion of the Atlantic Ocean which sends its breakers up on the beach of Sandport. But he had found it difficult, nay, impossible just now, to bring him back, for the wind had gradually died away until there was not a breath of it left. Mr. Nugent, to whom nautical experiences were as new as the very nautical suit of blue flannel which he wore, rather liked the calm; it was such a relief to the monotony of rolling waves. He took out a cigar and lighted it, and then he remarked:

"I can easily imagine how a wind might come before you sailors might want it, but I don't see how Christmas could come too soon."

"It come wunst on me when things couldn't 'a' looked more onready fur it," said Silas.

"How was that?" asked Mr. Nugent, settling himself a little more comfortably on the hard thwart. "If it's a story, let's have it. This is a good time to spin a yarn."

"Very well," said old Silas. "I'll spin her."

The bare-legged boy, whose duty it was to stay forward and mind the jib, came aft as soon as he smelt a story, and took a nautical position which was duly studied by Mr. Nugent, on a bag of ballast in the bottom of the boat.

"It's nigh on to fifteen year ago," said Silas, "that I was on the bark, *Mary Auguster*, bound for Sydney, New South Wales, with a cargo of canned goods. We was somewhere about longitood a hundred an' seventy, latitood nothin', an' it was the twenty-second o' December, when we was ketched by a reg'lar typhoon which blew straight along, end on, fur a day an' a half. It blew away the storm sails; it blew away every yard, spar, shroud, an' every strand o' riggin', an' snapped the masts off, close to the deck; it blew away all the boats; it blew away the cook's caboose, an' everything else on deck; it blew off the hatches, an' sent 'em spinnin' in the air, about a mile to leeward; an' afore it got through, it washed away the cap'n an' all the crew 'cept me an' two others. These was Tom Simmons, the second mate, an' Andy Boyle, a chap from the Andirondack Mountins, who'd never been to sea afore. As he was a landsman he ought, by rights, to 'a' been swep' off by the wind an' water, consid'rin' that the cap'n an' sixteen good seamen had gone a'ready. But he had hands eleven inches long, an' that give him a grip which no typhoon could git the better of. Andy had let out that his father was a miller up there in York State, an' a story had got round among the crew that his gran'father an' great gran'father was millers too; an' the way the fam'ly got such big hands come from their habit of scoopin' up a extry quart or two of meal or flour for themselves when they was levelin' off their customers' measures. He was a good-natered feller, though, an' never got riled when I'd tell him to clap his flour-scoops onter a halyard.

"We was all soaked, an' washed, an' beat, an' battered. We held on some way or other till the wind blowed itself out, an' then we got on our legs an' began to look about us to see how things stood. The sea had washed into the open hatches till the vessel was more'n half full of water, an' that had sunk her so deep that she must 'a looked like a canal boat loaded with gravel. We hadn't had a thing to eat or drink durin' that whole blow, an' we was pretty ravenous. We found a keg of water which was all right, and a box of biscuit, which was what you might call soft tack, for they was soaked through and through with sea-water. We eat a lot of them so, fur we couldn't wait, an' the rest we spread on the deck to dry, fur the sun was now shinin' hot enough to bake bread. We couldn't go below much, fur there was a pretty good swell on the sea, and things was floatin' about so's to make it dangerous. But we fished out a piece of canvas, which we rigged up agin the stump of the mainmast so that we could have somethin' that we could sit down an' grumble under. What struck us all the hardest was that the bark was loaded with a whole cargo of jolly things to eat, which was just as good as ever they was, fur the water couldn't git through the tin cans in which they was all put up; an' here we was with nothin' to live on but them salted biscuit. There was no way of gittin' at any of the ship's stores, or any of the fancy prog, fur everythin' was stowed away tight under six or seven feet of water, an' pretty nigh all the room that was left between decks was filled up with extry spars, lumber boxes, an' other floatin' stuff. All was shiftin', an' bumpin', an' bangin' every time the vessel rolled.

"As I said afore, Tom was second mate, an' I was bo's'n. Says I to Tom, 'The thing we've got to do is to put up some kind of a spar with a rag on it for a distress flag, so that we'll lose no time bein' took off.' 'There's no use a-slavin' at anythin' like that,' says Tom, 'fur we've been blowed off the track of traders, an' the more we work the hungrier we'll git, an' the sooner will them biscuit be gone.'

"Now when I heerd Tom say this I sot still, and began to consider. Being second mate, Tom was, by rights, in command of this craft; but it was easy enough to see that if he commanded there'd never be nothin' for Andy an' me to do. All the grit he had in him he'd used up in holdin' on durin' that typhoon. What he wanted to do now was to make himself comfortable till the time come for him to go to Davy Jones's Locker; an' thinkin', most likely, that Davy couldn't make it any hotter fur him than it was on that deck, still in latitood nothin' at all, fur we'd been blowed along the line pretty nigh due west. So I calls to Andy, who was busy turnin' over the biscuits on the deck. 'Andy,' says I, when he had got under the canvas, 'we's goin' to have a 'lection fur skipper. Tom here is about played out. He's one candydate, an' I'm another. Now, who do you vote fur? An', mind yer eye, youngster, that you don't make no mistake.' 'I vote fur you,' says Andy. 'Carried unanermous!' says I. 'An' I want you to take notice that I'm cap'n of what's left of the *Mary Auguster*, an' you two has got to keep your minds on that, an' obey orders.' If Davy Jones was to do all that Tom Simmons said when he heard this, the old chap would be kept busier than he ever was yit. But I let him growl his growl out, known' he'd come round all right, fur there wasn't no help fur it, consid'rin' Andy an' me was two to his one. Pretty soon we all went to work, an' got up a spar from below which we rigged to the stump of the foremast, with Andy's shirt atop of it.

"Them sea-soaked, sun-dried biscuit was pretty mean prog, as you might think, but we eat so many of 'em that afternoon an' 'cordingly drank so much water that I was obliged to put us all on short rations the next day. 'This is the day before Christmas,' says Andy Boyle, 'an' to-night will be Christmas Eve, an' it's pretty tough fur us to be sittin' here with not even so much hard tack as we want, an' all the time thinkin' that the hold of this ship is packed full of the gayest kind of good things to eat.' 'Shut up about Christmas!' says Tom Simmons. 'Them two youngsters of mine, up in Bangor, is havin' their toes and noses pretty nigh froze, I 'spect, but they'll hang up their stockin's all the same to-night, never thinkin' that their dad's bein' cooked alive on an empty stomach.' 'Of course they wouldn't hang 'em up,' says I, 'if they knowed what a fix you was in, but they don't know it, an' what's the use of grum-blin' at 'em for bein' a little jolly?' 'Well,' says Andy, 'they couldn't be more jollier than I'd be if I could git at some of them fancy fixin's down in the hold. I worked well on to a week at 'Frisco puttin' in them boxes, an' the names of the things was on the outside of most of 'em, an' I tell you what it is, mates, it made my mouth water, even then, to read 'em, an' I wasn't hungry nuther, havin' plenty to eat three times a day. There was roast beef, an' roast mutton, an' duck, an' chicken, an' soup, an' peas, an' beans, an' termaters, an' plum-puddin', an' mince-pie—' 'Shut up with your mince-pie!' sung out Tom Simmons. 'Isn't it enough to have to gnaw on these salt chips, without hearin' about mince-pie?' 'An' more'n that,' says Andy, 'there was canned peaches, an' pears, an' plums, an' cherries.'

"Now these things did sound so cool an' good to me on that broilin' deck, that I couldn't stand it, an' I leans over to Andy, an' I says: 'Now look-a here, if you don't shut up talkin' about them things what's stowed below, an' what we can't git at, nohow, overboard you go!' 'That would make you short-handed.' says Andy, with a grin. 'Which is more'n you could say,' says I, 'if you'd chuck Tom an' me over'—alludin' to his eleven-inch grip. Andy didn't say no more then, but after a while he comes to me as I was lookin' round to see if anything was in sight, an' says he, 'I s'pose you ain't got nuthin' to say again my divin' into the hold just aft of the foremast, where there seems to be a bit of pretty clear water, an' see if I can't git up something?' 'You kin do it, if you like,' says I, 'but it's at your own risk. You can't take out no insurance at this office.' 'All right then,' says Andy, 'an' if I git stove in by floatin' boxes, you an' Tom'll have to eat the rest of them salt crackers.' 'Now, boy,' says I—an' he wasn't much more, bein' only nineteen year old—'you'd better keep out o' that hold. You'll just git yourself smashed. An' as to movin' any of them there heavy boxes, which must be swelled up as tight as if they was part of the ship, you might as well try to pull out one of the *Mary Auguster*'s ribs.' 'I'll try it,' says Andy, 'fur to-morrer is Christmas, an' if I kin help it I ain't goin' to be floatin' atop of a Christmas dinner without eatin' any on it.' I let him go, fur he was a good swimmer and diver, an' I did hope he might root out somethin' or other, fur Christmas is about the worst day in the year fur men to be starvin' on, and that's what we was a-comin' to.

"Well, fur about two hours Andy swum, an' dove, an' come up blubberin', an' dodged all sorts of floatin' an' pitchin' stuff, fur the swell was still on; but he couldn't even be so much as sartain that he'd found the canned vittles. To dive down through hatchways, an' among broken bulkheads, to hunt fur any partiklar kind o' boxes under seven feet of sea-water, ain't no easy job; an' though Andy says he got hold of the end of a box that felt to him like the big 'uns he'd noticed as havin' the meat pies in, he couldn't move it no more'n if it had been the stump of the foremast. If we could have pumped the water out of the hold we could have got at any part of the cargo we wanted, but as it was, we couldn't even reach the ship's stores, which, of course, must have been mostly spiled anyway; whereas the canned vittles was just as good as new. The pumps was all smashed, or stopped up, for we tried 'em, but if they hadn't a-been we three couldn't never have pumped out that ship on three biscuit a day, and only about two days' rations at that.

"So Andy he come up, so fagged out that it was as much as he could do to get his clothes on, though they wasn't much, an' then he stretched himself out under the canvas an' went to sleep, an' it wasn't long afore he was talking about roast turkey an' cranberry sass, an' punkin pie, an' sech stuff, most of which we knowed was under our feet that present minute. Tom Simmons he just b'iled over, an' sung out: 'Roll him out in the sun and let him cook! I can't stand no more of this!' But I wasn't goin' to have Andy treated no sech way as that, fur if it hadn't been fur Tom Simmons' wife an' young uns, Andy'd been worth two of him to anybody who was consid'rin' savin' life. But I give the boy a good punch in the ribs to stop his dreamin', fur I was as hungry as Tom was, and couldn't stand no nonsense about Christmas dinners.

"It was a little arter noon when Andy woke up, an' he went outside to stretch himself. In about a minute he give a yell that made Tom and me jump. 'A sail!' he hollered, 'a sail!' An' you may bet your life, young man, that 'twasn't more'n half a second before us two had scuffled out from under that canvas, an' was standin' by Andy. 'There she is!' he shouted, 'not a mile to win'ard.' I give one look, an' then I sings out: 'Tain't a sail! It's a flag of distress! Can't you see, you land-lubber, that that's the Stars and Stripes upside down?' 'Why, so it is,' said Andy, with a couple of reefs in the joyfulness of his voice. An' Tom, he began to growl as if somebody had cheated him out of half a year's wages.

"The flag that we saw was on the hull of a steamer that had been driftin' down on us while we was sittin' under our canvas. It was plain to see she'd been caught in the typhoon too, fur there wasn't a mast or a smoke stack on her; but her hull was high enough out of the water to catch what wind there was, while we was so low-sunk that we didn't make no way at all. There was people aboard, and they saw us, an' waved their hats an' arms, an' Andy an' me waved ours, but all we could do was to wait till they drifted nearer, fur we hadn't no boats to go to 'em if we'd 'a' wanted to.

"'I'd like to know what good that old hulk is to us,' said Tom Simmons. 'She can't take us off.' It did look to me somethin' like the blind leadin' the blind; but Andy sings out: 'We'd be better off aboard of her, fur she ain't waterlogged, an', more'n that, I don't s'pose her stores are all soaked up in salt water.' There was some sense in that, and when the steamer had got to within half a mile of us, we was glad to see a boat put out from her with three men in it. It was a queer boat, very low, an' flat, an' not like any ship's boat I ever see. But the two fellers at the oars pulled stiddy, an' pretty soon the boat was 'longside of us, an' the three men on our deck. One of 'em was the first mate of the other wreck, an' when he found out what was the matter with us, he spun his yarn, which was a longer one than ours. His vessel was the *Water Crescent*, nine hundred tons, from 'Frisco to Melbourne, and they had sailed about six weeks afore we did. They was about two weeks out when some of their machinery broke down, an' when they got it patched up it broke agin' worse than afore, so that they couldn't do nothin' with it. They kep' along under sail for about a month, makin' mighty poor headway till the typhoon struck 'em, an' that cleaned their decks off about as slick as it did ours, but their hatches wasn't blowed off, an' they didn't ship no water wuth mentionin', an' the crew havin' kep' below, none on 'em was lost. But now they was clean out of provisions and water, havin' been short when the break-down happened, fur they had sold all the stores they could spare to a French brig in distress that they overhauled when about a week out. When they sighted us they felt pretty sure they'd git some provisions out of us. But when I told the mate what a fix we was in his jaw dropped till his face was as long as one of Andy's hands. Howsomdever he said he'd send the boat back fur as many men as it could bring over, and see if they couldn't get up some of our stores. Even if they was soaked with salt water, they'd be better than nothin'. Part of the cargo of the *Water Crescent* was tools an' things fur some railway contractors out in Australier, an' the mate told the men to bring over some of them irons that might be used to fish out the stores. All their ship's boats had been blowed away, an' the one they had was a kind of shore boat for fresh water, that had been shipped as part of the cargo, an' stowed below. It couldn't stand no kind of a sea, but there wasn't nothin' but a swell on; an' when it came back it had the cap'n in it, an' five men, besides a lot of chains an' tools.

"Them fellers an' us worked pretty nigh the rest of the day, an' we got out a couple of bar'ls of water, which was all right, havin' been tight bunged; an' a lot of sea biscuit, all soaked an' sloppy, but we only got a half bar'l of meat, though three or four of the men stripped an' dove for more'n an hour. We cut up some of the meat, an' eat it raw, an' the cap'n sent some over to the other wreck, which had drifted past us to leeward, an' would have gone clean away from us if the cap'n hadn't had a line got out an' made us fast to it while we was workin' at the stores.

"That night the cap'n took us three, as well as the provisions we'd got out, on board his hull, where the 'commodations was consid'able better than they was on the half-sunk *Mary Auguster*. An' afore we turned in he took me aft, an' had a talk with me as commandin' off'cer of my vessel. 'That wreck o' yourn,' says he, 'has got a vallyble cargo in it, which isn't spiled by bein' under water. Now, if you could get that cargo into port it would put a lot of money in your pocket, fur the owners couldn't git out of payin' you fur takin' charge of it, an' havin' it brung in. Now I'll tell you what I'll do. I'll lie by you, an' I've got carpenters aboard that'll put your pumps in order, an' I'll set my men to work to pump out your vessel. An' then, when she's afloat all right, I'll go to work agin at my vessel, which I didn't s'pose there was any use o' doin'; but whilst I was huntin' round amongst our cargo to-day I found that some of the machinery we carried might be worked up so's to take the place of what is broke in our engin'. We've got a forge aboard an' I believe we can make these pieces of machinery fit, an' git goin' agin. Then I'll tow you into Sydney, an' we'll divide the salvage money. I won't git nothin' for savin' my vessel, coz that's my bizness; but you wasn't cap'n o' yourn, an' took charge of her a purpose to save her, which is another thing.'

"I wasn't at all sure that I didn't take charge of the *Mary Auguster* to save myself an' not the vessel, but I didn't mention that, an' asked the cap'n how he expected to live all this time. 'Oh, we kin git at your stores easy enough,' says he, 'when the water's pumped out.' 'They'll be mostly spiled,' says I. 'That don't matter,' says he, 'man'll eat anythin', when they can't git nothin' else.' An' with that he left me to think it over.

"I must say, young man, an' you kin b'lieve me if you know anythin' about sech things, that the idee of a pile of money was mighty temptin' to a feller like me, who had a girl at home ready to marry him, and who would like nothin' better'n to have a little house of his own, an' a little vessel of his own, an' give up the other side of the world altogether. But while I was goin' over all this in my mind, an' wonderin' if the cap'n ever could git us into port, along comes Andy Boyle, and sits down beside me. 'It drives me pretty nigh crazy,' says he, 'to think that to-morrer's Christmas, an' we've got to feed on that sloppy stuff we fished out of our stores, an' not much of it nuther, while there's all that roast turkey, an' plum-puddin', an' mince-pie, a-floatin' out there just before our eyes, an' we can't have none of it.' 'You hadn't oughter think so much about eatin', Andy!' says I, 'but if I was talkin' about them things I wouldn't leave out canned peaches. By George! Of a hot Christmas like this is goin' to be, I'd be the jolliest Jack on the ocean if I could git at that canned fruit.' 'Well, there's a way,' says Andy, 'that we might git some of 'em. A part of the cargo of this ship is stuff for blastin' rocks; catridges, 'lectric bat'ries, an' that sort of thing; an' there's a man aboard who's goin' out to take charge of 'em. I've been talkin' to this bat'ry man, an' I've made up my mind it'll be easy enough to lower a little catridge down among our cargo, an' blow out a part of it.' 'What ud be the good of it,' says I, 'blowed into chips?' 'It might smash some,' he said, 'but others would be only loosened, an' they'd float up to the top, where we could get 'em, 'specially them as was packed with pies, which must be pretty light.' 'Git out, Andy,' says I, 'with all that stuff!' An' he got out.

"But the idees he'd put into my head didn't git out, an' as I laid on my back on the deck, lookin' up at the stars, they sometimes seemed to put themselves into the shape of little houses, with a little woman cookin' at the kitchen fire, an' a little schooner layin' at anchor just off shore; an' then agin they'd hump themselves up till they looked like a lot of new tin cans with their tops off, an' all kinds of good things to eat inside, specially canned peaches—the big white kind—soft an' cool, each one split in half, with a holler in the middle filled with juice. By George, sir, the very thought of a tin can like that made me beat my heels agin the deck. I'd been mighty hungry, an' had eat a lot of salt pork, wet an' raw, an' now the very idee of it, even cooked, turned my stomach. I looked up to the stars agin, an' the little house an' the little schooner was clean gone, an' the whole sky was filled with nothin' but bright new tin cans.

"In the mornin', Andy, he come to me agin. 'Have you made up your mind,' says he, 'about gittin' some of them good things for Christmas dinner?' 'Confound you!' says I, 'you talk as if all we had to do was to go an' git 'em.' 'An' that's what I b'lieve we kin do,' says he, 'with the help of that bat'ry man.' 'Yes,' says I, 'an' blow a lot of the cargo into flinders, an' damage the *Mary Auguster* so's she couldn't never be took into port.' An' then I told him what the cap'n had said to me, an' what I was goin' to do with the money. 'A little catridge,' says Andy, 'would do all we want, an' wouldn't hurt the vessel nuther. Besides that, I don't b'lieve what this cap'n says about tinkerin' up his engin'. Tain't likely he'll ever git her runnin' agin, nor pump out the *Mary Auguster* nuther. If I was you I'd a durned sight ruther have a Christmas dinner in hand than a house an' wife in the bush.' 'I ain't thinkin' o' marryin' a girl in Australier,' says I. An' Andy he grinned, an' said I wouldn't marry nobody if I had to live on spiled vittles till I got her.

"A little after that I went to the cap'n, an' I told him about Andy's idea, but he was down on it. 'It's your vessel, an' not mine,' says he, 'an' if you want to try to git a dinner out of her I'll not stand in your way. But it's my 'pinion you'll just damage the ship, an' do nothin'.' Howsomdever I talked to the bat'ry man about it, an' he thought it could be done, an' not hurt the ship nuther. The men was all in favor of it, for none of 'em had forgot it was Christmas day. But Tom Simmons, he was agin it strong, for he was thinkin' he'd git some of the money if we got the *Mary Auguster* into port. He was a selfish-minded man, was Tom, but it was his nater, an' I s'pose he couldn't help it.

"Well, it wasn't long before I began to feel pretty empty, an' mean, an' if I'd a wanted any of the prog we got out the day afore, I couldn't have found much, for the men had eat it up nearly all in the night. An' so, I just made up my mind without any more foolin', an' me, and Andy Boyle, an' the bat'ry man, with some catridges an' a coil of wire, got into the little shore boat, and pulled over to the *Mary Auguster.* There we lowered a small catridge down the main hatch-way, an' let it rest down among the cargo. Then we rowed back to the steamer, uncoilin' the wire as we went. The bat'ry man clumb up on deck, an' fixed his wire to a 'lectric machine, which he'd got all ready afore we started. Andy and me didn't git out of the boat; we had too much sense for that, with all them hungry fellers waitin' to jump in her; but we just pushed a little off, an' sot waitin', with our mouths a waterin', for him to touch her off. He seemed to be a long time about it, but at last he did it, an' that instant there was a bang on board the *Mary Auguster* that made my heart jump. Andy an' me pulled fur her like mad, the others a-hollerin' after us, an' we was on deck in no time. The deck was all covered with the water that had been throwed up; but I tell you, sir, that we poked an' fished about, an' Andy stripped an' went down, an' swum all round, an' we couldn't find one floatin' box of canned goods. There was a lot of splinters, but where they come from we didn't know. By this time my dander was up, an' I just pitched around savage. That little catridge wasn't no good, an' I didn't intend to stand any more foolin'. We just rowed back to the other wreck, an' I called to the bat'ry man to come down, an' bring some bigger catridges with him, fur if we was goin' to do anythin' we might as well do it right. So he got down with a package of bigger ones, an' jumped into the boat. The cap'n he called out to us to be keerful, an' Tom Simmons leaned over the rail, an' swored, but I didn't pay no 'tension to nuther of 'em, an' we pulled away.

"When I got aboard the *Mary Auguster* I says to the bat'ry man: 'We don't want no nonsense this time, an' I want you to put in enough catridges to heave up somethin' that'll do fur a Christmas dinner. I don't know how the cargo is stored, but you kin put one big catridge 'midship, another for'ard, an' another aft, an' one or nuther of 'em oughter fetch up somethin'.' Well, we got the three catridges into place. They was a good deal bigger than the one we first used, an' we j'ined 'em all to one wire, an' then we rowed back, carryin' the long wire with us. When we reached the steamer, me an' Andy was a goin' to stay in the boat as we did afore, but the cap'n sung out that he wouldn't allow the bat'ry to be touched off till we come aboard. 'Ther's got to be fair play,' says he. 'It's your vittles, but it's my side that's doin' the work. After we've blasted her this time you two can go in the boat, an' see what there is to get hold of, but two of my men must go along.' So me an' Andy had to go on deck, an' two big fellers was detailed to go with us in the little boat when the time come; an' then the bat'ry man, he teched her off.

"Well, sir, the pop that followed that tech was somethin' to remember. It shuck the water, it shuck the air, an' it shuck the hull we was on. A reg'lar cloud of smoke, an' flyin' bits of things rose up out of the *Mary Auguster*. An' when that smoke cleared away, an' the water was all bilin' with the splash of various sized hunks that come rainin' down from the sky, what was left of the *Mary Auguster* was sprinkled over the sea like a wooden carpet for water birds to walk on.

"Some of the men sung out one thing, an' some another, an' I could hear Tom Simmons swear, but Andy an' me said never a word, but scuttled down into the boat, follered close by the two men who was to go with us. Then we rowed like devils for the lot of stuff that was bobbin' about on the water, out where the *Mary Auguster* had been. In we went, among the floatin' spars and ship's timbers, I keepin' the things off with an oar, the two men rowin', an' Andy in the bow.

"Suddenly Andy give a yell, an' then he reached himself for'ard with sech a bounce that I thought he'd go overboard. But up he come in a minnit, his two 'leven-inch hands gripped round a box. He sot down in the bottom of the boat with the box on his lap, an' his eyes screwed on some letters that was stamped on one end. 'Pidjin pies!' he sings out. 'Tain't turkeys, nor 'tain't cranberries. But, by the Lord Harry, it's Christmas pies all the same!' After that Andy didn't do no more work but sot holdin' that box as if it had been his fust baby. But we kep' pushin' on to see what else there was. It's my 'pinion that the biggest part of that bark's cargo was blown into mince meat, an' the most of the rest of it was so heavy that it sunk. But it wasn't all busted up, an' it didn't all sink. There was a big piece of wreck with a lot of boxes stove into the timbers, and some of these had in 'em beef ready biled an' packed into cans, an' there was other kinds of meat, an' dif'rent sorts of vegetables, an' one box of turtle soup. I look at every one of 'em as we took 'em in, an' when we got the little boat pretty well loaded I wanted to still keep on searchin', but the men, they said that shore boat ud sink if we took in any more cargo, an' so we put back, I feelin' glummer'n I oughter felt, fur I had begun to be afeared that canned fruit, such as peaches, was heavy, an' li'ble to sink.

"As soon as we had got our boxes aboard, four fresh men put out in the boat, an' after awhile they come back with another load; an' I was mighty keerful to read the names on all the boxes. Some was meat pies, an' some was salmon, an' some was potted herrin's an' some was lobsters. But nary a thing could I see that ever had growed on a tree.

"Well, sir, there was three loads brought in, altogether, an' the Christmas dinner we had on the for'ard deck of that steamer's hull was about the jolliest one that was ever seen of a hot day aboard of a wreck in the Pacific Ocean. The cap'n kept good order, an' when all was ready the tops was jerked off the boxes, and each man grabbed a can an' opened it with his knife. When he had cleaned it out, he tuk another without doin' much questionin' as to the bill of fare. Whether anybody got pidjin pie 'cept Andy, I can't say, but the way we piled in Delmoniker prog would 'a' made people open their eyes as was eatin' their Christmas dinners on shore that day. Some of the things would 'a' been better, cooked a little more, or het up, but we was too fearful hungry to wait for that, an' they was tip-top as they was.

"The cap'n went out afterwards, an' towed in a couple of bar'ls of flour that was only part soaked through, an' he got some other plain prog that would do fur futur use; but none of us give our minds to stuff like this arter the glorious Christmas dinner that we'd quarried out of the *Mary Auguster*. Every man that wasn't on duty went below, and turned in for a snooze. All 'cept me, an' I didn't feel just altogether satisfied. To be sure I'd had an A 1 dinner, an' though a little mixed, I'd never eat a jollier one on any Christmas that I kin look back at. But, fur all that, there was a hanker inside o' me. I hadn't got all I'd laid out to git, when we teched off the *Mary Auguster*. The day was blazin' hot, an'

77

a lot of the things I'd eat was pretty peppery. 'Now,' thinks I, 'if there had a-been just one can o' peaches sech as I see shinin' in the stars last night,' an' just then, as I was walkin' aft, all by myself, I seed lodged on the stump of the mizzenmast, a box with one corner druv down among the splinters. It was half split open, an' I could see the tin cans shinin' through the crack. I give one jump at it, an' wrenched the side off. On the top of the first can I seed was a picture of a big white peach with green leaves. That box had been blowed up so high that if it had come down anywhere 'cept among them splinters it would a smashed itself to flinders, or killed somebody. So fur as I know, it was the only thing that fell nigh us, an' by George, sir, I got it! Then we went aft, an' eat some more. 'Well,' says Andy, as we was a-eatin', 'how d'ye feel now about blowin' up your wife, an' your house, an' that little schooner you was goin' to own?'

"'Andy,' says I, 'this is the joyfulest Christmas I've had yit, an' if I was to live till twenty hundred I don't b'lieve I'd have no joyfuller, with things comin' in so pat, so don't you throw no shadders.'

"'Shadders,' says Andy, 'that ain't me. I leave that sort of thing fur Tom Simmons.'

"'Shadders is cool,' says I, 'an' I kin go to sleep under all he throws.'

"Well, sir," continued old Silas, putting his hand on the tiller and turning his face seaward, "if Tom Simmons had kept command of that wreck, we all would 'a' laid there an' waited an' waited till some of us was starved, an' the others got nothin' fur it, fur the cap'n never mended his engin', an' it was more'n a week afore we was took off, an' then it was by a sailin' vessel, which left the hull of the *Water Crescent* behind her, just as she would 'a' had to leave the *Mary Auguster* if that jolly old Christmas wreck had a-been there.

"An' now sir," said Silas, "d'ye see that stretch o' little ripples over yander, lookin' as if it was a lot o' herrin' turnin' over to dry their sides? Do you know what that is? That's the supper wind. That means coffee, an' hot cakes, an' a bit of br'iled fish, an' pertaters, an' p'raps—if the old woman feels in a partiklar good humor—some canned peaches, big white uns, cut in half, with a holler place in the middle filled with cool, sweet juice."

The Dual Personality of Slick Dick Nickerson

Frank Norris

I

O n a certain morning in the spring of the year, the three men who were known as the Three Black Crows called at the office of "The President of the Pacific and Oriental Flotation Company," situated in an obscure street near San Francisco's water-front. They were Strokher, the tall, blond, solemn, silent Englishman; Hardenberg, the American, dry of humour, shrewd, resourceful, who bargained like a Vermonter and sailed a schooner like a Gloucester cod-fisher; and in their company, as ever inseparable from the other two, came the little colonial, nicknamed, for occult reasons, "Ally Bazan," a small, wiry man, excitable, vociferous, who was without fear, without guile and without money.

When Hardenberg, who was always spokesman for the Three Crows, had sent in their names, they were admitted at once to the inner office of the "President." The President was an old man, bearded like a prophet, with a watery blue eye and a forehead wrinkled like an orang's. He spoke to the Three Crows in the manner of one speaking to friends he has not seen in some time.

"Well, Mr. Ryder," began Hardenberg. "We called around to see if you had anything fer us this morning. I don't mind telling you that we're at liberty jus' now. Anything doing?"

Ryder fingered his beard distressfully. "Very little, Joe; very little."

"Got any wrecks?"

"Not a wreck."

Hardenberg turned to a great map that hung on the wall by Ryder's desk. It was marked in places by red crosses, against which were written certain numbers and letters. Hardenberg put his finger on a small island south of the Marquesas group and demanded: "What might be H. 33, Mr. President?"

"Pearl Island," answered the President. "Davidson is on that job."

"Or H. 125?" Hardenberg indicated a point in the Gilbert group.

"Guano deposits. That's promised."

"Hallo! You're up in the Aleutians. I make out. 20 A.—what's that?"

"Old government telegraph wire—line abandoned—finest drawn-copper wire. I've had three boys at that for months."

"What's 301? This here, off the Mexican coast?"

The President, unable to remember, turned to his one clerk: "Hyers, what's 301? Isn't that Peterson?"

The clerk ran his finger down a column: "No, sir; 301 is the Whisky Ship."

"Ah! So it is. I remember. *You* remember, too, Joe. Little schooner, the *Tropic Bird*—sixty days out from Callao—five hundred cases of whisky aboard—sunk in squall. It was thirty years ago. Think of five hundred cases of thirty-year-old whisky! There's money in that if I can lay my hands on the schooner. Suppose you try that, you boys—on a twenty per cent. basis. Come now, what do you say?"

"Not for *five* per cent," declared Hardenberg. "How'd we raise her? How'd we know how deep she lies? Not for Joe. What's the matter with landing arms down here in Central America for Bocas and his gang?"

"I'm out o' that, Joe. Too much competition."

"What's doing here in Tahiti—No. 88? It ain't lettered."

Once more the President consulted his books.

"Ah!—88. Here we are. Cache o' illicit pearls. I had it looked up. Nothing in it."

"Say, Cap'n!"—Hardenberg's eye had traveled to the upper edge of the map—"whatever did you strike up here in Alaska? At Point Barrow, s'elp me Bob! It's 48 b."

The President stirred uneasily in his place. "Well, I ain't quite worked that scheme out, Joe. But I smell the deal. There's a Russian post along there some'eres. Where they catch sea-otters. And the skins o' sea-otters are selling this very day for seventy dollars at any port in China."

"I s'y," piped up Ally Bazan, "I knows a bit about that gyme. They's a bally kind o' Lum-tums among them Chinese as sports those syme skins on their bally clothes—as a mark o' rank, d'ye see."

"Have you figured at all on the proposition, Cap'n?" inquired Hardenberg.

"There's risk in it, Joe; big risk," declared the President nervously. "But I'd only ask fifteen per cent."

"You *have* worked out the scheme, then."

"Well—ah—y'see, there's the risk, and—ah—" Suddenly Ryder leaned forward, his watery blue eyes glinting: "Boys, it's a *jewel*. It's just your kind. I'd a-sent for you, to try on this very scheme, if you hadn't shown up. You kin have the *Bertha Millner*—I've a year's charter o' her from Wilbur—and I'll only ask you fifteen per cent of the net profits—*net*, mind you."

"I ain't buyin' no dead horse, Capt'n," returned Hardenberg, "but I'll say this: we pay no fifteen per cent."

"Banks and the Ruggles were daft to try it and give me twenty-five."

"An' where would Banks land the scheme? I know him. You put him on that German cipher-code job down Honolulu way, an' it cost you about a thousand before you could pull out. We'll give you seven an' a half."

"Ten," declared Ryder, "ten, Joe, at the very least. Why, how much do you suppose just the stores would cost me? And Point Barrow—why, Joe, that's right up in the Arctic. I got to run the risk o' you getting the *Bertha* smashed in the ice."

"What do *we* risk?" retorted Hardenberg; and it was the monosyllabic Strokher who gave the answer:

"Chokee, by Jove!"

"Ten is fair. It's ten or nothing," answered Hardenberg.

"Gross, then, Joe. Ten on the gross—or I give the job to the Ruggles and Banks."

"Who's your bloomin' agent?" put in Ally Bazan.

"Nickerson. I sent him with Peterson on that *Mary Archer* wreck scheme. An' you know what Peterson says of him—didn't give him no trouble at all. One o' my best men, boys."

"There have been," observed Strokher stolidly, "certain stories told about Nickerson. Not that *I* wish to seem suspicious, but I put it to you as man to man."

"Ay," exclaimed Ally Bazan. "He was fair nutty once, they tell me. Threw some kind o' bally fit an' come aout all skew-jee'd in his mind. Forgot his nyme an' all. I s'y, how abaout him, anyw'y?"

"Boys," said Ryder, "I'll tell you. Nickerson—yes, I know the yarns about him. It was this way—y'see, I ain't keeping anything from you, boys. Two years ago he was a Methody preacher in Santa Clara. Well, he was what they call a revivalist, and he was holding forth one blazin' hot day out in the sun when all to once he goes down, *flat,* an' don't come round for the better part o' two days. When he wakes up he's *another person;* he'd forgot his name, forgot his job, forgot the whole blamed shooting-match. *And he ain't never remembered them since.* The doctors have names for that kind o' thing. It seems it does happen now and again. Well, he turned to an' began sailoring first off—soon as the hospitals and medicos were done with him—an' him not having any friends as you might say, he was let go his own gait. He got to be third mate of some kind o' dough-dish down Mexico way; and then I got hold o' him an' took him into the Comp'ny. He's been with me ever since. He ain't got the faintest kind o' recollection o' his Methody days, an' believes he's always been a sailorman. Well, that's *his* business, ain't it? If he takes my orders an' walks chalk, what do I care about his Methody game? There, boys, is the origin, history and development of Slick Dick Nickerson. If you take up this sea-otter deal and go to Point Barrow, naturally Nick has got to go as owner's agent and representative of the Comp'ny. But I couldn't send a easier fellow to get along with. Honest, now,

I couldn't. Boys, you think over the proposition between now and tomorrow an' then come around and let me know."

And the upshot of the whole matter was that one month later the *Bertha Millner,* with Nickerson, Hardenberg, Strokher and Ally Bazan on board, cleared from San Francisco, bound—the papers were beautifully precise—for Seattle and Tacoma with a cargo of general merchandise.

As a matter of fact, the bulk of her cargo consisted of some odd hundreds of very fine lumps of rock—which as ballast is cheap by the ton—and some odd dozen cases of conspicuously labeled champagne.

The Pacific and Oriental Flotation Company made this champagne out of Rhine wine, effervescent salts, raisins, rock candy and alcohol. It was from the same stock of wine of which Ryder had sold some thousand cases to the Coreans the year before.

II

"Not that I care a curse," said Strokher, the Englishman. "But I put it to you squarely that this voyage lacks that certain indescribable charm."

The *Bertha Millner* was a fortnight out, and the four adventurers— or, rather, the three adventurers and Nickerson—were lame in every joint, red-eyed from lack of sleep, half-starved, wholly wet and unequivocally disgusted. They had had heavy weather from the day they bade farewell to the whistling buoy off San Francisco Bay until the moment when even patient, docile, taciturn Strokher had at last—in his own fashion—rebelled.

"Ain't I a dam' fool? Ain't I a proper lot? Gard strike me if I don't chuck fer fair after this. Wot'd I come to sea fer—an' this 'ere go is the worst I *ever* knew—a baoat no bigger'n a bally bath-tub, head seas, livin' gyles the clock 'round, wet food, wet clothes, wet bunks. Caold till, by cricky! I've lost the feel o' mee feet. An' wet for? For the bloomin' good chanst o' a slug in mee guts. That's wat for."

At little intervals the little vociferous colonial, Ally Bazan—he was red-haired and speckled-capered with rage, shaking his fists.

But Hardenberg only shifted his cigar to the other corner of his mouth. He knew Ally Bazan, and knew that the little fellow would have jeered at the offer of a first-cabin passage back to San Francisco in the swiftest, surest, steadiest passenger steamer that ever wore paint. So he remarked: "I ain't ever billed this promenade as a Coney Island picnic, I guess."

Nickerson—Slick Dick, the supercargo—was all that Hardenberg, who captained the schooner, could expect. He never interfered, never questioned; never protested in the name or interests of the Company when Hardenberg "hung on" in the bleak, bitter squalls till the *Bertha* was rail under and the sails hard as iron.

If it was true that he had once been a Methody revivalist no one, to quote Alla Bazan, "could a' smelled it off'n him." He was a black-bearded, scrawling six-footer, with a voice like a steam siren and a fist like a sledge. He carried two revolvers, spoke of the Russians at Point Barrow as the "Boomskys," and boasted if it came to *that* he'd engage to account for two of them, would shove their heads into their boot-legs and give them the running scrag, by God so he would!

Slowly, laboriously, beset in blinding fogs, swept with icy rains, buffeted and mauled and man-handled by the unending assaults of the sea, the *Bertha Millner* worked her way northward up that iron coast— till suddenly she entered an elysium.

Overnight she seemed to have run into it: it was a world of green, wooded islands, of smooth channels, of warm and steady winds, of cloudless skies. Coming on deck upon the morning of the *Bertha*'s first day in this new region, Ally Bazan gazed open-mouthed. Then: "I s'y!" he yelled. "Hey! By crickey! Look!" He slapped his thighs. "S'trewth! This is 'eavenly."

Strokher was smoking his pipe on the hatch combings. "Rather," he observed. "An' I put it to you—we've deserved it."

In the main, however, the northward flitting was uneventful. Every fifth day Nickerson got drunk—on the Company's Corean champagne. Now that the weather had sweetened, the Three Black Crows had less to do in the way of handling and nursing the schooner. Their plans when the "Boomskys" should be reached were rehearsed over and over again. Then came spells of card and checker playing, story-telling, or hours of silent inertia when, man fashion, they brooded over pipes in a patch of sun, somnolent, the mind empty of all thought.

But at length the air took on a keener tang; there was a bite to the breeze, the sun lost his savour and the light of him lengthened till Hardenberg could read off logarithms at ten in the evening. Great-coats and sweaters were had from the chests, and it was no man's work to reef when the wind came down from out the north.

Each day now the schooner was drawing nearer the Arctic Circle. At length snow fell, and two days later they saw their first iceberg.

Hardenberg worked out their position on the chart and bore to the eastward till he made out the Alaskan coast—a smudge on the horizon. For another week he kept this in sight, the schooner dodging the bergs that by now drove by in squadrons, and even bumping and butling through drift and slush ice.

Seals were plentiful, and Hardenberg and Strokher promptly revived the quarrel of their respective nations. Once even they slew a mammoth bull walrus—astray from some northern herd—and played poker for the tusks. Then suddenly they pulled themselves sharply together, and, as it were, stood "attention."

For more than a week the schooner, following the trend of the far-distant coast, had headed eastward, and now at length, looming out of the snow and out of the mist, a somber bulwark, black, vast, ominous, rose the scarps and crags of that which they came so far to see—Point Barrow.

Hardenberg rounded the point, ran in under the lee of the land and brought out the chart which Ryder had given him. Then he shortened sail and moved west again till Barrow was "hull down" behind him. To the north was the Arctic, treacherous, nursing hurricanes, ice-sheathed; but close aboard, not a quarter of a mile off his counter, stretched a gray and gloomy land, barren, bleak as a dead planet, inhospitable as the moon.

For three days they crawled along the edge keeping their glasses trained upon every bay, every inlet. Then at length, early one morning, Ally Bazan, who had been posted at the bows, came scrambling aft to Hardenberg at the wheel. He was gasping for breath in his excitement.

"Hi! There we are," he shouted. "O Lord! Oh, I s'y! Now we're in fer it. That's them! That's them! By the great jumpin' jimminy Christmas, that's them fer fair! Strike me blind for a bleedin' gutter-cat if it eyent. O Lord! S'y, I gotta to get drunk. S'y, what-all's the first jump in the bally game now?"

"Well, the first thing, little man," observed Hardenberg, "is for your mother's son to hang the monkey onto the safety-valve. Keep y'r steam and watch y'r uncle."

"Scrag the Boomskys," said Slick Dick encouragingly.

Strokher pulled the left end of his viking mustache with the fingers of his right hand.

"We must now talk," he said.

A last conference was held in the cabin, and the various parts of the comedy rehearsed. Also the three looked to their revolvers.

"Not that I expect a rupture of diplomatic relations," commented Strokher; "but if there's any shooting done, as between man and man, I choose to do it."

"All understood, then?" asked Hardenberg, looking from face to face. "There won't be no chance to ask questions once we set foot ashore."

The others nodded.

It was not difficult to get in with the seven Russian sea-otter fishermen at the post. Certain of them spoke a macerated English, and through these Hardenberg, Ally Bazan and Nickerson—Strokher remained on board to look after the schooner—told to the "Boomskys" a lamentable tale of the reported wreck of a vessel, described by Hardenberg, with laborious precision, as a steam whaler from San Francisco —the *Tiber* by name, bark-rigged, seven hundred tons burden, Captain Henry Ward Beecher, mate Mr. James Boss Tweed. They, the visitors, were the officers of the relief-ship on the lookout for castaways and survivors.

But in the course of these preliminaries it became necessary to restrain Nickerson—not yet wholly recovered from a recent incursion into the store of Corean champagne. It presented itself to his consideration as facetious to indulge (when speaking to the Russians) in strange and elaborate distortions of speech.

"And she sunk-avitch in a hundred fathom o' water-owski."

"—All on board-erewski."

"—hell of dam' bad storm-onavna."

And he persisted in the idiocy till Hardenberg found an excuse for taking him aside and cursing him into a realization of his position.

In the end—inevitably—the schooner's company were invited to dine at the post.

It was a strange affair—a strange scene. The coast, flat, gray, dreary beyond all power of expression, lonesome as the interstellar space, and quite as cold, and in all that limitless vastness of the World's Edge, two specks—the hut, its three windows streaming with light, and the tiny schooner rocking in the offing. Over all flared the pallid incandescence of the auroras.

The Company drank steadily, and Strokher, listening from the schooner's quarterdeck, heard the shouting and the songs faintly above the wash and lapping under the counter. Two hours had passed since the moment he guessed that the feast had been laid. A third went by. He grew uneasy. There was no cessation of the noise of carousing. He even fancied he heard pistol shots. Then after a long time the noise by degrees wore down; a long silence followed. The hut seemed deserted; nothing stirred; another hour went by.

Then at length Strokher saw a figure emerge from the door of the hut and come down to the shore. It was Hardenberg. Strokher saw him wave his arm slowly, now to the left, now to the right, and he took down the wig-wag as follows: "Stand—in—closer—we—have—the—skins."

III

During the course of the next few days Strokher heard the different versions of the affair in the hut over and over again till he knew its smallest details. He learned how the "Boomskys" fell upon Ryder's champagne like wolves upon a wounded buck, how they drank it from "enameled-ware" coffee-cups, from tin dippers, from the bottles themselves; how at last they even dispensed with the tedium of removing the corks and knocked off the heads against the table-ledge and drank from the splintered bottoms; how they quarreled over the lees and dregs, how

ever and always fresh supplies were forthcoming, and how at last Hardenberg, Ally Bazan and Slick Dick stood up from the table in the midst
of the seven inert bodies; how they ransacked the place for the priceless
furs; how they failed to locate them; how the conviction grew that this
was the wrong place after all, and how at length Hardenberg discovered
the trap-door that admitted to the cellar, where in the dim light of the
uplifted lanterns they saw, corded in tiny bales and packages, the costli-
est furs known to commerce.

Ally Bazan had sobbed in his excitement over that vision and did
not regain the power of articulate speech till the "loot" was safely stowed
in the 'tween-decks and Hardenberg had given order to come about.

"Now," he had observed dryly, "now, lads, it's Hongkong—or bust."

The tackle had fouled aloft and the jib hung slatting over the sprit
like a collapsed balloon.

"Cast off up there, Nick!" called Hardenberg from the wheel.

Nickerson swung himself into the rigging, crying out in a mincing
voice as, holding to a rope's end, he swung around to face the receding
hut: "By-bye-skevitch. We've had *such* a charming evening. *Do* hope-sky
we'll be able to come again-off." And as he spoke the lurch of the *Bertha*
twitched his grip from the rope. He fell some thirty feet to the deck, and
his head carromed against an iron cleat with a resounding crack.

"Here's luck," observed Hardenberg, twelve hours later, when Slick
Dick, sitting on the edge of his bunk, looked stolidly and with fishy eyes
from face to face. "We wasn't quite short-handed enough, it seems."

"Dotty for fair. Dotty for fair," exclaimed Ally Bazan; "clean off 'is
nut. I s'y, Dick-ol'-chap, wyke-up, naow. Buck up. Buck up. 'Ave a
drink."

But Nickerson could only nod his head and murmur: "A few more
—consequently—and a good light—" Then his voice died down to
unintelligible murmurs.

"We'll have to call at Juneau," decided Hardenberg two days later.
"I don't figure on navigating this 'ere bath-tub to no Hongkong what-
soever, with three hands. We gotta pick up a couple o' A.B.'s in Juneau,
if so be we can."

"How about the loot?" objected Strokher. "If one of those hands gets between decks he might smell—a sea-otter, now. I put it to you he might."

"My son," said Hardenberg, "I've handled A.B.'s before;" and that settled the question.

During the first part of the run down, Nickerson gloomed silently over the schooner, looking curiously about him, now at his comrades' faces, now at the tumbling gray-green seas, now—and this by the hour —at his own hands. He seemed perplexed, dazed, trying very hard to get his bearings. But by and by he appeared, little by little, to come to himself. One day he pointed to the rigging with an unsteady forefinger, then, laying the same finger doubtfully upon his lips, said to Strokher: "A ship?"

"Quite so, quite so, me boy."

"Yes," muttered Nickerson absently, "a ship—of course."

Hardenberg expected to make Juneau on a Thursday. Wednesday afternoon Slick Dick came to him. He seemed never more master of himself. "How did I come aboard?" he asked.

Hardenberg explained.

"What have we been doing?"

"Why, don't you remember?" continued Hardenberg. He outlined the voyage in detail. "Then you remember," he went on, "we got up there to Point Barrow and found where the Russian fellows had their post, where they caught sea-otters, and we went ashore and got 'em all full and lifted all the skins they had—"

" 'Lifted'? You mean *stole* them."

"Come here," said the other. Encouraged by Nickerson's apparent convalescence, Hardenberg decided that the concrete evidence of things done would prove effective. He led him down into the 'tween-decks. "See now," he said. "See this packing-case"—he pried up a board—"see these 'ere skins. Take one in y'r hand. Remember how we found 'em all in the cellar and hyked 'em out while the beggars slept?"

"Stole them? You say we got—that is *you* did—got somebody intoxicated and stole their property, and now you are on your way to dispose of it."

"Oh, well, if you want to put it thataway. Sure we did."

"I understand—Well—Let's go back on deck. I want to think this out."

The *Bertha Millner* crept into the harbour of Juneau in a fog, with ships' bells tolling on every side, let go her anchor at last in desperation and lay up to wait for the lifting. When this came the Three Crows looked at one another wide-eyed. They made out the drenched town and the dripping hills behind it. The quays, the custom house, the one hotel, and the few ships in the harbour. There were a couple of whalers from 'Frisco, a white, showily painted passenger boat from the same port, a Norwegian bark, and a freighter from Seattle grimy with coal-dust. These, however, the *Bertha's* company ignored. Another boat claimed all their attention. In the fog they had let go not a pistol-shot from her anchorage. She lay practically beside them. She was the United States revenue cutter *Bear*.

"But so long as they can't *smell* sea-otter skin," remarked Hardenberg, "I don't know that we're any the worse."

"All the syme," observed Ally Bazan, "I don't want to lose no bloomin' tyme a-pecking up aour bloomin' A.B.'s."

"I'll stay aboard and tend the baby," said Hardenberg with a wink. "You two move along ashore and get what you can—Scoovies for choice. Take Slick Dick with you. I reckon a change o' air might buck him up."

When the three had gone, Hardenberg, after writing up the painfully doctored log, set to work to finish a task on which the adventurers had been engaged in their leisure moments since leaving Point Barrow. This was the counting and sorting of the skins. The packing-case had been broken open, and the scanty but precious contents littered an improvised table in the hold. Pen in hand, Hardenberg counted and ciphered and counted again. He could not forbear a chuckle when the net result was reached. The lot of the skins—the pelt of the sea-otter is ridiculously small in proportion to its value—was no heavy load for the average man. But Hardenberg knew that once the "loot" was safely landed at the Hongkong pierhead the Three Crows would share between them close upon ten thousand dollars. Even—if they had luck, and could dispose of the skins singly or in small lots—that figure might be doubled.

"And I call it a neat turn," observed Hardenberg. He was aroused by the noise of hurried feet upon the deck, and there was that in their sound that brought him upright in a second, hand on hip. Then, after a second, he jumped out on deck to meet Ally Bazan and Strokher, who had just scrambled over the rail.

"Bust. B-u-s-t!" remarked the Englishman.

"'Ere's 'ell to pay," cried Ally Bazan in a hoarse whisper, glancing over at the revenue cutter.

"Where's Nickerson?" demanded Hardenberg.

"That's it," answered the colonial. "That's where it's 'ell. Listen naow. He goes ashore along o' us, quiet and peaceable like, never battin' a eye, we givin' him a bit o' jolly, y' know, to keep him chirked up as ye might s'y. But so soon as ever he sets foot on shore, abaout faice he gaoes, plumb into the Custom's orfice. I s'ys, 'Wot all naow, messmite? Come along aout o' that.' But he turns on me like a bloomin' babby an s'ys he: 'Hands orf, wretch!' Ay, them's just his words. Just like that, 'Hands orf, wretch!' And then he nips into the orfice an' marches fair up to the desk an' sy's like this—we heerd him, havin' followed on to the door—he s'ys, just like this:

"'Orfficer, I am a min'ster o' the gospel, o' the Methodis' denomin-eye-tion, an' I'm deteyined agin my will along o' a pirate ship which has robbed certain parties o' val-able goods. Which syme I'm pre-pared to attest afore a no'try publick, an' lodge informeye-tion o' crime. An',' s'ys he, 'I demand the protection o' the authorities an' arsk to be directed to the American consul.'

"S'y, we never wyted to hear no more, but hyked awye hot foot. S'y, wot all now. Oh, mee Gord! eyen't it a rum gao for fair? S'y, let's get aout o' here, Hardy, dear."

"Look there," said Hardenberg, jerking his head toward the cutter, "how far'd we get before the customs would 'a' passed the tip to *her* and she'd started to overhaul us? That's what they feed her for—to round up the likes o' us."

"We got to do something rather soon," put in Strokher. "Here comes the custom house dinghy now."

As a matter of fact, a boat was putting off from the dock. At her stern fluttered the custom house flag.

"Bitched—bitched for fair!" cried Ally Bazan.

"Quick, now!" exclaimed Hardenberg. "On the jump! Overboard with that loot!—or no. Steady! That won't do. There's that dam' cutter. They'd see it go. Here!—into the galley. There's a fire in the stove. Get a move on!"

"Wot!" wailed Ally Bazan. "Burn the little joker. Gord, I *can't*, Hardy, I *can't*. It's agin human nature."

"You can do time in San Quentin, then, for felony," retorted Strokher as he and Hardenberg dashed by trim, their arms full of the skins. "You can do time in San Quentin else. Make your choice. I put it to you as between man and man."

With set teeth, and ever and again glancing over the rail at the oncoming boat, the two fed their fortune to the fire. The pelts, partially cured and still fatty, blazed like crude oil, the hair crisping, the hides melting into rivulets of grease. For a minute the schooner reeked of the smell and a stifling smoke poured from the galley stack. Then the embers of the fire guttered and a long whiff of sea wind blew away the reek. A single skin, fallen in the scramble, still remained on the floor of the galley. Hardenberg snatched it up, tossed it into the flames and clapped the door to. "Now, let him squeal," he declared. "You fellows, when that boat gets here, let *me* talk; keep your mouths shut or, by God, we'll all wear stripes."

The Three Crows watched the boat's approach in a silence broken only once by a long whimper from Ally Bazan. "An' it was a-workin' out as lovely as Billy-oh," he said, "till that syme underbred costermonger's swipe remembered he was Methody—an' him who, only a few d'ys back, went raound styin' 'scrag the "Boomskys"!' A couple o' thousand pounds gone as quick as look at it. Oh, I eyn't never goin' to git over this."

The boat came up and the Three Crows were puzzled to note that no brass-buttoned personage sat in the stern-sheets, no harbour police glowered at them from the bow, no officer of the law fixed them with the eye of suspicion. The boat was manned only by a couple of freight-handlers in woolen Jerseys, upon the breasts of which were affixed the two letters, "C. H."

"Say," called one of the freight-handlers, "is this the *Bertha Mill-ner?*"

"Yes," answered Hardenberg, his voice at a growl. "An' what might you want with her, my friend?"

"Well, look here," said the other, "one of your hands came ashore mad as a coot and broke into the house of the American Consul, and resisted arrest and raised hell generally. The inspector says you got to send a provost guard or something ashore to take him off. There's been several mix-ups among ships' crews lately and the town—"

The tide drifted the boat out of hearing, and Hardenberg sat down on the capstan head, turning his back to his comrades. There was a long silence. Then he said:

"Boys, let's go home. I—I want to have a talk with President Ryder."

She met him first in August at an ice-cream social given by her friend Robert. She did not pay too much attention to him then, or no more than she was paying to the other guests—which is to say quite a lot, being who she was, a listener, an observer; but she didn't single him out for special attention. That would come later. In August she had only recently returned from hospital and was still feeling a bit strange, things alternately too fuzzy or almost unbearably clear, so she had been given a *chaise-longue* on the veranda and a glass of punch and was told to relax and enjoy herself.

There were three ice-cream-makers in action, everyone taking turns with cranking, including her daughter, who had never done this before. She was half asleep from the sunshine and punch and murmur of voices when she heard someone say, "Ah, here comes the man now; here comes the Emperor of Ice Cream himself, here's the expert." After some talk and laughter inside the house, where Robert's daughter was strumming a guitar and a group of her friends were softly singing, a smiling man with a round, benevolent face—the kind of face she used to imagine she saw on the man in the moon—came out onto the

Elevation

Audrey Thomas

veranda carrying a large covered basket. With a magician's flourish he pulled out Mason jars full of fruits and nuts and jewelled syrups, holding each one up to the light before placing it on the round table by the door. He said that the ferry had been late, and he and Robert embraced warmly. Nobody introduced him but he seemed to know most of the crowd already. (The next day she found out from Robert that one of the women there was his ex-wife, his second ex-wife to be exact, but she didn't remember the woman at all.)

She watched him through half-closed eyes, watched him being warm and friendly, never staying in one place very long, sitting down and then jumping up to take a turn with the ice-cream or volunteering to go up to the fish camp for more ice. At one point he spoke to her daughter, who was filling two bowls with blackberry ice-cream. "Save room for some of my fresh peach," he said to her, smiling. His voice, if not exactly southern, was certainly country. Her daughter explained that one bowl was for her mother and he looked around to see which woman that was. "Over there," her daughter said, "on the *chaise.*" He smiled again but didn't hurry over, only came and sat down just as she was thinking she'd had enough and better be getting home. He spoke to her briefly in that soft country accent and told her what a pretty daughter she had.

She thought to herself that it would be perfect if his name were Floyd or Earle and he ran a gas station somewhere in Oregon or Montana; but since he was one of Robert's friends it wouldn't be that simple. Robert's friends all seemed to live lives of carefully orchestrated poverty, although she felt that there was money behind them, perhaps trust funds from dead grandmothers, something like that. And education too. If you asked the right questions, it usually turned out that they'd been to Berkeley or Yale or Columbia. You wouldn't know it to look at them, of course; that was part of the game. They were weavers, makers of stained glass, painters or writers or musicians. That is, when asked, what they said they did; but they had done something else first, and for a long time, something which, if it were talked about at all, was shrugged off with a laugh, part of a past they were quite willing to forget. Robert sold wood-stoves and wore a T-shirt that said "Split wood, not atoms" on the back. He had jars of different flours and dried fruits on shelves in the entrance way. One was labelled NFM in his neat handwriting. When people asked, he said "Not for Munchies. Those are special, just for me." They were peyote buttons.

He also kept a few rust-coloured hens, who ranged freely in the yard during the daytime. Lately he had taken up EST.

("Humming-birds," Robert says to her on the phone the next day, when she calls to thank him for the party. "His name is Clayton and he studies humming-birds." "As a hobby?" she asks, thinking that would fit right in with Robert and his friends. Some ex-engineer with a private income who was now "into" humming-birds. Robert laughs, "Hardly. He's a zoologist. He's obsessed by them." "How interesting," she says. So is he one of you or not, she wants to say.)

She and Robert have not been close friends for very long, although she had heard his name often enough and seen him at the Friday market or on the ferries. Two summers earlier she had even spent an afternoon at the beach with a group of women and children, including Robert's wife (now ex-) and her daughter. Robert interested her, not romantically, but as an example of something. The American Boy— Man, perhaps—the Eternal Boy. It was something to do with his smile and a certain innocence. There had been several of these boy-men at the ice-cream social: charming, interesting to sit next to. But perhaps scary to spend your life with. Most of them were Americans, as Robert was, as she had been once, technically, but had never really felt herself to be. Lying in bed the night of the ice-cream social, she had thought to herself, "They're all so American," then wondered what on earth she had meant by that. And she realized that she hadn't been in love with an American since she was nineteen years old.

(That one had dropped her after a steamy evening in a car in Cambridge, Massachusetts, when he had whispered, "Oh God, I want to make love to you," and she had given the wrong answer, she had answered, "I think that would be lovely." Whereupon he had sat up and turned on the ignition and taken her straight back to her hotel. Nice girls didn't say things like that. He never really forgave her and they soon broke up.)

The Americans she had met here on the island and in Canada generally were charming, for the most part. They led admirable and enviable lives—kept goats or chickens, cooked on woodstoves (Robert was a superb cook, as was—she was to discover later—Clayton). They joined Amnesty International and supported Greenpeace; they often lived in hand-built houses and almost always had fruit trees and vegetable gardens. They had friendly rivalries to see who had the first peas up. Yet for some vague reason which, she admitted, might lie within herself, they made her uneasy. Robert's house was beautiful and orderly. He baked his own bread (even ground his own flour), planted Iceland poppies in among the rocks. And yet. And yet.

(One thing about Clayton—he made this clear early on—he didn't come from any well-to-do family like Robert's or some of those others. His father had been a railwayman and proud of it. Nothin' fancy about him, no sir! Just his fancy brain.)

The following winter, during the rather dreary months, when it was too wet to do more than look at seed catalogues and there wasn't much going on socially, she and Robert and some of their other friends decided to hold pot-luck suppers every other Saturday. This turned out to be a lot of fun, and in March she dreamed up the idea of a welcome-to-springtime party to which everyone would have to bring something green. Robert had a new girlfriend as well as a winter beard, so he said he was going to dye it green and have Susan shave it off at the party. "Sounds a little too much like Samson and Delilah to me," she said, "but do it, do it. We can all sit around and watch." Then she suggested he invite his friend Clayton to come over. "He can bring some pistachio ice-cream."

That night was the beginning of their friendship—if that's what it was. At one point Clayton, who was quite stoned when he arrived and spent a long time going from room to room in her small house, picking up objects, looking at what she had put up on the walls, told a story about his daughter, who lived with her mother somewhere in the States. She had been accidentally left in a coffin when her class was having a workshop on dying and death. She heard the class leave and then the teacher, and then there she was, all alone. He told how she didn't panic, knowing the teacher would remember and come back, just kept saying to herself, "Now then Em'ly, now then Em'ly," and taking deep breaths the way he'd taught her to do when she was in a tight situation and feel-in kinda scared. The teacher was surprised, when she rushed back in a panic, to find Emily sound asleep.

She looked at her own daughter, who was a little younger than the Emily in the story. "Bullshit," she mouthed, and her daughter grinned. (But still they both admired his dark and curly hair.)

Now it is May and he is over on the island to catch some humming-birds for his research project. She has seen him several times since March and they have exchanged telephone calls and letters. She knows that he has neat black notebooks going back years—each year is clearly labelled on the spine. They contain memories, dreams, reflections, thoughts on per-ception, on language, on decision-making. There are maps and drawings and the occasional letter from an old girlfriend. The notebooks are not personal, although they contain some intensely personal details. She real-izes with a shock that he expects to be famous. They are something he is sure will be read and admired by strangers at some point in the future. He talks about rates of accomplishment and degrees of involvement, dis-cusses optimal foraging, nectar availability, genetic longevity. She copies down some phrases that appeal to her, such as this remark by William Bateson: "The brain can receive only news of difference."

She begins to realize that if he is studying humming-birds, she is studying him. She is fascinated by people with obsessions, having one or two of her own. In one place he writes, "There is a whole world let loose in my head right now," and she smiles at his excitement.

The first time she really talks to him about his work, she asks him how much a humming-bird weighs. He forages in his pockets, then shakes his head and says, "Well, I guess this will have to do." He holds out her hand, palm up, and places a dime on it. She notices that it is an old Franklin D. Roosevelt dime. "Imagine that there are two of these," he says. Later Robert tells her that Clayton often does this—rummages in his pocket but can only come up with one dime instead of two. So what she feels that day is half the weight of a humming-bird.

His hands flutter when he talks—they soar and dip. He says things like, "Let's see if this idea gets off the ground." His big interest is decision-making—that's what he needs the birds for, that's why he is over here today with his two graduate students. Dinner will be early, so that they will be free to deal with the birds at dusk.

The feeders they have brought along are nasty plastic things with red plastic flowers arranged around nectar holes. The flowers look like strange, brightly lipsticked mouths. She is surprised that the birds are taken in, but it's the nectar they're after—their interest is not aesthetic. She imagines drinking from one of those things as the equivalent of eating a good picnic lunch off paper plates. And many people have feeders over here, some of them of equal ugliness. It amuses her when he says that you must never feed humming-birds honey; they get a disease like thrush, and the throat closes over. She wonders how many humming-birds died over here in the sixties, when nobody would've been caught dead using sugar.

She asks about the colour red. It seems to be important to vertebrates, he says. A male robin will go absolutely crazy at a large patch of red. He "sees" it as the breast of an enormous robin. She thinks of those heavily lipsticked mouths. She thinks of the red satin dresses of Hollywood sirens. She thinks of how when she was young she and her friends played a game where you counted a hundred red convertibles and then the next man you saw was the man you were going to marry.

The birds will be taken to the city and then out to the university, where they will participate in a study on decision-making. He has always before studied humming-birds in high meadows; he does not like the idea of capturing them, but it's necessary. "Consistent choice," he writes in his journal, "implies the ability to discriminate between alternatives and also suggests preference for some alternatives over others." The longer she knows him, the more she tries to come to some decisions of her own.

"Do you ever see them hesitate?" she asks.

"The birds? Why of course."

He has given her some of his papers to read. She finds it heavy going. There are many words she simply does not understand. She keeps a piece of paper by her right hand as she reads, just as she does when she's reading a book or a newspaper in French, and writes down all the words she doesn't know. And in her notebook she writes down things about him, the story of the dime, the way his hands flutter and fly, the way he started telling her about what keeps an airplane up and then suddenly said, "When I was flying to X to get my vasectomy undone . . ."

One day she comes across a phrase she particularly likes. "On the immediate level of events occurring in meadows." She is not sure what it means but she likes the sound of it. "On the immediate level of events occurring in meadows."

He loves Vancouver for its sidewalks and umbrellas. There were no sidewalks in the small town he came from and a real man would never carry an umbrella. They built the highway to Panama City right past his front door. He and his friends used to go up on a hill with handfuls of rocks and throw them at the earth-moving machines, pretending they were grenades, blowing up the whole damn works. Trucks rolled past the house all night.

"What is 'sessile'?" she asks.

"Rooted to one point," he says, "like a tree. Fastened down. Occupying a single point on a plane. We also occupy points on a plane, but the points we occupy can be different at different times. However, unless we use machines, the points are continuous; they exist on the same plane. That plane represents our freedom."

"We live in two dimensions," he says, "not like a fish or a bird. It's volume that makes the difference."

She reads him John Donne's poem where the soul of the beloved is the fixed foot of the compass around which the lover moves. And then, embarrassed, she closes the book and says, "I don't really like them, you know—humming-birds. They seem more like insects than birds. And they dive at you. And at each other. They seem very aggressive."

"Oh they are, they are," he cries, "they have to be! But what I'm seeing with the humming-birds is that they pack themselves into the available resource space and take whatever advantage they can."

"Sounds just like man," she says, and he smiles. His face really does "light up" when he smiles, she thinks. He really is the man in the moon.

"Rufous humming-birds," she writes in her notebook. "Calliope."

He won't sit still. He moves around her kitchen, checking it out, seeing what spices she has, whether she uses "real" coffee. Talking all the time. "In some language or other," he says, "the word for 'eat' changes depending on whether you are standing or sitting, indoors or out, et cetera. And some primitive languages are predominantly verbs."

"Well, *sit down* then," she wants to say, "and *shut up.*" When he gets really wound up, his small-town accent becomes more and more pronounced, as if saying to her, to the world, "I'm not really an intellectual, I'm still just a boy from Chico, California."

"This coffee's real good," he says.

Gradually his childhood takes shape for her, takes on flesh. She thinks she likes his mother best so far. His mother had a Whammo slingshot she kept on a nail by the kitchen door. And a little pile of pebbles on the windowsill. Whenever a dog came into her vegetable garden, she'd grab the slingshot and let fly. She was a terrific shot and could get the dog in the left hind leg every time. He had a slingshot, too, and went robin hunting. He'd line up the dead robins in the ditch between the back alley and the garden. Just study them, see how they were put together. Later, when he was a bit older, he had a .22 rifle and loaded it with a hollowpoint .22 shell. He shot a bird, a stellar jay, as it flew directly above him. "It rained guts and blood and bones all over me and something went click right then. Something about killing for the hell of it or even just for study. I have a hard time with that one, I surely do."

His mother goes to his father's grave, puts flowers on it and just stands there. He wonders what she is thinking, what remembering. He smiles. She can see that he's fond of his mother.

She decides to be motherly herself and make gingerbread with whipped cream. Her whole house smells of spices. Her daughter is staying overnight with friends, so at five o'clock she puts the cake in her basket, together with a bottle of wine, and walks the short distance to where he and his two students are staying. They are fixing the nets to long, thin poles. The nets are black and very fine, and for just a few minutes, at dusk, they will become invisible. They are like the nets her mother used to put over the blackcurrant bushes. (But those were to keep the birds away.)

He is very excited and gives her a hug. He is pleased to see that she has brought her notebook. "I've brought gingerbread and whipped cream and wine as well," she says.

"Good girl."

After all the nets and feeders are in place, up here above the sea and down below, across the road in the meadow, they sit down to eat. The stew is delicious, but the air is full of tension. He can hardly wait to get started. At dusk the three men hurry out, but she decides to sit a while by the Franklin stove.

Soon he is back, running, grabbing her hand, insisting she come and watch; so they run down the path in the gathering darkness, then stand, hand in hand in the meadow, hardly breathing, waiting. Soon she hears the strange buzzing whine but cannot see the bird.

"There's one," he whispers, then drops her hand, moves forward quickly to pluck it off the net.

He comes back to her, his hands together, cupped gently around the bird, holding it out to her as though he is about to offer her a drink of water. His hands are shaking. Or is the bird doing it to him, frantic—is it really the bird's heart beating?

"Do you want to hold it?" he whispers. "Hold out your hands."

She puts her hands behind her back. "No. I don't want to."

Still holding the humming-bird he leans over and kisses her.

"I don't like it either," he whispers. "I don't like this part of it at all."

The Divine Right of Kings

Bill Gaston

This time Marcie yelled for a Kleenex. She yelled again, adding to her order—Roger was to boil some water for her root tea. He could never get the tea's Japanesy name right so they both called it her root tea. She'd brought a big bag of it on vacation, as if she knew she'd be needing it. When anything went wrong with her body, like now, she drank it constantly.

As he would beer. Roger started her root water, then reached into the tiny fridge and removed a cold beer, which he replaced with a warm one from the box. There was room in there for just one, on its side, squishing the lettuce.

As he took a sip, part of him was alarmed that it was only ten in the morning. But it was a medicinal sip, like the hillgranny with her rheumatizz tonic. Medicinal because already, as he sipped, one of his five kids was banging in the screen door to announce boredom and demand the impossible. Medicinal, because the other four would follow with— here they were now, stomping in, they were upon him. Medicinal, because Marcie's back had chosen Prince Edward Island to collapse and keep her in bed, where she could neither enjoy her vacation nor let him enjoy his.

He would sip, no guzzling. Maybe one beer an hour, which, if buffered with occasional food, would dull the edges, the urges to violence, yet allow the watchful eye of a good parent. Little Jess these days toddled at a sprint and had grown a precocious death wish and a hound's nose for the poisonous, the electric. At the other end of the ladder, first-born Ben's sneer told Roger that his thirteen-year-old was on the verge of the sort of trouble that would involve police. The other three, the noisy, fleshy, middle part of the family, were in the transition zone between infantile stupidity and indiscriminate hatred.

Roger had sipped it down to empty.

"Sweetheart? Roger? Can—"

"YES."

Her root tea was boiling. He was slicing and handing out greasy coins of garlic sausage, the kids' eyes glazing over and their hands and faces slick with it already.

"Okay. *Outside* with that."

"What, honey?"

"Coming."

He caught little Jess by the shoulder, and while she struggled against his hold he licked his thumb and rubbed from her forehead what looked to be dried barbecue sauce. He considered tasting it to check, but didn't.

"Roger?"

"COM—"

With her cute naughty-game look, Jess had whirled and punched him in the throat.

A reprieve in the guise of an errand, Marcie asked him to go see how Ruby was doing. Letting the screen door squeal and bang behind him, sounding how he felt, Roger heard Marcie begin to read a story-book, could envision the clustered brood. Then shrieks of No! My leg! as someone sat on or wrestled close to her, sending fire up her back. Roger walked faster.

Doctors said take two to start, so Roger had guzzled a couple between trips with her root tea, snack, salt for her snack, not-that-magazine-sorry-the-other-one. As he crossed the lawn to Ruby's, his yeasty rise wasn't as joyful as it was disorienting, given that the sun hadn't yet clanged high noon.

Ruby, the owner of Seaside Farm and Resort, had all week been fretting and lying down a lot, hence Marcie's concern. Ruby's fret involved the imminent arrival of an English lord. Because any actual lord choosing this place was highly unlikely, and because Ruby was ninety-one, none of the other guests paid attention to her flutterings. But as far as Roger and Marcie could see, Ruby was never wrong. She was an energetic, happy, bright, utterly improbable old lady and so Roger figured there might in fact be a lord on his way. But what an image.

Seaside Farm and Resort, as they'd assessed it at first sight, was Hopefully Not Awful. By day three it was Actually Not Bad, mostly in light of it being After all the Cheapest Place on the Island. The tiny cabins were fifty years old and smelled their age, but it was a camp-smell, summery, a bygone sort of mildew. There was a sprawling lawn for children's hysterical, flapping games. A horse to seduce with apples, chickens to chase. Best of all, from a safety point of view, the sea was a five-minute walk, and the beach so gradual that it took another three minutes' hard wading to get deep enough to drown. Marcie and Roger had calculated over beer that, adding in the oxygen factor, they therefore had a twelve-minute grace period before their children suffered any brain damage. And this was if the kids set out to try to drown. So more like fifteen minutes. In any case enough time for two starved parents to crack off a semi-decent one. At this realization, Marcie deemed the place Great. Some levity before her back took her down.

But it wasn't a place a lord would choose. Lord no. No phone, TV, not even radio. Mismatched paint and old amber fly strips. Hot-plate. Fridgeen fit for salad makings and a single beer, not the massive roasts and puddings or whatever an English lord would demand for his table.

Roger hoped he and his family weren't part of some noble research on Commonwealth poverty; or some kind of self-betterment experiment, a butlerless camp-out. Or worse, an experiment in slumming. He pictured his swarming family, their dirty faces. Little Jess peeing wherever she happened to be. The father drinking beer at ten in the morning.

He stood at the door of Ruby's big farmhouse, burping quietly. Hoping he didn't smell too much of beer, he rapped and entered. Ruby was country casual. She badgered guests to "drop in, and I mean it." All were invited to "visit the henhouse back of the big house and get your breakfast eggs." Roger and Ben had in fact done this, Ben's sneer faltering in awe of the sign tacked over the chicken-shelves: "Wash your eggs, and leave one for me, Ruby." Ben looked a little scared by it.

Ruby was having a lie-down on the couch.

"Hi there, Ruby."

"Why, hello, Roger. Thanks, I'm just fine."

Hearing was her one sense scuffed by age.

"Any word on the lord?"

"Sorry?"

"ANY WORD ON THE LORD?"

"Oh, why yes, yes." Ruby smiled, a lifting and flowering of wrinkles, but her eyes stayed worried. "His secretary, a man—his secretary is a man!—called from London in England last night to say His Lordship was landing right in Charlottetown this morning. So he's already here." Ruby's smile had slowly been falling, and now it was gone. "The lord is on the island, Roger."

"Well, good. Great."

"Oh dear. I keep—" She stopped breathing.

"Ruby?"

"Why has he picked here? There has to be a mistake."

"He can come to the party tonight. We'll put on a Beatles tape. In his honour." Roger saw she hadn't got his little joke when she looked up at him in fresh panic.

"Oh my. A Beatles? Is that what he—? Do you have one? My grandson could ask around I suppose. A Beatles?"

By late afternoon various guests had done this and that until eventually a few tables were organized in the shade of the big linden tree. A tiny tape deck was stuck to the end of a thick yellow extension cord.

Lawn darts and a kite. A beer cooler, at present empty and ajar and holding a purring cat. Passing it by with ashtrays, staggering a little, Roger wondered if his Ben, given this chance, would lock that lid on that cat.

The party was for Ray 'n' Viv, of New Jersey. Exactly thirty years ago they had honeymooned at none other than Seaside Farm and Resort, which, Ray announced in yells, "HASN'T CHANGED A BIT. THANK CHRIST." Ray 'n' Viv were thin, and dressed in identical pastels, parodies of American crass. They were accompanied by their thirty-year-old son, Ray. "HERE WE ARE," Ray Sr. would announce, arm ambushing Jr.'s shoulders, "HERE WE ARE, RAY 'N' RAY." He was also given to pointing to his cabin and stating that little Ray here was likely the result of the honeymoon "there in that cottage, that one you're looking at, CAN YOU BELIEVE IT—RIGHT THROUGH THAT WINDOW." No one, least of all Ray Jr., wanted to picture anything through that window.

Ray Jr. showed public disgust at his father's vulgarity, and spoke to others softly, quickly, and like an intellectual. "Dad—Dad and Mum— *refuse* to experience any other of the island's aspects—any alternatives— there *are* remote spots, tranquil—oddities, not overrun—in any case, *I'm* going."

Dad, eavesdropping from across a lawn, yelled, "So experience. Go." EXPERIENCE. GO.

Viv was the most energetic in helping set up her own party, and Roger felt a taint in this. Though, true, the guests were beached-out and tired, and without Viv's help it might not have gotten going at all. But emerging from his cabin, Roger met the unnerving sight of Viv, fiftyish, and Ruby, almost twice that, wrestling an oil-drum barbecue across the grounds. Both women were covered with rust and soot by the time Roger arrived to help with the final five feet.

Rubber-legged, winded, he set his end down. He had just had an active five minutes with Marcie. Opening a beer in the kitchen, he'd answered another of her calls to find her lying there on the bed, eyeing him dreamily. On her chest was a paperback with a florid, romantic cover. All five children were out raiding the party's potato-chip bowls. Through nothing more verbal than eye contact, Marcie had Roger approach, take down his pants, position himself just so on the bed, and nip-her-neck, the way she loved, while she took him in hand. Roger wondered if this was a reward for his week of suffering service. Or had she just been surprised by a dirty book? Or was this Marcie proving to both of them that, even prone and half-dead, she could turn him into a quivering boy? A minute in, Roger didn't care what her motive was. A minute after that, after he'd exhaled like a dying man and Marcie had given him her naughty-game look and then painfully rolled over for a nap, Roger stood up and zipped up, retrieved his beer from the kitchen, went out to help wrestle the barbecue, and then witnessed the arrival by taxi of Lord Andrew, Lady Amelia, and their two noblechildren, Kate and Andrew.

He watched poor Ruby shudder at seeing them de-car, watched her suck it up and approach and greet them. She did well, old-fashioned graces coming through as she shook hands and dipped heads. He watched her slip money into the cabby's hand to get him to bring the luggage. It seemed they would be staying in the big house. Roger watched for any lordly reaction to the place, but their glancings around showed only stunned neutrality. They must be, in their language, frightfully tired.

They made their way to the house. The lord, past middle age, looked like a boy who'd been hopeless at soccer but had been forced to play anyway. He wore his belted pants up over his paunch, like an old nerd. The lady, her hair greasy and hanging, looked half his age. At the moment Roger thought this, she swung her head his way, finding Roger across twenty yards of grass. She met his eye. Hers flashed, and Roger saw that she was beautiful, slyly so. Even after what he'd just been through with Marcie, he felt a stirring. More than that, he saw that she was brilliant, and that he would never have secrets from her.

It turned out that Ray Jr. was a slavering anglophile. He knew all the royals' names, for instance, and was the only man Roger knew who'd watched The Wedding (Roger was unclear which) start to finish. When the lord appeared at eight to join the party, Ray Jr. was on him like mosquitoes, his probings angled and furtive and quick. Seeing his son's interest, Ray Sr. decided to be interested too, but his questions were for the benefit of others, and asked in an extra-rancid voice.

"SO. SO SIR ANDREW." The trace of a smirk, and a hint of quotes around the name. "YOU LIVE IN A CASTLE OR WHAT."

"Just 'Andrew', please." Sir Andrew smiled gently. He looked tentative on his feet, as if they were too tender for this rough land. "Hardly a castle. We have a flat in Chelsea, and we keep a place in Oxford, though—"

"CALL IT WHAT YOU WANT, IT WAS TRAGIC. IT WAS A TRAGEDY. IN MY OPINION SHE WAS A LOVELY PERSON."

"One assumes you mean the late Lady D—"

"A REAL HUMAN BEING. I mean, LAND MINES? COME ON."

"Indeed. It was with great—"

"ROUGH TIME FOR THE QUEEN, HUH?"

"Ah. Well, I suppose, yes. . . ." The lord's brows furrowed. Ray Jr. looked as though, had there been a weapon handy, his father would be dead.

"I mean, 'RANDY ANDY'? And, and—THAT FRECKLED ONE, ON THE DIETS? FREDDIE? FERGIE!"

"Yes. Indeed. Indeed."

"YOU EVER, YOU KNOW, TALK TO THE QUEEN ABOUT ALL THAT?" At this, Ray Sr. lurched across the gap between chairs to punch his son's shoulder. Ray Jr., who had decided to die himself, died.

"I am hardly"—the lord had a diplomat's perfect smile—"what could be termed a *confidant* of Her Majesty. At most, I have had occasion, during committee work for the House, to consult about certain, one might say largely 'bureaucratic' matters which—"

"HOUSE OF LORDS, right? Jesus, the HOUSE OF LORDS." Ray smiled at everyone and shook his head.

Since Ray Jr. was staring off, dead, and not up to it, Roger considered saying something to shut the bozo up, to show the lord they weren't all stupid and, more than that, to show him that Canadians weren't as stupid as Americans. Then it dawned on Roger that the man was simply asking the questions everyone else wanted to ask but was too scared and sophisticated to.

"Andrew?" God, Roger was asking the lord a question.

"Yes?"

"Care for a beer? I'm on a mission home, refill the cooler." He jerked a thumb back at his cabin.

"Ah. Yes, please. Excellent."

Roger nodded and spun around and away. He felt a surge of pride. He hadn't sounded either eager or repressed, and the lord had seemed like a decent guy relieved to have been treated like a decent guy.

Marcie was still asleep, so he rattled in the beer quietly. He filled a bag with one cold, eleven warm Red Dog. Recrossing the lawn he devised a theory dividing up the Canadians in their response to this lord. Being Canadian, all were afraid of him, but while one half avoided him under the guise of aloofness, the other half was so afraid that, under the guise of bravery, they actually spoke to him. In voices barely audible they conveyed the most inane sentiments. Bashing Red Dogs into the ice of the cooler, Roger, proudly a part of neither group, listened.

"Sir. Welcome. To PEI."

"Thank you."

"Is this, is this your first time to Canada? I, I doubt it, in that you no doubt travel, a lot, probably. . . . But, is it?"

"It's my first visit to this particular province."

"Ah! And, and. . . ."

"I like Prince Edward Island very much. Quite scenic."

"Isn't it though? It *is* a charming island."

"The brochures were modest."

Ruby was right, there must have been a mistake. How had this man with the same honorific as Jesus Christ ended up here? Roger approached him now with two bottles proffered. From the corner of his eye he saw that Lady Amelia had arrived under the linden tree, a child on either side of her.

"Andrew. I have a cold one and a warm one. Your call."

The lord's look was puzzled. Roger tried again.

"It's humble canuck beer but I thought you might like it like at home. Room temp."

"What a splendid label."

"Red Dog."

"I believe I'll opt for the chilled. Do as the natives, and all that."

Roger handed him the cold one. The warm one felt suddenly warmer in his hand. This one he would definitely sip. Was the wife, the Lady, smiling at him? Yes, but it was her eyes, just her eyes doing the smiling. She was a foxy one. Bit of a looker. "Looker," Jesus. A few minutes with these people and here he was talking Brit.

The lord was again stalled. Someone had handed him a mug, and he stood helplessly eyeing it and the unopened beer.

"Twist top," Roger said. He demonstrated on the wet mouth of his own half-empty bottle.

Lord Andrew regarded the Red Dog with suspicion, then with adventure. He took a firm grip, actually took a breath, and twisted. At the bottle's hissy burp he visibly startled, and announced, "Oh dear!"

He poured the beer proudly, glugging it in from straight over top until he had one inch of beer and seven of foam, and a soaked hand. To all this he said, "Good head." His eyes had the determined but vacant look of a man who makes no mistakes.

And here Roger witnessed a gesture he instantly recognized to be foreign to this country. What the lord did with his emptied bottle was hold it out to his side, tilted at an expectant angle, positioned for a servant's removal. Here the bottle hung, waiting, servants an ocean away. Perturbed at this negligence, Lord Andrew gave the bottle a little waggle. Roger stood spellbound. The waggle was bored and impatient and habitual, not unlike Cinderella's stepmother's bellwork. When the lord awoke to where he was, he had another little startle and then, all by himself, placed the bottle on the picnic table. Lord Ordinary. Lord of White Pudding. Roger wondered if the "divine right of kings" had ever and in any way applied to lords as well, a blue blood trickle-down. But he had decided to like Lord Andrew, above the cheap affection given novelties. The man was gentle, and meant well. An innocent. An old lamb. Odd how the worldly can be of a different world than the actual. And the party already seemed to be turning away from him, growing louder around him while not including him, a cage of crude noise. Hysterical with relief that her poor resort had survived royalty, Ruby bounced on the spot like an ancient girl. Ray Sr., fighting everyone's noise and winning, shouted the details of the seduction that had led to Jr.'s conception. He had hold of his wife's wrist, thrusting it at the lord to show the size of her wedding ring, which according to his yells had had lots to do with her carnal swoon.

Roger found himself approaching Lady Amelia. She sat at the end of a bench at the party's farthest edge. Her attendance looked dutiful, in that English way. At her flanks, her children sat in a virtual stupor of duty, bug-eyed with fatigue, head-thick with lag.

"Get you something to drink?" Of all the guests he'd been here longest and it was natural to play host. He had caught himself on the verge of saying, Can I be of service.

"A brandy or something? A scotch?" Her smile was almost too lovely.

"Have to ask Ruby if she has anything like that. I was offering, I guess, your basic beer, or beer." He nodded to the kids. "Or lemonade."

"Three lemonades would be perfect." She dipped down to whisper something about "lemon squash" to her children, who weren't at all moved by the news.

"I could ask Ruby about the brandy." Already into the mission, he looked up for the old lady.

"No, it's—"

Both of them were suddenly laughing, having located Ruby in the crowd, plunging her face into the chip bowl and taking one up on her tongue, possibly demonstrating to the children how a great blue heron stabs a fish. She pointed her face at the moon and gulped the chip down. Roger and Lady Amelia shared an "isn't life absurd and wonderful" look.

"No, I shouldn't. I'm just here for the moment. Lemon is my ticket tonight." She looked at him marvelling over what she had just said. "I'm Amelia by the way."

"Amelia." He felt his tongue's liquid dance. Amelia Bye the Waye. He shook her hand. A give of bones in flesh.

"And you're?"

" 'Lady Amelia'. . . ."

"No, that's me."

"No, I know. Sorry. Roger."

"Hello. Roger."

She said his name as he pivoted for the lemon squash, and though she said it nicely enough it sounded to his ears like the name of a wide-faced serf who lived in his own shit a mile's trudge from the manor. He found three plastic cups, one of them used (that would be for one of the kids), and tried not to spill the lemonade he poured, pausing to finger a dead bug from one (the other kid's). He was tired and drunk and knew he was in deep danger. He hadn't been so instantly afraid of a woman since high school, and that woman was lying on her bad back in a cabin fifty yards away.

With one of his middle-children whining and clamped to his leg, trying to go to sleep on it, Roger delivered the drinks. Amelia's eyes, thanking him under the fragrant linden tree, were almost unbearable. Her mouth offered a wry little smile that could have meant—everything. Shall we do it, slowly, now, on the beach? You have a child on your leg. Lemon squash, how nice, do you love me?

Looking at her, Roger felt on the verge of some sort of idiocy when, luckily, Ray Sr. roared up for introductions. He had a humiliated but excited Jr. by the arm.

As practised as Andrew, Amelia was gracious. When Ray Sr. learned that her young lad was also an Andrew—that is, a Jr.—he shouted at the stricken boy, "ANDREW TWO! ANDY THE SECOND! ANDY JUNIOR! ALL RIGHT!" and ran off to claim kinship with the lord.

"I have to—I want to apologize—for Dad." The Jr. Ray was on her. "He doesn't understand how to—he doesn't, he doesn't respect proper distance."

"Your father is an absolute blast, don't be silly."

"Mummy?" Young Andrew, about eight, looked near tears. "Mummy? May we go up now?"

"He doesn't—as your people might say—know his place."

"Oh nonsense. He's fine." Her lovely smile fixing all. Roger could see in her eyes her accurate assessment of Jr. Ray, that here was a thirty-year-old on a sulking vacation with his parents.

"Mummy?" Little Andrew's voice was Christopher Robin's. "You could stay, Mummy. I could go alone. I could read my new book."

"Ah—the young lord." Ray Jr. swivelled his hunger to the boy and stooped to reverently shake his hand. "How do you do—Sir."

"I am not a lord. My father is a lord."

"Ah—but you will be—one day."

"When my father dies." The boy's look turned severe, and his lower lip began to tremble.

"That's right!—and on that day—you will ascend—with all rights and privileges—to the House of—"

"Andrew, let's be off, your book is a good idea." Amelia stood, putting her shoulder into Ray Jr.'s chest. "I have a book too. Kate, come along, bring your squash."

With that, she made off with her children, leaving Roger and Ray Jr. staring after her.

"Long flight," Roger suggested.

"She's a—bitch." Ray's look was that of the newly hatched traitor.

At the porch, the lemon-light of the wrought-iron lamp suggesting mist, Amelia swung her face over her shoulder. "Thank you, Roger."

Ra-jah. Roger closed his eyes. Amelia could save him. Rajahhh. His own name sounded like the very breath of elegant sex. She could save him from all this. The middle-child had fallen asleep at his feet, arms limp around his ankle.

He gathered his brood to take home to bed. This took an hour and several beer and much shouting and violent wrestlings-to-the-grass. Son Ben had beer on his breath, little Jess candle wax in her hair, and one of the middle ones was wearing someone else's clothes. It had begun to rain.

Job done, veering past Marcie's bedroom door, Roger was beckoned. Marcie had a new book folded on her lap. Eyeing it, Roger stumbled. But all she had for him was a little speech. It was heavy-handed and clear. She knew his state.

"Roger. You don't remember this. We promised Ruby a clambake before we left. Tomorrow's our last day, so tomorrow we dig clams. Low tide is in the morning. If you can walk—"

"What y'mean fie can walk?"

"—if you can walk, go invite the lord and lady to dig with us. They'll love it. Don't argue."

"They're bloody asleep." Jesus, an English accent.

"Their light's on." Marcie pointed out her window at the big house. So from her cell she had been keeping tabs, and had her own version of things.

Before he knew what was what, knowing only that he must not think anything at all, he'd passed Ruby asleep on her couch and was knocking on their door, Her door. And good God here she was, framed in doorway light. Smiling yet professionally unsurprised, as if expecting something, something "raucous." He thought of the words, Naughty Victorian.

"Hello. 'Roger,' wasn't it?"

"Hi, jus' wanted to mention the party."

"The, the party?"

Pah-ty. Lovely. Speak some more. He waited. Victorians like her— their floor-length frills and scented rooms and chamber music and life one big happy euphemism—thought of absolutely nothing except hard sex. He didn't want to think ill of her, this Lady Amelia here, because she was friendly, and funny, and wise, all of those, but you couldn't help but look at her, and then at poor old Andrew, pale and paunchy and sixty, a gormless lord. She was probably good to him, but come on. There was no way you could look at her and see "Lady Amelia." She should be someone called Lisette, Lisette Barker, the dangerous one in your grade eleven class, Lisette who you lusted after in fear until one night, both of you drunk at a party, you fall into each other's arms, you can't believe your luck, but you're up to the task, Lord Jesus yes you are, your time is steamy and thick and your moans are broken only by laughter incredulous in the discovery that pleasure can be so pleasant. Lisette Barker. You are too tame for her fire and after a month she dumps you, and five months after that she's married to a criminal.

"Hello?" Lady Amelia was hunching to peer into Roger's stare. "Are we, are we done?"

"Clams."

"Excuse me?"

"Clam digging. Clams for the party, the one tomorrow night."

"Ah, another party. And clamming?"

"No, the clamming's during the day. To get clams for the party. Clambake. Old-fashioned, for Ruby. We thought maybe your kids, your children, or maybe even you yourself, might like to—" Roger came back into his brain, and smiled. "—to slog around in some mud with us, forage for molluscs."

"Lady Amelia" laughed beautifully. "I haven't had an invitation like that in ages. Lord Andrew and I and the children would be most delighted." May-ost de-lahted. God, she was mocking herself. He loved her. She wasn't a gold-digger. He was ashamed of himself. Desperately poor, she had had to marry the dull noble in order to pay off her parents' medical bills.

Despite the drawing-room acceptance her look was wryly confidential, sexually bittersweet. Her eyes flashed a metallic lustre, a kind of makeup you couldn't buy.

"Another party. My word." Pah-ty. She looked in no hurry to leave her door sill.

"It's all we do here. Canada."

He wanted to lean in, touch his cheek to hers and close his eyes. She could save him, and he could save her. Look at her, feverish with dreams of escape. This golden cage.

"Well, splendid. And the clamming."

"Good. Low tide's at, I'll check. Ruby has pails and shovels in the barn. The smaller one. The one behind the, you know, the bigger one. Barn."

"Fine. Are you all right to drive?"

"I'm not dr—I'm staying with you, I mean here. In one of the. . . ." He saw her smile. God, she was a wily one. Lady Sardonic. His stagger had been so small he'd hardly noticed it himself. "Got me."

"Gotcha. Good-night then, Roger." She smiled again, not yet turning into her room, royal euphemism all over her face. Roger looked past her at the bed in there, no lord in it. Was he asleep somewhere else? Did they have two rooms?

Recognizing certain death when he saw it, he turned away first. "Night. 'Amelia.' "

Even asleep he knew the day was too bright. He suffered a morning dream that Marcie was bravely out of bed and had a weird hat on, a bonnet. He awoke in the middle of a sincere moan, passing out again when the moan ran out of breath. His waking continued on and off like this for an hour, when several children were sent in to jump on him, shouting, *"Clams!"*

His only clean shirt, the one he'd avoided up till now, was very white and orange, brighter than the day, and hurt to wear. Marcie was in fact up, and she did have a ball cap on her head. From the side of his face Roger witnessed his children eating a breakfast of potato chips and butter. He heard them leave for the beach, dragging shovels on the road behind them, loud but too slow for sparks. He could smell the low tide that waited for him out there. He knew he would soon be in the middle of that smell, digging up the little meat pouches that created it.

Head in hands, elbows on table, he teetered over his coffee. A walk, the beach. Gravelly sucking shovel sounds under the hot sun. Why did he find himself thinking of Malcolm Lowry, the Brit who drank and wrote here and then went home to England to die? Wait—England, Canada, last night, the Lord. The Lady. Amelia.

He rose shaking, Lowry-like, feebly trusting that in action, in walking, his pain would fade to the background. He got outside, but the pain simply grew bigger than the day. Walking felt like flying, in that he might go down. He squinted past tourists and villagers, he suffered the mixed aroma of coconut oil and manure. He didn't know why, but it was important that he arrive before her, that he have at least a half pail of clams before she got there. He pictured himself bent over her—the clamless lord looking on—bent over her, showing her how to dig.

The simple vista of sea and sky—two blues meeting in the middle of his vision, bisecting it cleanly—did ease his pain. As did the breeze on his face. What hurt was the crowd out there on the flats. Scattered on the hard sand, hunting the area at their feet, intense even at this distance. They looked like Dali's version of farmers, addled lost naked farmers, working a dead, timeless, skin-bald field.

They were all here. All of them. Marcie. His children. Old Ruby. Ray 'n' Ray 'n' Viv. The lord, Lord Nothing, and his two Pooh kids. And Her. The Lady. Lady Much. She who knew him to his depths. She who would save him. Was she reading his thoughts even now? Soothing them? This breeze on his face was from her.

He arrived in their midst in the middle of a vague argument, and it looked as if its two main participants were, good God, Amelia and Marcie. They were digging side by side.

"It's *not* that they look frightful, though they do. It's that they'll go *bad*." Lady Amelia bent and tugged a fleshy bullet from the hole at her feet and plopped it into her half-full pail.

"Not in an hour or two," Marcie said. "Just keep them under a bit of water." Marcie finished a hole but, careful of her back, pointed down and little Jess ran in to grab the clam. She dropped it into her mom's pail, singing "Boop!" as it hit.

"Well *we* won't be eating them, I shouldn't think."

It was odd but her voice sounded different, pinched, no throaty lustre. Perhaps it was all this sunlight.

The genteel fight had to do with damaged clams. It seemed that Amelia had been leaving any shovel-broken clams by the wayside, and Marcie had been disturbed by the waste, the needless killing. At her request, son Ben was retracing their path with a bucket, picking them up. Roger could hear him moaning, "Bring out yer dead. Bring out yer dead."

He knew he was staring at her. Amazing how clothing could keep a body secret. Lady Amelia's wasn't a "bad" body. Of course it wasn't. But it was a weird body. And no doubt surprise made it seem weirder than it probably actually was. But her pelvis was a bulb, as wide front-to-back as it was hip-to-hip. A machined pearness. Her limbs were perfectly tubular, with no hint of muscle. The effect was that she looked like a big, unformed, unused baby. But what was this to-do about bodies anyway? Here at middle age, spirit and desire could do the trick.

Neither woman had seen him yet. They were discussing bivalve nervous systems, Amelia saying that compassion for clams was absurd, they had no feeling whatever, they had shells for godsake, and Marcie suggesting that since we didn't know for sure how it felt to be a clam, to be on the safe side we shouldn't unthinkingly torture them.

In fear of being made to comment, Roger turned away, but Marcie saw him.

"Speaking of nervous systems, it's ROGER—DODGER!"

Right at him, as loud as she could. Marcie could be such a teenager.

His hand involuntarily cupping the side of his head, he tried not to squint as he talked, as he whispered.

"You're up. How's the back?"

"I bored it to death." His wife laughed, reckless, fresh, indeed like a teenager. "I don't care anymore. I wanted to be here."

Jess ran in for a new clam when her mother pointed, and Roger thought he saw Marcie wince to move her arm. Marcie in her baseball cap. He liked her in that cap.

"Good morning, Roger." Ra-jah. "Have we recovered?"

"Hi. No." An awkward pause. "How are you and yours?"

"Just *mah*velous. Ruby gave us our breakfast, which was nice indeed, a *love*ly breakfast, just wonderful, and it's so very nice out today. *Lovely. Very* nice indeed."

"Well. Good."

She met his eye but her look was nothing but a nice-breakfast look. How was it that her baby-body made her words seem unwise as well? Her flesh looked pale, newly freed. Clammy. She still hadn't washed her hair—the European influence? Hair like strips of greased metal had a way of accentuating the wide babyishness of things.

"It *is* quite, I don't know, *wonder*ful here. When we return from the beach I really *do* think I'm going to write a postcard to my sister all about how nice Canada is. Because really it's all quite lovely indeed." She smiled off into this lovely near future, apparently believing in it.

Roger stood looking at her. Who was this woman?

"Lucky you don't feel worse," Marcie said to him, perhaps misreading his face. "Amelia was telling me Andrew went on a bit of a rampage last night. Got into some Canadian Club with Ray."

"Andrew *so* wanted to fetch you out of bed but I wouldn't let him," Amelia added.

"Ray has a headache." Marcie nodded at the silent figure leaning on his shovel, breathing hard for no apparent reason. Nearby, Ray Jr. strolled with his mother, hand in hand. "But His Lordship," Marcie nodded in another direction, "seems okay."

"Odd how he manages," said Amelia. "I don't know that he slept at all." She gazed off at him, looking blandly worried. "He does enjoy his vacations."

At water's edge, Lord Andrew was briskly striding through flat tongues of surf. Now he turned their way. He looked almost rakish in his straw hat, his sleeveless jean vest, his white cotton pants rolled to the knees. Quite alone, he was laughing, a booming laugh. Roger saw that he had a cell phone at his ear. As he neared them they could hear his voice, rich and eager.

"I do wish he'd do some clamming," said Lady Amelia, petulant but cowardly.

Roger removed his gaze from her flesh when he found himself thinking of wind-dried porridge. He looked out to sea. He considered lifting a shovel. The lord's exclamations joined the stew of his consciousness: ". . . get out of it, man! . . . that's fantastic! . . . I'm phoning Bob! Well yes, I am . . . I'm phoning Bob!"

Roger smelled the sun on Marcie's skin before he felt her touch. She leaned a cocked elbow on his shoulder, supporting herself on him, careful to keep her wet and gritty hands away. One leg touched his along its entire length.

"How's your head?" Her voice soft, penetrating his mess.

"I'll live." He took another breath, as if testing this theory. "Back's a bit better?"

"A bit. I'm fine."

"That's great." It did make him feel lighter, this news, even though she was leaning harder on him.

"If we go around stuck together like this," Marcie smiled lazily, "me the head, you the body, neither of us will be a burden on society."

"Right."

As if on cue, little Jess joined them, literally, by sitting on Roger's foot and wrapping her arms around both their legs.

"Walk!" she commanded.

The lord had been dialling and talking to an operator, and Roger caught the words *"North* Vancouver. Yes." He was twenty feet away, still walking toward them, his ear to the phone, grinning in mischief and anticipation. He didn't look like a man who hadn't slept.

"Bob? Bob! . . . Yes! . . . Actually, Prince Edward Island! . . . Bob, listen! . . . Gino astral projected! . . . No! . . . Yes! . . . Well that's what he said!"

Lord Andrew marched past them and kept going, acknowledging no one. They watched him, heads turning in unison as he passed.

"Well I know. . . . Well of course. . . . Well who isn't dreaming, you silly fucker! That's what it's about! . . . Right. Well of course. Ah, good show. Do call him, yes."

They watched him walk away. He stomped through a tide pool like a child doing a puddle. They could hear his laughter, but no longer his words.

"Andrew has this, he has this pack of *friends,"* Amelia was saying, a sudden frenzy of apology. "It's more like, more like a sort of *club.* Spread out all over. I don't much like them, I truly don't."

But Roger and Marcie had turned away from her, had been dragged away, actually, as another child joined the family sculpture, pulling on it until it began to move jerkily along the sand. A further child leapt aboard Roger's other leg, and then another clutched his waist. They made a grotesquely tall and impractical crab, spastically skittling, threatening to topple. They all screamed as they did fall at Ben's casual push, good son Ben who held his mother firm and safe while pushing the rest of them down. Ben and mother stood regarding the squirming pile, Ben looking down in dire judgement of his father.

"Think he'll fit in here?" Ben asked his mother, holding up the pail of wounded clams.

One of the middle ones joined the judgement, yelling, "Dog-pile on Daddy!"

The heap of children shifted its purpose and its mass, climbing up onto their father. They twisted and wrestled and punched and shrieked reptilian, and Ben joined in, and so did Marcie with a foot, working gritty toes beneath his waistband, and Roger was screaming louder than all of them, sand chafing his skin, little hands pummelling his pain away, beating him out of himself, saving him once again.

Winter Idyll

Thomas Raddall

Most of the inshore fishermen
tied up their boats at
Hagan's Wharf, which was
old and rotten and unfit for anything
else, and was convenient to the dock
of the cold storage company, where
they bought bait and gasoline, and
sold their catch. Mostly they were
bachelors working in pairs, owning a
motorboat on the halves; and they
lived on board, cooking meals over a
tiny stove, sleeping in narrow bunks.
When a boat fisherman married, his
wife usually persuaded him to sell his
share and go to sea in the schooners,
which fished on the Banks and made
a better living for their hands. It
meant long trips, of course, and
loneliness; but the wife put up with
that, or rejoiced in it, according to
her inclinations; and the schooner
crews despised the inshore men for
their poverty and their feckless way
of life—and envied their independence and nights in port.

So the motorboats lying six
abreast at Hagan's were a floating
Bachelors' Hall, a joy to Water Street
and a sin and sorrow to the clergy
and police. At night it looked snug
and romantic, with yellow lamplight
gleaming from the small cabin windows, and smoke curling up from
stubby tin chimneys into the electric
glare of the cold storage plant; and

you could hear an accordion, a fiddle, a mouth organ, men's voices in song, and often the laughter of girls. But the fishing boys paid for their fun with long hard days on the sea. They fished on the edge of soundings, twenty miles off the coast, and were out of their bunks before daylight, summer and winter, starting cold engines, chugging out to sea in the chill dark to set their trawls before daybreak, when the fish were hungriest.

Setting and hauling a mile of trawl was a morning's work. In the afternoon they came in and tossed their catch up to the wharf with long fish-forks, and got their credit slips at the office. Then they refueled their boats and bought frozen herring or mackerel for bait; and they overhauled their trawls, replacing worn gangings, resetting hundreds of hooks and touching up their points with a file, baiting them with chunks of frozen fish, and coiling all down very neatly in the tubs for the morrow. They never worked less than twelve hours a day, and seldom cleared more than two dollars a day each, but they would do nothing else.

Summer was a good time with long daylight and warm weather, and there were fat fees sometimes from sportsmen eager to angle for the big Nova Scotia tuna. But fall came quickly and then winter and the long bleak spring, a slow dragging of rough weather across the calendar that hardened the souls in their hard bodies. When winter gales blew they lay at Hagan's in the cramped and frowsty boats, with cabin slides shut against the cold, and the little stoves going; smoking, sleeping, cooking meals that were nearly always fish.

When they had money they tramped up to the movie theatre, where their rubber boots, spangled with fish scales, and their unwashed duffel trousers and mackinaws filled the gallery with the reek of their trade. Or they joined with schooner men and sailors and firemen from the steamers, and livened the nights of Water Street. But they were not roisterers all. There were men like the two McClures, lean gray bachelors who drank a tot of rum—no more—each Saturday night, and went to church of a Sunday. And there was big Peter Grant, of the *Albacore* who neither drank nor smoked, and would not look at a woman.

Peter lived frugally and was called "Fish-an'-'taters" by some, though not in his hearing, for he weighed well over two hundred and none of it was fat. He moved deliberately, as a big man learns to move in a small boat, and he talked deliberately in a mild unmusical voice. He did not talk much. His grey eyes were bright and intelligent, and his big clean face was a healthy reddish brown, like a ripe russet fresh from the tree. If he had a home he never mentioned it. He had come to the town at eighteen, a poor boy from the village around the cape, picking up a living along the waterfront.

At that time—it was just after the armistice of '18—the inshore fishermen used open boats, with a one-lung gasoline engine, a riding sail aft, and a makeshift whaleback of canvas at the bow for shelter. Peter had seen the advent of bigger boats, the Cape Island kind, with cabins and bunks and stoves, and powerful four and six-cylinder engines for fast runs in from the grounds. He had the born fisherman's instinct for finding fish in the sea, and he followed that instinct in weather that often kept the other men tied to the wharf. His *Albacore* was the best kept boat in the fleet, and he was pointed out on the waterfront as a phenomenon, a man who had made money at inshore fishing.

Peter was thirty when he met and fell in love with Clissie Telfair, who was nine. She lived in a grubby tenement on Water Street with other smaller Telfairs and hard hopeless Ma Telfair and drunken Pa Telfair, the stevedore. The Telfair kids haunted the wharves, begging dimes from the fishermen, cadging food at the steamer galleys, a litter of human rats.

Clissie came down Hagan's Wharf one summer afternoon to fish for sculpins. She was a frail thing, all blue eyes and soiled tow pigtails, with a pale face dusted with freckles by the waterfront sun.

Peter stood in his boat and flung up a plump young halibut fresh from the Outer Ground. "Take that home, kid."

"Ya! Fish!" sneered Clissie, making a nose at him and the fish. " 'At's all Pa ever brings home. Fish! Beh-beh-beh!"

"Then what's your cod-line for?"

"Fun," she said, and looked at him under her long lashes. "I hear tell you live on fish an' 'taters. Zat so? Whyn't you buy grub in cans? You got money."

"Who says so?"

She indicated the rest of the fleet with her chin.

"I see." He took a quarter dollar from his pocket and passed it up to her. "You buy somethin' in a can, then, kid, an' give me back that halibut. I won't see it wasted."

She took the coin gravely, and after a moment's hesitation picked up the split shining fish by the tail and dropped it down to him. From the top of the cabin house he watched her skipping up the wharf to the store of Newfie Nance, who sold cigarettes and sweets as a front for her main stock-in-trade.

After that she appeared frequently in the afternoon, dangling thin legs over the wharf edge, the cod line in her fingers, while Peter and old Haines his partner baited trawls for the next day's work. He gave her no more money, seeing where the first had gone, but kept a bag of candy in his locker and tossed a few pieces to her. She never asked for it, and never offered thanks for what she got. But she chased off the other urchins when they came around Peter's boat.

One day the town truant officer raided the waterfront and gathered Clissie and two other young Telfairs into the toils of school. Ma Telfair protested shrilly that her kids hadn't a rag to their backs nor shoes to their feet, and what did the School Board propose to do about that? The officer reported to the Women's Institute, and the Telfair kids were taken uptown in a car—their first experience in an automobile—and issued their first new clothes.

So Clissie went to school and opened her eyes upon another world. She became very quiet and studious, and the Institute ladies were fond of pointing her out as a sample of what could be done with the Water Street tribe.

When she left school at fifteen the Institute got her a job as housemaid somewhere amongst the plush homes towards Harbor Point. Each week she had one afternoon off, which she spent at home. On that day she never failed to come down the wharf just as Peter finished his trawls, picking her way carefully amongst the fish scraps and dockside litter in her new high-heeled shoes.

Peter boggled at tossing candy to the fine bird she had become, but on her birthday he sent up to the house where she worked a big box of chocolates. And one Christmas, big and brown and uncomfortable in a shiny suit of blue serge reach-me-downs, he escorted her to thirty-five cent seats in the Empire Theatre and later to the Rose Room for ice cream, and gave her ten dollars in an envelope.

"Get yourself somethin' for Christmas, Clissie—from me."

About that time old Haines sold Peter his share in the boat and went off to live with a daughter somewhere. The fleet wondered who Peter would take for his second hand. At thirty-eight he was set in his ways, and some of those ways were queer, like scrubbing out his cabin once a week, and taking a bucket-bath, stripped, every three or four days winter and summer. He made visitors spit in the stove and spare the floor, and was death on drinking and what he called "tom-catting around." When the partner came he turned out to be a half-brother, a shabby youngster with a glib tongue, a perpetual cigarette and some dubious experience as a hanger-on about a small country garage. The fleet marvelled, and bet on how long it would last.

When Calvin saw Clissie he uttered a piercing whistle and asked loudly, for Clissie's ears, "Who's the peach?" She was parlor-maid in a bank manager's household, and because the banker's wife had a petite figure and a passion for new raiment, Clissie inherited and wore rather well clothes that housemaids rarely possess. She was not pretty but her eyes were large and blue, and she had learned the art of curling her soft yellow hair with an electric iron in a bedroom. She was still slight of figure, but during the past three years her body had undergone a subtle and charming change. And the change was still going on. It must be, Peter thought, the good food she got at the banker's.

"Clissie," he mumbled, "this is my young brother Calvin."

Clissie stood on the wharf edge smiling down at them and showing a lot of taut chiffon stocking. Peter felt embarrassed, wondering if he should tell her she wasn't a little girl any more. But Calvin stared and admired.

Finally Calvin urged, "Come down, kid, an' be sociable." He put up a hand for her small grasp and she jumped to the cabin roof, her flimsy skirt ballooning. She sat on a locker in the cabin, prattling backstairs gossip of a harmless kind and preening her fine feathers for their admiration. The floor space was so narrow that Peter and Calvin on the locker opposite had to swing their knees to make room for hers.

It was the first time she had been invited to enter the cabin of the *Albacore* and she was delighted. She exclaimed over the dinky stove and the pot locker, and the way everything was fastened against the roll of the boat in a seaway; and she liked the hanging brass lamp, and the small rectangular windows set just above the level on the foredeck, and marvelled how big Peter got in and out through the cabin slide, so small it was.

"It's like living in a doll's house," she announced, as if she had ever seen a doll's house except in other people's houses.

From other housemaids she had learned to make free use of her mistress' toilet table. She rejected rouge, remembering Newfie Nance, and put nothing on her pale cheeks but a little powder to hide the freckles about her nose; but she lavished her lips with Mrs. Banker's lipstick, a bright scarlet stuff chosen to match that giddy woman's finger nails. In the pallid oval of her face the mouth was like the long red slash of a bait-knife. Peter looked on those lips and felt his own go dry. And the fragrance that hung in the cabin, a fragrance that was half Clissie and half her mistress' perfume, sent a queer hunger all through him. It was a new experience and he sat laughing woodenly, mumbling something now and then, while Calvin ran off with the conversation. Did she dance? Clissie must come with him to Froler's next Saturday night. Did she ever go to the movies?

Calvin took her to these and other entertainments, and on Sundays went for walks with her outside the town. Above his bunk he tacked a snapshot of himself and Clissie sitting on grass somewhere; their eyes were closed against the sunshine and he had pulled Clissie's head down to his shoulder. They were laughing.

Peter was stirred to words at the sight of it.

"Calvin, I've knowed Clissie a long time. Since she was a kid. She ain't like the others off Water Street. You know what I mean. Calvin, I couldn't stand to know that anybody was messin' around with Clissie."

"Aw!" The cigarette in Calvin's fingers made a thin blue arc in air.

"Take Clissie off your mind, Pete. She wasn't born yesterday. Clissie knows all the answers. They don't come any wiser than Clissie." He paused. Then, airily, "I got a notion to marry Clissie. Next spring, maybe. Maybe after New Year. I dunno."

"You dunno," echoed Peter.

He wondered how Calvin would support a wife. Money ran through his agile tobacco-stained fingers. He was fond of liquor amongst other things, and boasted of his prowess with the back-town girls, who were easy but not free.

The boat fleet watched, but Peter took it all resignedly.

"The son o' my mother," he said once.

The son of his mother was far from a total loss to Peter, however. He had a certain cunning with gasoline engines. And he was full of ideas. There was the matter of a windshield, for instance.

"A what?" Peter said.

"Well, a kind o' hood built right across the after end o' the cabin roof, to keep the wind an' spray off o' the feller at the wheel. All these boats got the wheel on the after side o' the house, an' there you stand, head an' shoulders above the level o' the roof, takin' the weather right in your face. You got to stand there, close to the engine hatch, so's you can get at the engine quick if you want. All right. But it never struck none o' you fellas to build a wind screen, with wooden side-pieces, say, an' a couple o' widths o' board overhead to keep off the rain."

"The others'd call us softies, Calvin."

"They'll imitate us quick enough, come winter."

"T'won't keep out rain with a follerin' wind."

"Pooh! Who minds a bit o' rain with the wind fair?"

Who indeed? He was glad to see Calvin taking such an interest in the boat. And they built the wind screen after Christmas, when a three-day gale kept the *Albacore* at moorings with the rest. It cost ten dollars in glass and putty and boards and paint, but its worth was proved when they put out for the grounds in the dark of a bitter January morning, with an easterly breeze whipping spray over the bow and the town thermometers showing ten below zero.

Peter steered, standing under the new hood, with one hand on the small brass steering wheel and the other clutching the mast to steady himself against the boat's pitch and roll. Four feet from his back the short rusty pipe of the exhaust stuck out of the engine hatch like a miniature funnel, trailing a reek of burnt gasoline aft. At five by the cabin clock they dropped anchor on the grounds, lit their flarepots— "old-fashioned," sniffed Calvin—and put off in the little yellow dory to set the trawls. The sea jostled them with a violence made worse for Calvin by the darkness; the hollows seemed black and ominous, and each crest was marked by a lacy glimmer that met the rising gunwale with a hiss and a slap, and flicked icy brine in their faces.

The oars and the sides of the dory were soon crusted with ice, and in the shimmer of false dawn their ice-spattered oilskins had a ghostly look. Their mittens were soon wet. They dipped their hands into the sea from time to time, to keep the wet wool from freezing hard.

Calvin sat in the stern, paying the coiled lines out of the tubs into the sea. The boat fleet had scattered along the grounds. Now and then on a heave of water they caught the far glimmer of a flare-pot, nothing more. The land lights were under the sea horizon to the west.

When they anchored their trawls in the first blanched light of day the *Albacore* looked like a small white chip in the distance, appearing and vanishing amongst the grey humps of the sea. No other boats were in sight. Eastward, hull down, a steamer daubed a black stripe across the face of the morning. It was cracking cold. A northeasterly breeze bit their cheeks and chapped their lips, already split and sore from other sea mornings.

Calvin's teeth were rattling when they got back to the motorboat. He had chosen to pay out the trawls because he hated the physical labor of rowing, but the after-man's job proved a cold one. Stiffly they clambered aboard. The steamer had gone. To the west, towards the invisible land, a white wreath lay along the horizon—vapor whipped off the sea's face by the stinging air. The fire had died in the stove. Peter lit wood and threw in some coal from the bucket. Calvin closed the cabin slide and went down on his knees beside the stove. He tore off his frozen mittens, two pairs, one inside the other, and they rattled on the floor like chunks of wood.

At eleven o'clock they put off in the dory and hauled the trawls, slinging cod and pollack off the hooks and into the bottom about their feet. The fish flapped wetly for a minute and then stiffened in the cold. The dripping trawl froze in a mass in the tubs as they coiled it down. It was a good haul. They pitched the catch into the *Albacore*'s hold with their fish-forks as the dory rose and fell alongside.

"Should go twenty, maybe twenty-three quintal," grunted Peter with satisfaction. They took the dory aboard and began cleaning the catch, Calvin splitting and Peter gutting. The big basket under the gutting-board spread fatly with the increasing weight of the dark cod livers, while a flock of gulls came up from nowhere and fought noisily for the refuse flying from Peter's busy left hand.

When that was done they were hungry. The sun and their bellies said it was well past dinner time. They got up the anchor and Calvin started the engine and steered for the land, while Peter prepared a dinner of cod steak and potatoes. The stove had two covers, one for the frying pan, one for the pot; an iron rail four inches high kept pot and pan from sliding off as the boat pitched.

The cabin slide was open a little for ventilation, and in the midst of his cooking Peter caught a strong whiff of the exhaust. The boat's westerly course had brought the wind astern and the new hood seemed to funnel the hot reek into the cabin. Peter was accustomed to exhaust fumes as he was used to the smell of fish, but a man couldn't enjoy his dinner with a taste of burnt gas in his mouth. He closed the slide and ate his dinner.

When he got up to call Calvin and take the wheel himself, he spun dizzily and sprawled on the floor, with his big right arm underneath. He felt himself drowning in a dark and evil-tasting sea that had no wetness to the skin but yet enfolded him and smothered him. At intervals of years it tossed him momentarily to a surface where the air was cool and sweet, and again sucked him down into depths as black as night. He wanted to cough but he could not, and the effort nearly split him between the eyes.

Outside in the bitter weather Calvin lay between the cabin slide and the engine hatch, very still, while the *Albacore* ran away with her herself. The boat was carrying a bit of port helm when his nerveless fingers left the wheel, and now she described a series of wide circles on the lonely grey sea. On the windward arc the man on deck and the man in the cabin stirred a little and moaned; but soon she was going west on the other arc and the hot exhaust blew around and over the silent Calvin and penetrated the cabin through the loose groove-and-tongue slide, and the men went back to their drowning in the strange dry sea.

When Peter came to the surface at last, and managed to stay there, he opened his eyes and saw only a blackness, and thought, *I'm blind.* But he felt a cold air on his face, and the cold persisted, and turned his skin to a stiff chilled mask. Then he was aware of his arm, crushed under his body's weight all this time. The arm screamed with pain, as if it lived separate from the rest of him and had a voice. He tried to get on his feet, but an invisible demon kept smiting him between the eyes with a hammer and he fell back, crying for mercy in a voice like the rubbing of sandpaper.

He tried again, and managed to get to his knees, with his right arm hanging useless to the floor and the hammerblows filling his brain with sparks. He crawled to the slide and after much drunken fumbling managed to pull it open.

Darkness on deck. But stars—real stars, in fixed and familiar constellations. Mystery! Were they back at Hagan's Wharf? Darkness and stars and a sleepy head were firmly associated in his mind with bedtime and the loom of the old wharf overhead. He wondered what he was doing out of his bunk dressed at that hour. The air pouring in through the open slide was like a wind from the Pole. He crawled to the stove and put his left hand to the iron. It was cold. The fire had been dead for hours.

The boat lurched and threw him on his side. He rolled over, to ease his arm, and lay for a time hearing the creak of woodwork and rattle of gadgets that could mean only one thing. It was impossible. But he crept again to the open slide and saw starlight on a wide expanse of water. He was astonished. He crawled out on deck—a terrible time getting over the weatherboard—and looked again. It was true! The *Albacore* was at sea in the night, and adrift. He gazed all round. No lights anywhere, nothing. He crawled to the gasoline tank and gave it a rap. It rang empty.

Into his blurred mind crept a vague alarm that took shape and put a word on his tongue. "Calvin!" He considered carefully, and plucked a fact out of the whirl in his head. Calvin had been at the wheel. Perhaps the son of his mother could explain.

"Calvin!" he said again in the rasping voice. He crept about the deck, while his arm shrieked, and found a bundle aft—oilskins, rubber boots, a cap, a stiff white face turned up to the stars. Something had brought Calvin out of the weird dry drowning as far as the fish hatch, where he had been sick all over the deck, and now lay like one dead. Why had he gone aft? To get away from something. But what?

Peter sat on his haunches and shook the bundle. It did not stir.

"You dead, Calvin?" Peter asked, very quietly and reasonably.

The son of his mother said nothing. His eyes and lips were closed and stiff. There was a faint flutter of breath in his nostrils now and then.

"You'll freeze out here," Peter said. His words rustled like frozen oilskins.

He made his way back to the cabin and by great effort, with painful concentration on every move, lit a fire in the stove with bits of an old herring box. While the fire crackled he tried once more to solve the mystery. Bits of sense eddied to the surface of his fermenting wits but he could not string them together. Then from the depths of his black mind, like a demon out of the Pit, swam a notion. The notion grinned and was plausible, like something alive. It whispered that one thing was certain and one alone—out there on the deck, in the killing cold of a January night, lay the creature who had shared his blankets and eaten his bread and stolen the heart of Clissie.

Into his aching mind sprang pictures as clear and hard as photographs; Clissie fishing for sculpins; Clissie in her new school clothes, her fine grown-up clothes; Clissie smiling at him under the pink lights of the Rose. Room ice cream parlor; Clissie opening his box of chocolates and next day crying down to him from the wharf edge, "Oh, Peter —those chocolates—you shouldn't!"; Calvin, the baby in his mother's arms, Calvin the loafer, the lady-killer, the noisy young drunkard;

Calvin who could make an engine tick like a watch, Calvin's slender clever fingers, Calvin's eyes aglow when he talked of the new weather screen or one of his crackpot schemes for getting rich quick.

And the little dark devil whispered, "What's he to you, after all?"

The son of his mother. He tried to call up pictures of the mother he had not seen in twenty years. Nothing came but vague sketches of a large widow woman, sharp of tongue, with a family too large for affection in detail, who had taken the village carpenter for her second husband and promptly presented the man with a child of his own begetting—in fact, with Calvin. Peter had left home about then, and never went back. He owed her nothing. He owed the carpenter's son nothing.

"Let him die, then," whispered the devil. "Think of Clissie," added the devil.

He thought of Clissie, of the placid blue eyes, the avid red mouth, the swing of her slim foot. The charming fairychild Clissie, the lovely half-woman Clissie, sprung like a flower from the muck of Water Street—for Calvin's plucking! Was it right? Was it fair?

The fire crackled in the stove. He rattled some coal on to the flames. He closed the cabin slide and crawled to the stove again, craving warmth. He was cold. Though oilskins, sweaters, heavy shirt and underwear, through duffel trousers and three pairs of thick country-wool socks he was cold to the marrow of his bones. The little stove spread its heat. It thawed his body and to some extent his brain, but it wakened the pain in his useless right arm. Ripples of agony ran up from the fingertips to the shoulder, with a final pang in the socket like the crack of a whip. He cried out and the sound startled him, as if it were some other voice—Calvin's, say—crying out there on the deck in the awful cold.

"Let him cry," snapped the devil. "Keep your mind on Clissie," the devil said. And the devil turned Peter's eyes towards the snapshot over Calvin's bunk. Clissie and the son of his mother, together, her head on Calvin's shoulder. Devils always out-do themselves, and this was a devilish mistake. For all Peter could see was the look on their faces, the happy young look of them, laughing into the sun.

He thrust the devil aside then—or was it only the cabin slide?—and crawled over the weatherboard to the deck. He pulled himself erect by the mast, but at the first step away from it he fell, and nearly went overboard as the boat rolled on a sea. On his knees, then, dragging the anguished arm, he made his way to the huddle that was Clissie's sweetheart and tried to drag it forward to the cabin's warmth. It would not move. He raised himself and tried to pick it up with his good arm, but his legs were water and he fell heavily, sometimes to the deck, sometimes on top of Calvin. These tumbles bruised him cruelly, for he could not save himself in falling and he was heavy. A ragged cut bled down his face for a time and then froze and was dry.

Gradually, because the devil was no longer there to make the pictures clear, he saw an alternative. He could bring warmth to Calvin. He crept back into the cabin, reached up painfully for blankets from the bunks, and dragged them out one at a time with his teeth. He laid the blankets on deck and rolled Calvin into them, over and over, like a log. It went so well that he tried to roll Clissie's sweetheart, blankets and all, along the deck to the cabin, but after getting him past the engine hatch he could not lift the dead weight over the weatherboard.

These efforts had tired him; but a new devil appeared now, a she-devil with Clissie's face, urging him to get the boat back to the coast, to harbor, to a doctor—a doctor for Calvin. But how? The gas tank was empty. The Clissie-devil reminded him scornfully of the spare fuel in a five-gallon can in the stern. He crept aft and worked the can out of its beckets. He tried to pick it up, and fell to the deck, striking his head. A gong clanged monotonously in his brain, and for a time he wept.

Then the Clissie-devil suggested rolling the thing as he had rolled the muffled body of Calvin. The can was round, with a wire handle at the top. He screwed the cover tight and laid the can on its side. He rolled it a couple of feet. Then the idle boat gave a surge and the can took charge.

Awkwardly, insanely, he pursued the heavy thing about the deck on his knees and left hand, dragging the tortured right. The can eluded him cunningly. He cornered it at last and got it over to the empty tank. He paused for strength, then. After a time he raised himself and got astride of the tank, gripping it with his knees. He reached down for the can with his left hand. There were several crashing failures. At last he swung it singlehanded to the tank top. Another pause. He unscrewed the tank and began to pour. The precious stuff spilled whenever the boat lurched, and the Clissie devil, always at his elbows, shrieked over the loss. But most of it went into the tank.

Now for the engine. It was an old automobile engine, gears and all. The electric starter kicked the engine over handsomely, considering how the cold had stiffened the grease and thickened the oil, but the cylinders would not fire. He kept the switch on, with the dead engine turning monotonously, and cried out to God to make the thing work.

God made no answer, but plaintively the Clissie-devil told him the battery would run down if he kept on like this. So he took the crank and began turning the engine by hand. Usually he could make the thing spin like a grindstone, and dockside loafers liked to watch a man as strong as that. It was different now. The crank slipped off the shaft several times, bruising his one good hand, and a long gash in his forefinger dripped blood over the handle and made matters worse. He persisted doggedly. At last the engine gave a dyspeptic belch and began to fire in a very ragged fashion.

He fumbled with choke and throttle, but the firing did not improve and he decided to let well enough alone. He slipped the engine into low gear. The boat began to move. Encouraged, he tried high gear, but the spluttering engine died. He regarded the crank and groaned. He switched on the starter and was relieved to hear the engine spluttering again. This time he put it in second gear and left it there.

The stars had gone, wiped off the sky by a sweep of clouds. He crawled into the cabin for the box compass. It was warm in there and he wanted to lie down, to rest his howling arm, to weep over his cuts and bruises, to stop somehow the gong in his head. The Clissie-devil dragged him outside. He set a course west, wondering thickly how far the *Albacore* had gone to sea. The air was dead calm but the forward movement of the boat gave the cold air the feel of a wind on his face, in spite of the screen. The exhaust fumes drifted aft.

In time—an age of time—he saw a flicker on the darkness ahead, the cloud reflection of a lighthouse, too far to be seen direct. He counted the flashes and intervals carefully, and shut his eyes and explored his memory. It must be the Port Murray light. He swung the helm, thankfully. It was something to know where he was. The Clissie-devil complained of the slow speed, and he told her aloud that the engine was sick like himself. He begged her to go away and leave him and the engine alone. She said nothing but hovered somehow in the corner of his eye, smiling mournfully.

Suddenly the engine changed its sound. It seemed to have thawed itself out and come to life, like Peter himself. He slipped the gear into high, shouting in triumph. The boat threw up a white V in the dark, rushing in towards the coast at twelve knots.

He picked up the flash of Cape Bald, closed it, steered the *Albacore* in under the sweeping white arm of it. Then appeared the gleam of the fairway buoy, and presently its bell rang clear above the gong in his head. And finally, bursting up like small bright flowers in the dark ahead, there appeared the lights of the town.

As he drew in he could see the glitter of the cold-storage wharf, the lone arc lamp at the end of Hagan's. The moored boats were dark. He looked for the flash and scurry of car headlights along the harbor road and saw nothing but the fixed white lamps of the highway. It must be very late.

He steered past Hagan's, straight for the cold-storage wharf, where there was a night watchman and a telephone. The snow on the docks and warehouse roofs sparkled under the lights, and icicles glittered all along the eaves, and every spire of the wharves wore a ballet skirt of ice where the tide rose and fell.

From habit he reversed his engine as the *Albacore* swept in; but the gong in his brain beat very loudly now, and the Clissie-devil had melted away like that other devil, and nothing was clear any more. He misjudged his distance and the boat fetched up with a crash, with broken-glass sounds from the spires where the crinkled ice-skirts were going to ruin. A fat old man ran out of the watchman's shack, swearing loudly into the night, and his astonished curses hung visible in small white puffs in the crisp air. But his mouth fell open as he looked down, seeing a giant with mad eyes and a bloody face crying up to him, "Doctor! Get a doctor for Calvin! Run, man!"

Peter was not conscious of much after that. Things came to him confusedly. Boots drumming. The frosty wharf planks crackling under-foot. Men's voices, and after some time a girl's voice crying, "I knew something was wrong! I knew it! Knew it!"

He felt them hoist his heavy body out of the boat in the bight of a rope. Then he was lying naked on the floor of the watchman's shack. The stove glowing. Somebody chafing his skin with hot blankets. The electric lights hurting his eyes. Calvin's face, all blue under the lights. Somebody phoning for the pulmotor from the chemical works. Old Doctor Springald grumbling, "Carbon monoxide, of course! Too care-less with your exhaust, all you fishermen. Hate to shove 'em under water and lose a bit of power, eh? Now I s'pose you'll all be building those death-contraptions around your steering wheels, just to cheat Davy Jones. When'll you learn?"

"My arm," Peter said.

"Traumatic paralysis, man—what we used to call Saturday Night Arm in the old saloon days—drunks going to sleep with an arm over the back of a chair and waking up yelling blue murder. It'll pass off in a week or so. So will the gas in your blood. The other chap got a worse dose he must have been right under that hood. But the cold was your worst enemy. Wonder you didn't freeze to death—it's twenty below, and you must have been unconscious a long time to get an arm like that."

But now a pair of slender silken knees appeared at Peter's shoulder, a pair of slim hands stroked his matted brown, hair, and Clissie's voice was crying, "Oh, Peter, Peter!" and sobbing that if he didn't get better she would die.

"Calvin," he muttered, fighting the gong. "You an' Calvin . . ."

"Ah, no! No!" Tears ran down her nose and sparkled in the light. "It's you, Peter. Always was, from the first time ever you spoke to me. After I got grown up—it took such a long time, growing up—you sort of stood me off, somehow. I—I couldn't get near to you any more—not the way I wanted. When Calvin came I could come and sit in your cabin, and all like that, and you didn't mind."

Doctor Springald told about it next evening over a hand of bridge, and the banker's wife was there.

"Heaven's!" she said. "My maid—such a refined little thing—and a fisherman twice her age! Clissie must be mad. I'll try to talk her out of it."

"I wouldn't if I were you," Doctor Springald said whimsically. "You're thinking of December-and-May and all that stuff and nonsense. This is a January idyl. Biologically speaking, it's a beautiful match, and the girl knows it. The man's an athlete, as hard and clean as carved oak. There's such a thing as bodily beauty in the human male—even at thirty-nine. D'you think she should have taken the younger man? That young rake'll be arthritic and booze-broken at thirty-five, and probably dead of TB at forty. She knows. Besides, the big fellow's a steady worker with a bank account. He'll treat her well, more gently than she wants, I fancy. After all, she's from Water Street. That breed is tough."

"And you think it's just that—the physical attraction of opposites, and a certain common sense on the part of the girl. No sentiment?"

"On Water Street," replied Doctor Springald, with a waterfront rasp in his voice, "there ain't no such thing."

I

None of them knew the colour of the sky. Their eyes glanced level, and were fastened upon the waves that swept toward them. These waves were of the hue of slate, save for the tops, which were of foaming white, and all of the men knew the colours of the sea. The horizon narrowed and widened, and dipped and rose, and at all times its edge was jagged with waves that seemed thrust up in points like rocks.

Many a man ought to have a bathtub larger than the boat which here rode upon the sea. These waves were most wrongfully and barbarously abrupt and tall, and each froth-top was a problem in small-boat navigation.

The cook squatted in the bottom, and looked with both eyes at the six inches of gunwale which separated him from the ocean. His sleeves were rolled over his fat forearms, and the two flaps of his unbuttoned vest dangled as he bent to bail out the boat. Often he said, "Gawd! that was a narrow clip." As he remarked it he invariably gazed eastward over the broken sea.

The oiler, steering with one of the two oars in the boat, sometimes raised himself suddenly to keep clear

The Open Boat

Stephen Crane

A Tale Intended to be after the Fact: Being the Experience of Four Men from the Sunk Steamer Commodore

of water that swirled in over the stern. It was a thin little oar, and it seemed often ready to snap.

The correspondent, pulling at the other oar, watched the waves and wondered why he was there.

The injured captain, lying in the bow, was at this time buried in that profound dejection and indifference which comes, temporarily at least, to even the bravest and most enduring when, willy-nilly, the firm fails, the army loses, the ship goes down. The mind of the master of a vessel is rooted deep in the timbers of her, though he command for a day or a decade; and this captain had on him the stern impression of a scene in the greys of dawn of seven turned faces, and later a stump of a top-mast with a white ball on it, that slashed to and fro at the waves, went low and lower, and down. Thereafter there was something strange in his voice. Although steady, it was deep with mourning, and of a quality beyond oration or tears.

"Keep 'er a little more south, Billie," said he.

"A little more south, sir," said the oiler in the stern.

A seat in his boat was not unlike a seat upon a bucking broncho, and by the same token a broncho is not much smaller. The craft pranced and reared and plunged like an animal. As each wave came, and she rose for it, she seemed like a horse making at a fence outrageously high. The manner of her scramble over these walls of water is a mystic thing, and, moreover, at the top of them were ordinarily these problems in white water, the foam racing down from the summit of each wave requiring a new leap, and a leap from the air. Then, after scornfully bumping a crest, she would slide and race and splash down a long incline, and arrive bob-bing and nodding in front of the next menace.

A singular disadvantage of the sea lies in the fact that after suc-cessfully surmounting one wave you discover that there is another behind it just as important and just as nervously anxious to do some-thing effective in the way of swamping boats. In a ten-foot dinghy one can get an idea of the resources of the sea in the line of waves that is not probable to the average experience which is never at sea in a dinghy. As each slaty wall of water approached, it shut all else from the view of the men in the boat, and it was not difficult to imagine that this particular wave was the final outburst of the ocean, the last effort of the grim water. There was a terrible grace in the move of the waves, and they came in silence, save for the snarling of the crests.

In the wan light the faces of the men must have been grey. Their eyes must have glinted in strange ways as they gazed steadily astern. Viewed from a balcony, the whole thing would doubtless have been weirdly picturesque. But the men in the boat had no time to see it, and if they had had leisure, there were other things to occupy their minds. The sun swung steadily up the sky, and they knew it was broad day because the colour of the sea changed from slate to emerald green streaked with amber lights, and the foam was like tumbling snow. The process of the breaking day was unknown to them. They were aware only of this effect upon the colour of the waves that rolled toward them.

In disjointed sentences the cook and the correspondent argued as to the difference between a life-saving station and a house of refuge. The cook had said: "There's a house of refuge just north of the Mosquito Inlet Light, and as soon as they see us they'll come off in their boat and pick us up."

"As soon as who sees us?" said the correspondent.

"The crew," said the cook.

"Houses of refuge don't have crews," said the correspondent. "As I understand them, they are only places where clothes and grub are stored for the benefit of ship-wrecked people. They don't carry crews."

"Oh, yes, they do," said the cook.

"No, they don't," said the correspondent.

"Well, we're not there yet, anyhow," said the oiler, in the stern.

"Well," said the cook, "perhaps it's not a house of refuge that I'm thinking of as being near Mosquito Inlet Light; perhaps it's a life-saving station."

"We're not there yet," said the oiler in the stern.

II

As the boat bounced from the top of each wave the wind tore through the hair of the hatless men, and as the craft plopped her stern down again the spray slashed past them. The crest of each of these waves was a hill, from the top of which the men surveyed for a moment a broad tumultuous expanse, shining and wind-riven. It was probably splendid, it was probably glorious, this play of the free sea, wild with lights of emerald and white and amber.

"Bully good thing it's an on-shore wind," said the cook. "If not, where would we be? Wouldn't have a show."

"That's right," said the correspondent.

The busy oiler nodded his assent.

Then the captain, in the bow, chuckled in a way that expressed humour, contempt, tragedy, all in one. "Do you think we've got much of a show now, boys?" said he.

Whereupon the three were silent, save for a trifle of hemming and hawing. To express any particular optimism at this time they felt to be childish and stupid, but they all doubtless possessed this sense of the situation in their minds. A young man thinks doggedly at such times. On the other hand, the ethics of their condition was decidedly against any open suggestion of hopelessness. So they were silent.

"Oh, well," said the captain, soothing his children, "we'll get ashore all right."

But there was that in his tone which made them think; so the oiler quoth, "Yes! if this wind holds."

The cook was bailing. "Yes! if we don't catch hell in the surf."

Canton-flannel gulls flew near and far. Sometimes they sat down on the sea, near patches of brown seaweed that rolled over the waves with a movement like carpets on a line in a gale. The birds sat comfortably in groups, and they were envied by some in the dinghy, for the wrath of the sea was no more to them than it was to a covey of prairie chickens a thousand miles inland. Often they came very close and stared at the men with black bead-like eyes. At these times they were uncanny and sinister in their unblinking scrutiny, and the men hooted angrily at them, telling them to be gone. One came, and evidently decided to alight on the top of the captain's head. The bird flew parallel to the boat and did not circle, but made short sidelong jumps in the air in chicken-fashion. His black eyes were wistfully fixed upon the captain's head. "Ugly brute," said the oiler to the bird. "You look as if you were made with a jackknife." The cook and the correspondent swore darkly at the creature. The captain naturally wished to knock it away with the end of the heavy painter, but he did not dare do it, because anything resembling an emphatic gesture would have capsized this freighted boat; and so, with his open hand, the captain gently and carefully waved the gull away. After it had been discouraged from the pursuit the captain breathed easier on account of his hair, and others breathed easier because the bird struck their minds at this time as being somehow gruesome and ominous.

In the meantime the oiler and the correspondent rowed. And also they rowed. They sat together in the same seat, and each rowed an oar. Then the oiler took both oars; then the correspondent took both oars; then the oiler; then the correspondent. They rowed and they rowed. The very ticklish part of the business was when the time came for the reclining one in the stern to take his turn at the oars. By the very last star of truth, it is easier to steal eggs from under a hen than it was to change seats in the dinghy. First the man in the stern slid his hand along the thwart and moved with care, as if he were of Sèvres. Then the man in the rowing-seat slid his hand along the other thwart. It was all done with the most extraordinary care. As the two sidled past each other, the whole party kept watchful eyes on the coming wave, and the captain cried: "Look out, now! Steady, there!"

The brown mats of seaweed that appeared from time to time were like islands, bits of earth. They were traveling, apparently, neither one way nor the other. They were, to all intents, stationary. They informed them in the boat that it was making progress slowly toward the land.

The captain, rearing cautiously in the bow after the dinghy soared on a great swell, said that he had seen the lighthouse at Mosquito Inlet. Presently the cook remarked that he had seen it. The correspondent was at the oars then, and for some reason he too wished to look at the lighthouse; but his back was toward the far shore, and the waves were important, and for some time he could not seize an opportunity to turn his head. But at last there came a wave more gentle than the others, and when at the crest of it he swiftly scoured the western horizon.

"See it?" said the captain.

"No," said the correspondent, slowly; "I didn't see anything."

"Look again," said the captain. He pointed. "It's exactly in that direction."

At the top of another wave the correspondent did as he was bid, and this time his eyes chanced on a small, still thing on the edge of the swaying horizon. It was precisely like the point of a pin. It took an anxious eye to find a lighthouse so tiny.

"Think we'll make it, Captain?"

"If this wind holds and the boat don't swamp, we can't do much else," said the captain.

The little boat, lifted by each towering sea and splashed viciously by the crests, made progress that in the absence of seaweed was not apparent to those in her. She seemed just a wee thing wallowing miraculously top up, at the mercy of five oceans. Occasionally a great spread of water, like white flames, swarmed into her.

"Bail her, cook," said the captain, serenely.

"All right, Captain," said the cheerful cook.

III

It would be difficult to describe the subtle brotherhood of men that was here established on the seas. No one said that it was so. No one mentioned it. But it dwelt in the boat, and each man felt it warm him. They were a captain, an oiler, a cook, and a correspondent, and they were friends—friends in a more curiously iron-bound degree than may be common. The hurt captain, lying against the water-jar in the bow, spoke always in a low voice and calmly; but he could never command a more ready and swiftly obedient crew than the motley three of the dinghy. It was more than a mere recognition of what was best for the common safety. There was surely in it a quality that was personal and heart-felt. And after this devotion to the commander of the boat, there was this comradeship, that the correspondent, for instance, who had been taught to be cynical of men, knew even at the time was the best experience of his life. But no one said that it was so. No one mentioned it.

"I wish we had a sail," remarked the captain. "We might try my

overcoat on the end of an oar, and give you two boys a chance to rest."
So the cook and the correspondent held the mast and spread wide the
overcoat; the oiler steered; and the little boat made good way with her
new rig. Sometimes the oiler had to scull sharply to keep a sea from
breaking into the boat, but otherwise sailing was a success.

Meanwhile the lighthouse had been growing slowly larger. It had
now almost assumed colour, and appeared like a little grey shadow on
the sky. The man at the oars could not be prevented from turning his
head rather often to try for a glimpse of this little grey shadow.

At last, from the top of each wave, the men in the tossing boat
could see land. Even as the lighthouse was an upright shadow on the
sky, this land seemed but a long black shadow on the sea. It certainly
was thinner than paper. "We must be about opposite New Smyrna," said
the cook, who had coasted this shore often in schooners. "Captain, by
the way, I believe they abandoned that life-saving station there about a
year ago."

"Did they?" said the captain.

The wind slowly died away. The cook and the correspondent were
not now obliged to slave in order to hold high the oar. But the waves
continued their old impetuous swooping at the dinghy, and the little
craft, no longer under way, struggled woundily over them. The oiler or
the correspondent took the oars again.

Shipwrecks are apropos of nothing. If men could only train them
and have them occur when the men had reached pink condition, there
would be less drowning at sea. Of the four in the dinghy none had slept
any time worth mentioning for two days and two nights previous to
embarking in the dinghy, and in the excitement of clambering about the
deck of a foundering ship they had also forgotten to eat heartily.

For these reasons, and for others, neither the oiler nor the correspondent was fond of rowing at this time. The correspondent wondered
ingenuously how in the name of all that was sane could there be people
who thought it amusing to row a boat. It was not an amusement; it was
a diabolical punishment, and even a genius of mental aberrations could
never conclude that it was anything but a horror to the muscles and a
crime against the back. He mentioned to the boat in general how the

amusement of rowing struck him, and the weary-faced oiler smiled in full sympathy. Previously to the foundering, by the way, the oiler had worked a double watch in the engine-room of the ship.

"Take her easy now, boys," said the captain. "Don't spend yourselves. If we have to run a surf you'll need all your strength, because we'll sure have to swim for it. Take your time."

Slowly the land arose from the sea. From a black line it became a line of black and a line of white—trees and sand. Finally the captain said that he could make out a house on the shore. "That's the house of refuge, sure," said the cook. "They'll see us before long, and come out after us."

The distant lighthouse reared high. "The keeper ought to be able to make us out now, if he's looking through a glass," said the captain. "He'll notify the life-saving people."

"None of those other boats could have got ashore to give word of this wreck," said the oiler, in a low voice, "else the life-boat would be out hunting us."

Slowly and beautifully the land loomed out of the sea. The wind came again. It had veered from the north-east to the south-east. Finally a new sound struck the ears of the men in the boat. It was the low thunder of the surf on the shore. "We'll never be able to make the lighthouse now," said the captain. "Swing her head a little more north, Billie."

"A little more north, sir," said the oiler.

Whereupon the little boat turned her nose once more down the wind, and all but the oarsman watched the shore grow. Under the influence of this expansion doubt and direful apprehension were leaving the minds of the men. The management of the boat was still more absorbing, but it could not prevent a quiet cheerfulness. In an hour, perhaps, they would be ashore.

Their backbones had become thoroughly used to balancing in the boat, and they now rode this wild colt of a dinghy like circus men. The correspondent thought that he had been drenched to the skin, but happening to feel in the top pocket of his coat, he found therein eight cigars. Four of them were soaked with sea-water; four were perfectly scatheless. After a search, somebody produced three dry matches; and thereupon the four waifs rode impudently in their little boat and, with an assurance of an impending rescue shining in their eyes, puffed at the big cigars, and judged well and ill of all men. Everybody took a drink of water.

IV

"Cook," remarked the captain, "there don't seem to be any signs of life about your house of refuge."

"No," replied the cook. "Funny they don't see us!"

A broad stretch of lowly coast lay before the eyes of the men. It was of low dunes topped with dark vegetation. The roar of the surf was plain, and sometimes they could see the white lip of a wave as it spun up the beach. A tiny house was blocked out black upon the sky. Southward, the slim lighthouse lifted its little grey length.

Tide, wind, and waves were swinging the dinghy northward. "Funny they don't see us," said the men.

The surf's roar was here dulled, but its tone was nevertheless thunderous and mighty. As the boat swam over the great rollers the men sat listening to this roar. "We'll swamp sure," said everybody.

It is fair to say here that there was not a life-saving station within twenty miles in either direction; but the men did not know this fact, and in consequence they made dark and opprobrious remarks concerning the eyesight of the nation's life-savers. Four scowling men sat in the dinghy and surpassed records in the invention of epithets.

"Funny they don't see us."

The light-heartedness of a former time had completely faded. To their sharpened minds it was easy to conjure pictures of all kinds of incompetency and blindness and, indeed, cowardice. There was the shore of the populous land, and it was bitter and bitter to them that from it came no sign.

"Well," said the captain, ultimately, "I suppose we'll have to make a try for ourselves. If we stay out here too long, we'll none of us have strength left to swim after the boat swamps."

And so the oiler, who was at the oars, turned the boat straight for the shore. There was a sudden tightening of muscles. There was some thinking.

"If we don't all get ashore," said the captain—"if we don't all get ashore, I suppose you fellows know where to send news of my finish?"

They then briefly exchanged some addresses and admonitions. As for the reflections of the men, there was a great deal of rage in them. Perchance they might be formulated thus: "If I am going to be drowned— if I am going to be drowned—if I am going to be drowned, why, in the name of the seven mad gods who rule the sea, was I allowed to come thus far and contemplate sand and trees? Was I brought here merely to have my nose dragged away as I was about to nibble the sacred cheese of life? It is preposterous. If this old ninny-woman, Fate, cannot do better than this, she should be deprived of the management of men's fortunes. She is an old hen who knows not her intention. If she has decided to drown me, why did she not do it in the beginning and save me all this trouble? The whole affair is absurd.—But no; she cannot mean to drown me. She dare not drown me. She cannot drown me. Not after all this work." Afterward the man might have had an impulse to shake his fist at the clouds. "Just you drown me, now, and then hear what I call you!"

The billows that came at this time were more formidable. They seemed always just about to break and roll over the little boat in a turmoil of foam. There was a preparatory and long growl in the speech of them. No mind unused to the sea would have concluded that the dinghy could ascend these sheer heights in time. The shore was still afar. The oiler was a wily surfman. "Boys," he said swiftly, "she won't live three minutes more, and we're too far out to swim. Shall I take her to sea again, Captain?"

"Yes; go ahead!" said the captain.

This oiler, by a series of quick miracles and fast and steady oarsmanship, turned the boat in the middle of the surf and took her safely to sea again.

There was a considerable silence as the boat bumped over the furrowed sea to deeper water. Then somebody in gloom spoke: "Well, anyhow, they must have seen us from the shore by now."

The gulls went in slanting flight up the wind toward the grey, desolate east. A squall, marked by dingy clouds and clouds brick-red like smoke from a burning building, appeared from the south-east.

"What do you think of those life-saving people? Ain't they peaches?"

"Funny they haven't seen us."

"Maybe they think we're out here for sport! Maybe they think we're fishin'. Maybe they think we're damned fools."

It was a long afternoon. A changed tide tried to force them southward, but wind and wave said northward. Far ahead, where coast-line, sea, and sky formed their mighty angle, there were little dots which seemed to indicate a city on the shore.

"St. Augustine?"

The captain shook his head. "Too near Mosquito Inlet."

And the oiler rowed, and then the correspondent rowed; then the oiler rowed. It was a weary business. The human back can become the seat of more aches and pains than are registered in books for the composite anatomy of a regiment. It is a limited area, but it can become the theatre of innumerable muscular conflicts, tangles, wrenches, knots, and other comforts.

"Did you ever like to row, Billie?" asked the correspondent.

"No," said the oiler; "hang it!"

When one exchanged the rowing-seat for a place in the bottom of the boat, he suffered a bodily depression that caused him to be careless of everything save an obligation to wiggle one finger. There was cold sea-water swashing to and fro in the boat, and he lay in it. His head, pillowed on a thwart, was within an inch of the swirl of a wave-crest, and sometimes a particularly obstreperous sea came inboard and drenched him once more. But these matters did not annoy him. It is almost certain that if the boat had capsized he would have tumbled comfortably out upon the ocean as if he felt sure that it was a great soft mattress.

"Look! There's a man on the shore!"

"Where?"

"There! See 'im? See 'im?"

"Yes, sure! He's walking along."

"Now he's stopped. Look! He's facing us!"

"He's waving at us!"

"So he is! By thunder!"

"Ah, now we're all right! Now we're all right! There'll be a boat out here for us in half an hour."

"He's going on. He's running. He's going up to that house there."

The remote beach seemed lower than the sea, and it required a searching glance to discern the little black figure. The captain saw a floating stick, and they rowed to it. A bath towel was by some weird chance in the boat, and, tying this on the stick, the captain waved it. The oarsman did not dare turn his head, so he was obliged to ask questions.

"What's he doing now?"

"He's standing still again. He's looking, I think.—There he goes again—toward the house.—Now he's stopped again."

"Is he waving at us?"

"No, not now; he was, though."

"Look! There comes another man!"

"He's running."

"Look at him go, would you!"

"Why, he's on a bicycle. Now he's met the other man. They're both waving at us. Look!"

"There comes something up the beach."

"What the devil is that thing?"

"Why, it looks like a boat."

"Why, certainly, it's a boat."

"No; it's on wheels."

"Yes, so it is. Well, that must be the life-boat. They drag them along shore on a wagon."

"That's the life-boat, sure."

"No, by God, it's—it's an omnibus."

"I tell you it's a life-boat."

"It is not! It's an omnibus. I can see it plain. See? One of these big hotel omnibuses."

"By thunder, you're right. It's an omnibus, sure as fate. What do you suppose they are doing with an omnibus? Maybe they are going around collecting the life-crew, hey?"

"That's it, likely. Look! There's a fellow waving a little black flag. He's standing on the steps of the omnibus. There come those other two fellows. Now they're all talking together. Look at the fellow with the flag. Maybe he ain't waving it!"

"That ain't a flag, is it? That's his coat. Why, certainly, that's his coat."

"So it is; it's his coat. He's taken it off and is waving it around his head. But would you look at him swing it!"

"Oh, say, there isn't any life-saving station there. That's just a winter-resort hotel omnibus that has brought over some of the boarders to see us drown."

"What's that idiot with the coat mean? What's he signalling, anyhow?"

"It looks as if he were tryin' to tell us to go north. There must be a life-saving station up there."

"No; he thinks we're fishing. Just giving us a merry hand. See? Ah, there, Willie!"

"Well, I wish I could make something out of those signals. What do you suppose he means?"

"He don't mean anything; he's just playing."

"Well, if he'd just signal us to try the surf again, or to go to sea and wait, or go north, or go south, or go to hell, there would be some reason in it. But look at him! He just stands there and keeps his coat revolving like a wheel. The ass!"

"There come more people."

"Now there's quite a mob. Look! Isn't that a boat?"

"Where? Oh, I see where you mean. No, that's no boat."

"That fellow is still waving his coat."

"He must think we like to see him do that. Why don't he quit it? It don't mean anything."

"I don't know. I think he is trying to make us go north. It must be that there's a life-saving station there somewhere."

"Say, he ain't tired yet. Look at 'im wave!"

"Wonder how long he can keep that up. He's been revolving his coat ever since he caught sight of us. He's an idiot. Why aren't they getting men to bring a boat out? A fishing-boat—one of those big yawls— could come out here all right. Why don't he do something?"

"Oh, it's all right now."

"They'll have a boat out here for us in less than no time, now that they've seen us."

A faint yellow tone came into the sky over the low land. The shadows on the sea slowly deepened. The wind bore coldness with it, and the men began to shiver.

"Holy smoke!" said one, allowing his voice to express his impious mood, "if we keep on monkeying out here! If we've got to flounder out here all night!"

"Oh, we'll never have to stay here all night! Don't you worry. They've seen us now, and it won't be long before they'll come chasing out after us."

The shore grew dusky. The man waving a coat blended gradually into this gloom, and it swallowed in the same manner the omnibus and the group of people. The spray, when it dashed uproariously over the side, made the voyagers shrink and swear like men who were being branded.

"I'd like to catch the chump who waved the coat. I feel like socking him one, just for luck."

"Why? What did he do?"

"Oh, nothing, but then he seemed so damned cheerful."

In the meantime the oiler rowed, and then the correspondent rowed, and then the oiler rowed. Grey-faced and bowed forward, they mechanically, turn by turn, plied the leaden oars. The form of the lighthouse had vanished from the southern horizon, but finally a pale star appeared, just lifting from the sea. The streaked saffron in the west passed before the all-merging darkness, and the sea to the east was black. The land had vanished, and was expressed only by the low and drear thunder of the surf.

"If I am going to be drowned—if I am going to be drowned—if I am going to be drowned, why, in the name of the seven mad gods who rule the sea, was I allowed to come thus far and contemplate sand and trees? Was I brought here merely to have my nose dragged away as I was about to nibble the sacred cheese of life?"

The patient captain, drooped over the water-jar, was sometimes obliged to speak to the oarsman.

"Keep her head up! Keep her head up!"

"Keep her head up, sir." The voices were weary and low.

This was surely a quiet evening. All save the oarsman lay heavily and listlessly in the boat's bottom. As for him, his eyes were just capable of noting the tall black waves that swept forward in a most sinister silence, save for an occasional subdued growl of a crest.

The cook's head was on a thwart, and he looked without interest at the water under his nose. He was deep in other scenes. Finally he spoke. "Billie," he murmured, dreamfully, "what kind of pie do you like best?"

V

"Pie!" said the oiler and the correspondent, agitatedly. "Don't talk about those things, blast you!"

"Well," said the cook, "I was just thinking about ham sandwiches and—"

A night on the sea in an open boat is a long night. As darkness settled finally, the shine of the light, lifting from the sea in the south, changed to full gold. On the northern horizon a new light appeared, a small bluish gleam on the edge of the waters. These two lights were the furniture of the world. Otherwise there was nothing but waves.

Two men huddled in the stern, and distances were so magnificent in the dinghy that the rower was enabled to keep his feet partly warm by thrusting them under his companions. Their legs indeed extended far under the rowing-seat until they touched the feet of the captain forward. Sometimes, despite the efforts of the tired oarsman, a wave came piling into the boat, an icy wave of the night, and the chilling water soaked them anew. They would twist their bodies for a moment and groan, and sleep the dead sleep once more, while the water in the boat gurgled about them as the craft rocked.

The plan of the oiler and the correspondent was for one to row until he lost the ability, and then arouse the other from his sea-water couch in the bottom of the boat.

The oiler plied the oars until his head drooped forward and the overpowering sleep blinded him; and he rowed yet afterward. Then he touched a man in the bottom of the boat, and called his name. "Will you spell me for a little while?" he said, meekly.

"Sure, Billie," said the correspondent, awaking and dragging himself to a sitting position. They exchanged places carefully, and the oiler, cuddling down in the sea-water at the cook's side, seemed to go to sleep instantly.

The particular violence of the sea had ceased. The waves came without snarling. The obligation of the man at the oars was to keep the boat headed so that the tilt of the rollers would not capsize her, and to preserve her from filling when the crests rushed past. The black waves were silent and hard to be seen in the darkness. Often one was almost upon the boat before the oarsman was aware.

In a low voice the correspondent addressed the captain. He was not sure that the captain was awake, although this iron man seemed to be always awake. "Captain, shall I keep her making for that light north, sir?"

The same steady voice answered him. "Yes. Keep it about two points off the port bow."

The cook had tied a life-belt around himself in order to get even the warmth which this clumsy cork contrivance could donate, and he seemed almost stove-like when a rower, whose teeth invariably chattered wildly as soon as he ceased his labour, dropped down to sleep.

The correspondent, as he rowed, looked down at the two men sleeping underfoot. The cook's arm was around the oiler's shoulders, and, with their fragmentary clothing and haggard faces, they were the babes of the sea—a grotesque rendering of the old babes in the wood.

Later he must have grown stupid at his work, for suddenly there was a growling of water, and a crest came with a roar and a swash into the boat, and it was a wonder that it did not set the cook afloat in his life-belt. The cook continued to sleep, but the oiler sat up, blinking his eyes and shaking with the new cold.

"Oh, I'm awfully sorry, Billie," said the correspondent, contritely.

"That's all right, old boy," said the oiler, and lay down again and was asleep.

Presently it seemed that even the captain dozed, and the correspondent thought that he was the one man afloat on all the oceans. The wind had a voice as it came over the waves, and it was sadder than the end.

There was a long, loud swishing astern of the boat, and a gleaming trail of phosphorescence, like blue flame, was furrowed on the black waters. It might have been made by a monstrous knife.

Then there came a stillness, while the correspondent breathed with open mouth and looked at the sea.

Suddenly there was another swish and another long flash of bluish light, and this time it was alongside the boat, and might almost been reached with an oar. The correspondent saw an enormous fin speed like a shadow through the water, hurling the crystalline spray and leaving the long glowing trail.

The correspondent looked over his shoulder at the captain. His face was hidden, and he seemed to be asleep. He looked at the babes of the sea. They certainly were asleep. So, being bereft of sympathy, he leaned a little way to one side and swore softly into the sea.

But the thing did not then leave the vicinity of the boat. Ahead or astern, on one side or the other, at intervals long or short, fled the long sparkling streak, and there was to be heard the *whirroo* of the dark fin. The speed and power of the thing was greatly to be admired. It cut the water like a gigantic and keen projectile.

The presence of this biding thing did not affect the man with the same horror that it would if he had been a picnicker. He simply looked at the sea dully and swore in an undertone.

Nevertheless, it is true that he did not wish to be alone with the thing. He wished one of his companions to awake by chance and keep him company with it. But the captain hung motionless over the water-jar, and the oiler and the cook in the bottom of the boat were plunged in slumber.

VI

"If I am going to be drowned—if I am going to be drowned—if I am going to be drowned, why, in the name of the seven mad gods who rule the sea, was I allowed to come thus far and contemplate sand and trees?"

During this dismal night, it may be remarked that a man would conclude that it was really the intention of the seven mad gods to drown him, despite the abominable injustice of it. For it was certainly an abominable injustice to drown a man who had worked so hard, so hard. The man felt it would be a crime most unnatural. Other people had drowned at sea since galleys swarmed with painted sails, but still—

When it occurs to a man that nature does not regard him as important, and that she feels she would not maim the universe by disposing of him, he at first wishes to throw bricks at the temple, and he hates deeply the fact that there are no bricks and no temples. Any visible expression of nature would surely be pelleted with his jeers.

Then, if there be no tangible thing to hoot, he feels, perhaps, the desire to confront a personification and indulge in pleas, bowed to one knee, and with hands supplicant, saying, "Yes, but I love myself."

A high cold star on a winter's night is the word he feels that she says to him. Thereafter he knows the pathos of his situation.

The men in the dinghy had not discussed these matters, but each had, no doubt, reflected upon them in silence and according to his mind. There was seldom any expression upon their faces save the general one of complete weariness. Speech was devoted to the business of the boat.

To chime the notes of his emotion, a verse mysteriously entered the correspondent's head. He had even forgotten that he had forgotten this verse, but it suddenly was in his mind.

A soldier of the Legion lay dying in Algiers;
There was lack of woman's nursing, there was dearth
of woman's tears;
But a comrade stood beside him, and he took that
comrade's hand,
And he said, "I never more shall see my own, my
native land."

In his childhood the correspondent had been made acquainted with the fact that a soldier of the Legion lay dying in Algiers, but he had never regarded the fact as important. Myriads of his school-fellows had informed him of the soldier's plight, but the dinning had naturally ended by making him perfectly indifferent. He had never considered it his affair that a soldier of the Legion lay dying in Algiers, nor had it appeared to him as a matter for sorrow. It was less to him than the breaking of a pencil's point.

Now, however, it quaintly came to him as a human, living thing. It was no longer merely a picture of a few throes in the breast of a poet, meanwhile drinking tea and warming his feet at the grate; it was an actuality—stern, mournful, and fine.

The correspondent plainly saw the soldier. He lay on the sand with his feet out straight and still. While his pale left hand was upon his chest in an attempt to thwart the going of his life, the blood came between his fingers. In the far Algerian distance, a city of low square forms was set against a sky that was faint with the last sunset hues. The correspondent, plying the oars and dreaming of the slow and slower movements of the lips of the soldier, was moved by a profound and perfectly impersonal comprehension. He was sorry for the soldier of the Legion who lay dying in Algiers.

The thing which had followed the boat and waited had evidently grown bored at the delay. There was no longer to be heard the slash of the cutwater, and there was no longer the flame of the long trail. The light in the north still glimmered, but it was apparently no nearer to the boat. Sometimes the boom of the surf rang in the correspondent's ears, and he turned the craft seaward then and rowed harder. Southward, some one had evidently built a watch-fire on the beach. It was too low and too far to be seen, but it made a shimmering, roseate reflection upon the bluff in back of it, and this could be discerned from the boat. The wind came stronger, and sometimes a wave suddenly raged out like a mountain cat, and there was to be seen the sheen and sparkle of a broken crest.

The captain, in the bow, moved on his water-jar and sat erect. "Pretty long night," he observed to the correspondent. He looked at the shore. "Those life-saving people take their time."

"Did you see that shark playing around?"

"Yes, I saw him. He was a big fellow, all right."

"Wish I had known you were awake."

Later the correspondent spoke into the bottom of the boat. "Billie!" There was a slow and gradual disentanglement. "Billie, will you spell me?"

"Sure," said the oiler.

As soon as the correspondent touched the cold, comfortable sea-water in the bottom of the boat and had huddled close to the cook's life-belt he was deep in sleep, despite the fact that his teeth played all the popular airs. This sleep was so good to him that it was but a moment before he heard a voice call his name in a tone that demonstrated the last stages of exhaustion. "Will you spell me?"

"Sure, Billie."

The light in the north had mysteriously vanished, but the correspondent took his course from the wide-awake captain.

Later in the night they took the boat farther out to sea, and the captain directed the cook to take one oar at the stern and keep the boat facing the seas. He was to call out if he should hear the thunder of the surf. This plan enabled the oiler and the correspondent to get respite together. "We'll give those boys a chance to get into shape again," said the captain. They curled down and, after a few preliminary chatterings and trembles, slept once more the dead sleep. Neither knew they had bequeathed to the cook the company of another shark, or perhaps the same shark.

As the boat caroused on the waves, spray occasionally bumped over the side and gave them a fresh soaking, but this had no power to break their repose. The ominous slash of the wind and the water affected them as it would have affected mummies.

"Boys," said the cook, with the notes of every reluctance in his voice, "she's drifted in pretty close. I guess one of you had better take her to sea again." The correspondent, aroused, heard the crash of the toppled crests.

As he was rowing, the captain gave him some whisky-and-water, and this steadied the chills out of him. "If I ever get ashore and anybody shows me even a photograph of an oar—"

At last there was a short conversation.

"Billie!—Billie, will you spell me?"

"Sure," said the oiler.

VII

When the correspondent again opened his eyes, the sea and the sky were each of the grey hue of the dawning. Later, carmine and gold was painted upon the waters. The morning appeared finally, in its splendour, with a sky of pure blue, and the sunlight flamed on the tips of the waves.

On the distant dunes were set many little black cottages, and a tall white windmill reared above them. No man, nor dog, nor bicycle appeared on the beach. The cottages might have formed a deserted village.

The voyagers scanned the shore. A conference was held in the boat. "Well," said the captain, "if no help is coming, we might better try a run through the surf right away. If we stay out here much longer we will be too weak to do anything for ourselves at all." The others silently acquiesced in this reasoning. The boat was headed for the beach. The correspondent wondered if none ever ascended the tall wind-tower, and if then they never looked seaward. This tower was a giant, standing with its back to the plight of the ants. It represented in a degree, to the correspondent, the serenity of nature amid the struggles of the individual— nature in the wind, and nature in the vision of men. She did not seem cruel to him then, nor beneficent, nor treacherous, nor wise. But she was indifferent, flatly indifferent. It is, perhaps, plausible that a man in this situation, impressed with the unconcern of the universe, should see the innumerable flaws of his life, and have them taste wickedly in his mind, and wish for another chance. A distinction between right and wrong seems absurdly clear to him, then, in this new ignorance of the grave-edge, and he understands that if he were given another opportunity he would mend his conduct and his words, and be better and brighter during an introduction or at a tea.

"Now, boys," said the captain, "she is going to swamp sure. All we can do is to work her in as far as possible, and then when she swamps, pile out and scramble for the beach. Keep cool now, and don't jump until she swamps sure."

The oiler took the oars. Over his shoulders he scanned the surf. "Captain," he said, "I think I'd better bring her about and keep her head-on to the seas and back her in."

"All right, Billie," said the captain. "Back her in." The oiler swung the boat then, and, seated in the stern, the cook and the correspondent were obliged to look over their shoulders to contemplate the lonely and indifferent shore.

The monstrous inshore rollers heaved the boat high until the men were again enabled to see the white sheets of water scudding up the slanted beach. "We won't get in very close," said the captain. Each time a man could wrest his attention from the rollers, he turned his glance toward the shore, and in the expression of the eyes during this contemplation there was a singular quality. The correspondent, observing the others, knew that they were not afraid, but the full meaning of their glances was shrouded.

As for himself, he was too tired to grapple fundamentally with the fact. He tried to coerce his mind into thinking of it, but the mind was dominated at this time by the muscles, and the muscles said they did not care. It merely occurred to him that if he should drown it would be a shame.

There were no hurried words, no pallor, no plain agitation. The men simply looked at the shore. "Now, remember to get well clear of the boat when you jump," said the captain.

Seaward the crest of a roller suddenly fell with a thunderous crash, and the long white comber came roaring down upon the boat.

"Steady now," said the captain. The men were silent. They turned their eyes from the shore to the comber and waited. The boat slid up the incline, leaped at the furious top, bounced over it, and swung down the long back of the wave. Some water had been shipped, and the cook bailed it out.

But the next crest crashed also. The tumbling, boiling flood of white water caught the boat and whirled it almost perpendicular. Water swarmed in from all sides. The correspondent had his hands on the gunwale at this time, and when the water entered at that place he swiftly withdrew his fingers, as if he objected to wetting them.

The little boat, drunken with this weight of water, reeled and snuggled deeper into the sea.

"Bail her out, cook! Bail her out!" said the captain.

"All right, Captain," said the cook.

"Now, boys, the next one will do for us sure," said the oiler. "Mind to jump clear of the boat."

The third wave moved forward, huge, furious, implacable. It fairly swallowed the dinghy, and almost simultaneously the men tumbled into the sea. A piece of life-belt had lain in the bottom of the boat, and as the correspondent went overboard he held this to his chest with his left hand.

The January water was icy, and he reflected immediately that it was colder than he had expected to find it off the coast of Florida. This appeared to his dazed mind as a fact important enough to be noted at the time. The coldness of the water was sad; it was tragic. This fact was somehow mixed and confused with his opinion of his own situation, so that it seemed almost a proper reason for tears. The water was cold.

When he came to the surface he was conscious of little but the noisy water. Afterward he saw his companions in the sea. The oiler was ahead in the race. He was swimming strongly and rapidly. Off to the correspondent's left, the cook's great white and corked back bulged out of the water; and in the rear the captain was hanging with his one good hand to the keel of the overturned dinghy.

There is a certain immovable quality to a shore, and the correspondent wondered at it amid the confusion of the sea.

It seemed also very attractive; but the correspondent knew that it was a long journey, and he paddled leisurely. The piece of life-preserver lay under him, and sometimes he whirled down the incline of a wave as if he were on a hand-sled.

But finally he arrived at a place in the sea where travel was beset with difficulty. He did not pause swimming to inquire what manner of current had caught him, but there his progress ceased. The shore was set before him like a bit of scenery on a stage, and he looked at it and understood with his eyes each detail of it.

As the cook passed, much farther to the left, the captain was calling to him, "Turn over on your back, cook! Turn over on your back and use the oar."

"All right, sir." The cook turned on his back, and, paddling with an oar, went ahead as if he were a canoe.

Presently the boat also passed to the left of the correspondent, with the captain clinging with one hand to the keel. He would have appeared like a man raising himself to look over a board fence if it were not for the extraordinary gymnastics of the boat. The correspondent marvelled that the captain could still hold to it.

They passed on nearer to shore—the oiler, the cook, the captain—and following them went the water-jar, bouncing gaily over the seas.

The correspondent remained in the grip of this strange new enemy—a current. The shore, with its white slope of sand and its green bluff topped with little silent cottages, was spread like a picture before him. It was very near to him then, but he was impressed as one who, in a gallery, looks at a scene from Brittany or Algiers.

He thought: "I am going to drown? Can it be possible? Can it be possible? Can it be possible?" Perhaps an individual must consider his own death to be the final phenomenon of nature.

But later a wave perhaps whirled him out of this small deadly current, for he found suddenly that he could again make progress toward the shore. Later still he was aware that the captain, clinging with one hand to the keel of the dinghy, had his face turned away from the shore and toward him, and was calling his name. "Come to the boat! Come to the boat!"

In his struggle to reach the captain and the boat, he reflected that when one gets properly wearied drowning must really be a comfortable arrangement—a cessation of hostilities accompanied by a large degree of relief; and he was glad of it, for the main thing in his mind for some moments had been horror of the temporary agony. He did not wish to be hurt.

Presently he saw a man running along the shore. He was undressing with most remarkable speed. Coat, trousers, shirt, everything flew magically off him.

"Come to the boat!" called the captain.

"All right, Captain." As the correspondent paddled, he saw the captain let himself down to bottom and leave the boat. Then the correspondent performed his one little marvel of the voyage. A large wave caught him and flung him with ease and supreme speed completely over the boat and far beyond it. It struck him even then as an event in gymnastics and a true miracle of the sea. An overturned boat in the surf is not a plaything to a swimming man.

The correspondent arrived in water that reached only to his waist, but his condition did not enable him to stand for more than a moment. Each wave knocked him into a heap, and the undertow pulled at him.

Then he saw the man who had been running and undressing, and undressing and running, come bounding into the water. He dragged ashore the cook, and then waded toward the captain; but the captain waved him away and sent him to the correspondent. He was naked—naked as a tree in winter; but a halo was about his head, and he shone like a saint. He gave a strong pull, and a long drag, and a bully heave at the correspondent's hand. The correspondent, schooled in the minor formulæ, said, "Thanks, old man." But suddenly the man cried, "What's that?" He pointed a swift finger. The correspondent said, "Go."

In the shallows, face downward, lay the oiler. His forehead touched sand that was periodically, between each wave, clear of the sea.

The correspondent did not know all that transpired afterward. When he achieved safe ground he fell, striking the sand with each particular part of his body. It was as if he had dropped from a roof, but the thud was grateful to him.

It seemed that instantly the beach was populated with men with blankets, clothes, and flasks, and women with coffee-pots and all the remedies sacred to their minds. The welcome of the land to the men from the sea was warm and generous; but a still and dripping shape was carried slowly up the beach, and the land's welcome for it could only be the different and sinister hospitality of the grave.

When it came night, the white waves paced to and fro in the moonlight, and the wind brought the sound of the great sea's voice to the men on the shore, and they felt that they could then be interpreters.

The Lost Salt Gift of Blood

Alistair MacLeod

Now in the early evening the sun is flashing everything in gold. It bathes the blunt grey rocks that loom yearningly out toward Europe and it touches upon the stunted spruce and the low-lying lichens and the delicate hardy ferns and the ganglia-rooted moss and the tiny tough rock cranberries. The grey and slanting rain squalls have swept in from the sea and then departed with all the suddenness of surprise marauders. Everything before them and beneath them has been rapidly, briefly, and thoroughly drenched and now the clear droplets catch and hold the sun's infusion in a myriad of rainbow colours. Far beyond the harbour's mouth more tiny squalls seem to be forming, moving rapidly across the surface of the sea out there beyond land's end where the blue ocean turns to grey in rain and distance and the strain of eyes. Even farther out, somewhere beyond Cape Spear lies Dublin and the Irish coast; far away but still the nearest land and closer now than is Toronto or Detroit to say nothing of North America's more western cities; seeming almost hazily visible now in imagination's mist.

Overhead the ivory white gulls wheel and cry, flashing also in the purity of the sun and the clean, freshly washed air. Sometimes they glide to the blue-green surface of the harbour, squawking and garbling; at times almost standing on their pink webbed feet as if they would walk on water, flapping their wings pompously against their breasts like over-conditioned he-men who have successfully passed their body-building courses. At other times they gather in lazy groups on the rocks above the harbour's entrance murmuring softly to themselves or looking also quietly out toward what must be Ireland and the vastness of the sea.

The harbour itself is very small and softly curving, seeming like a tiny, peaceful womb nurturing the life that now lies within it but which originated from without; came from without and through the narrow, rock-tight channel that admits the entering and withdrawing sea. That sea is entering again now, forcing itself gently but inevitably through the tightness of the opening and laving the rocky walls and rising and rolling into the harbour's inner cove. The dories rise at their moorings and the tide laps higher on the piles and advances upward toward the high-water marks upon the land; the running moon-drawn tides of spring.

Around the edges of the harbour brightly coloured houses dot the wet and glistening rocks. In some ways they seem almost like defiantly optimistic horseshoe nails: yellow and scarlet and green and pink; buoyantly yet firmly permanent in the grey unsundered rock.

At the harbour's entrance the small boys are jigging for the beautifully speckled salmon-pink sea trout. Barefootedly they stand on the tide-wet rocks flicking their wrists and sending their glistening lines in shimmering golden arcs out into the rising tide. Their voices mount excitedly as they shout to one another encouragement, advice, consolation. The trout fleck dazzlingly on their sides as they are drawn toward the rocks, turning to seeming silver as they flash within the sea.

It is all of this that I see now, standing at the final road's end of my twenty-five-hundred-mile journey. The road ends here—quite literally ends at the door of a now abandoned fishing shanty some six brief yards in front of where I stand. The shanty is grey and weatherbeaten with two boarded-up windows, vanishing wind-whipped shingles and a heavy rusted padlock chained fast to a twisted door. Piled before the twisted door and its equally twisted frame are some marker buoys, a small pile of rotted rope, a broken oar and an old and rust-flaked anchor.

The option of driving my small rented Volkswagen the remaining six yards and then negotiating a tight many-twists-of-the-steering-wheel turn still exists. I would be then facing toward the west and could simply retrace the manner of my coming. I could easily drive away before anything might begin.

Instead I walk beyond the road's end and the fishing shanty and begin to descend the rocky path that winds tortuously and narrowly along and down the cliff's edge to the sea. The small stones roll and turn and scrape beside and beneath my shoes and after only a few steps the leather is nicked and scratched. My toes press hard against its straining surface.

As I approach the actual water's edge four small boys are jumping excitedly upon the glistening rocks. One of them has made a strike and is attempting to reel in his silver-turning prize. The other three have laid down their rods in their enthusiasm and are shouting encouragement and giving almost physical moral support: "Don't let him get away, John," they say. "Keep the line steady." "Hold the end of the rod up." "Reel in the slack." "Good." "What a dandy!"

Across the harbour's clear water another six or seven shout the same delirious messages. The silver-turning fish is drawn toward the rock. In the shallows he flips and arcs, his flashing body breaking the water's surface as he walks upon his tail. The small fisherman has now his rod almost completely vertical. Its tip sings and vibrates high above his head while at his feet the trout spins and curves. Both of his hands are clenched around the rod and his knuckles strain white through the water-roughened redness of small-boy hands. He does not know whether he should relinquish the rod and grasp at the lurching trout or merely heave the rod backward and flip the fish behind him. Suddenly he decides upon the latter but even as he heaves his bare feet slide out from beneath him on the smooth wetness of the rock and he slips down into the water. With a pirouetting leap the trout turns glisteningly and tears itself free. In a darting flash of darkened greenness it rights itself within the regained water and is gone. "Oh damn!" says the small fisherman, struggling upright onto his rock. He bites his lower lip to hold back the tears welling within his eyes. There is a small trickle of blood coursing down from a tiny scratch on the inside of his wrist and he is wet up to his knees. I reach down to retrieve the rod and return it to him.

Suddenly a shout rises from the opposite shore. Another line zings tautly through the water throwing off fine showers of iridescent droplets. The shouts and contagious excitement spread anew. "Don't let him get away!" "Good for you." "Hang on!" "Hang on!"

I am caught up in it myself and wish also to shout some enthusiastic advice but I do not know what to say. The trout curves up from the water in a wriggling arch and lands behind the boys in the moss and lichen that grow down to the sea-washed rocks. They race to free it from the line and proclaim about its size.

On our side of the harbour the boys begin to talk. "Where do you live?" they ask and is it far away and is it bigger than St. John's? Awkwardly I try to tell them the nature of the North American midwest. In turn I ask them if they go to school. "Yes," they say. Some of them go to St. Bonaventure's which is the Catholic school and others go to Twilling Memorial. They are all in either grade four or grade five. All of them say that they like school and that they like their teachers.

The fishing is good they say and they come here almost every evening. "Yesterday I caught me a nine-pounder," says John. Eagerly they show me all of their simple equipment. The rods are of all varieties as are the lines. At the lines' ends the leaders are thin transparencies terminating in grotesque three-clustered hooks. A foot or so from each hook there is a silver spike knotted into the leader. Some of the boys say the trout are attracted by the flashing of the spike; others say that it acts only as a weight or sinker. No line is without one.

"Here, sir," says John, "have a go. Don't get your shoes wet." Standing on the slippery rocks in my smooth-soled shoes I twice attempt awkward casts. Both times the line loops up too high and the spike splashes down far short of the running, rising life of the channel.

"Just a flick of the wrist, sir," he says, "just a flick of the wrist. You'll soon get the hang of it." His hair is red and curly and his face is splashed with freckles and his eyes are clear and blue. I attempt three or four more casts and then pass the rod back to the hands where it belongs.

And now it is time for supper. The calls float down from the women standing in the doorways of the multicoloured houses and obediently the small fishermen gather up their equipment and their catches and prepare to ascend the narrow upward-winding paths. The sun has descended deeper into the sea and the evening has become quite cool. I recognize this with surprise and a slight shiver. In spite of the advice given to me and my own precautions my feet are wet and chilled within my shoes. No place to be unless barefooted or in rubber boots. Perhaps for me no place at all.

As we lean into the steepness of the path my young companions continue to talk, their accents broad and Irish. One of them used to have a tame sea gull at his house, had it for seven years. His older brother found it on the rocks and brought it home. His grandfather called it Joey. "Because it talked so much," explains John. It died last week and they held a funeral about a mile away from the shore where there was enough soil to dig a grave. Along the shore itself it is almost solid rock and there is no ground for a grave. It's the same with people they say. All week they have been hopefully looking along the base of the cliffs for another sea gull but have not found one. You cannot kill a sea gull they say, the government protects them because they are scavengers and keep the harbours clean.

The path is narrow and we walk in single file. By the time we reach the shanty and my rented car I am wheezing and badly out of breath. So badly out of shape for a man of thirty-three; sauna baths do nothing for your wind. The boys walk easily, laughing and talking beside me. With polite enthusiasm they comment upon my car. Again there exists the possibility of restarting the car's engine and driving back the road that I have come. After all, I have not seen a single adult except for the women calling down the news of supper. I stand and fiddle with my keys.

The appearance of the man and the dog is sudden and unexpected. We have been so casual and unaware in front of the small automobile that we have neither seen nor heard their approach along the rock-worn road. The dog is short, stocky and black and white. White hair floats and feathers freely from his sturdy legs and paws as he trots along the rock looking expectantly out into the harbour. He takes no notice of me. The man is short and stocky as well and he also appears as black and white. His rubber boots are black and his dark heavy worsted trousers are supported by a broadly scarred and blackened belt. The buckle is shaped like a dory with a fisherman standing in the bow. Above the belt there is a dark navy woollen jersey and upon his head a toque of the same material. His hair beneath the toque is white as is the three-or-four-day stubble on his face. His eyes are blue and his hands heavy, gnarled, and misshapen. It is hard to tell from looking at him whether he is in his sixties, seventies, or eighties.

"Well, it is a nice evening tonight," he says, looking first at John and then to me. "The barometer has not dropped so perhaps fair weather will continue for a day or two. It will be good for the fishing."

He picks a piece of gnarled grey driftwood from the roadside and swings it slowly back and forth in his right hand. With desperate anticipation the dog dances back and forth before him, his intense eyes glittering at the stick. When it is thrown into the harbour he barks joyously and disappears, hurling himself down the bank in a scrambling avalanche of small stones. In seconds he reappears with only his head visible, cutting a silent but rapidly advancing V through the quiet serenity of the harbour. The boys run to the bank's edge and shout encouragement to him—much as they had been doing earlier for one another. "It's farther out," they cry, "to the right, to the right." Almost totally submerged, he cannot see the stick he swims to find. The boys toss stones in its general direction and he raises himself out of the water to see their landing splashdowns and to change his wide-waked course.

"How have you been?" asks the old man, reaching for a pipe and a pouch of tobacco and then without waiting for an answer, "perhaps you'll stay for supper. There are just the three of us now."

We begin to walk along the road in the direction that he has come. Before long the boys rejoin us accompanied by the dripping dog with the recovered stick. He waits for the old man to take it from him and then showers us all with a spray of water from his shaggy coat. The man pats and scratches the damp head and the dripping ears. He keeps the returned stick and thwacks it against his rubber boots as we continue to walk along the rocky road I have so recently travelled in my Volkswagen.

Within a few yards the houses begin to appear upon our left. Frame and flat-roofed, they cling to the rocks looking down into the harbour. In storms their windows are splashed by the sea but now their bright colours are buoyantly brave in the shadows of the descending dusk. At the third gate, John, the man, and the dog turn in. I follow them. The remaining boys continue on; they wave and say, "So long."

The path that leads through the narrow whitewashed gate has had its stone worn smooth by the passing of countless feet. On either side there is a row of small, smooth stones, also neatly whitewashed, and seeming like a procession of large white eggs or tiny unbaked loaves of bread. Beyond these stones and also on either side, there are some cast-off tires also whitewashed and serving as flower beds. Within each whitened circumference the colourful low-lying flowers nod; some hardy strain of pansies or perhaps marigolds. The path leads on to the square green house, with its white borders and shutters. On one side of the wooden doorstep a skate blade has been nailed, for the wiping off of feet, and beyond the swinging screen door there is a porch which smells saltily of the sea. A variety of sou'westers and rubber boots and mitts and caps hang from the driven nails or lie at the base of the wooden walls.

Beyond the porch there is the kitchen where the woman is at work. All of us enter. The dog walks across the linoleum-covered floor, his nails clacking, and flings himself with a contented sigh beneath the wooden table. Almost instantly he is asleep, his coat still wet from his swim within the sea.

The kitchen is small. It has an iron cookstove, a table against one wall and three or four handmade chairs of wood. There is also a wooden rocking-chair covered by a cushion. The rockers are so thin from years of use that it is hard to believe they still function. Close by the table there is a wash-stand with two pails of water upon it. A wash-basin hangs from a driven nail in its side and above it is an old-fashioned mirrored medicine cabinet. There is also a large cupboard, a low-lying couch, and a window facing upon the sea. On the walls a barometer hangs as well as two pictures, one of a rather jaunty young couple taken many years ago. It is yellowed and rather indistinct; the woman in a long dress with her hair done up in ringlets, the man in a serge suit that is slightly too large for him and with a tweed cap pulled rakishly over his right eye. He has an accordion strapped over his shoulders and his hands are fanned out on the buttons and keys. The other picture is of the Christ-child. Beneath it is written, "Sweet Heart of Jesus Pray for Us."

The woman at the stove is tall and fine featured. Her grey hair is combed briskly back from her forehead and neatly coiled with a large pin at the base of her neck. Her eyes are as grey as the storm scud of the sea. Her age, like her husband's, is difficult to guess. She wears a blue print dress, a plain blue apron and low-heeled brown shoes. She is turning fish within a frying pan when we enter.

Her eyes contain only mild surprise as she first regards me. Then with recognition they glow in open hostility which in turn subsides and yields to self-control. She continues at the stove while the rest of us sit upon the chairs.

During the meal that follows we are reserved and shy in our lonely adult ways; groping for and protecting what perhaps may be the only awful dignity we possess. John, unheedingly, talks on and on. He is in the fifth grade and is doing well. They are learning percentages and the mysteries of decimals; to change a percent to a decimal fraction you move the decimal point two places to the left and drop the percent sign. You always, always do so. They are learning the different breeds of domestic animals: the four main breeds of dairy cattle are Holstein, Ayrshire, Guernsey, and Jersey. He can play the mouth organ and will demonstrate after supper. He has twelve lobster traps of his own. They were originally broken ones thrown up on the rocky shore by storms. Ira, he says nodding toward the old man, helped him fix them, nailing on new lathes and knitting new headings. Now they are set along the rocks near the harbour's entrance. He is averaging a pound a trap and the "big" fishermen say that that is better than some of them are doing. He is saving his money in a little imitation keg that was also washed up on the shore. He would like to buy an outboard motor for the small reconditioned skiff he now uses to visit his traps. At present he has only oars.

"John here has the makings of a good fisherman," says the old man. "He's up at five most every morning when I am putting on the fire. He and the dog are already out along the shore and back before I've made tea."

"When I was in Toronto," says John, "no one was ever up before seven. I would make my own tea and wait. It was wonderful sad. There were gulls there though, flying over Toronto harbour. We went to see them on two Sundays."

After the supper we move the chairs back from the table. The woman clears away the dishes and the old man turns on the radio. First he listens to the weather forecast and then turns to short wave where he picks up the conversations from the offshore fishing boats. They are conversations of catches and winds and tides and of the women left behind on the rocky shores. John appears with his mouth organ, standing at a respectful distance. The old man notices him, nods, and shuts off the radio. Rising, he goes upstairs, the sound of his feet echoing down to us. Returning he carries an old and battered accordion. "My fingers have so much rheumatism," he says, "that I find it hard to play anymore."

Seated, he slips his arms through the straps and begins the squeezing accordion motions. His wife takes off her apron and stands behind him with one hand upon his shoulder. For a moment they take on the essence of the once young people in the photograph. They begin to sing:

Come all ye fair and tender ladies
Take warning how you court your men
They're like the stars on a summer's morning
First they'll appear and then they're gone.

I wish I were a tiny sparrow
And I had wings and I could fly
I'd fly away to my own true lover

And all he'd ask I would deny.

Alas I'm not a tiny sparrow
I have not wings nor can I fly
And on this earth in grief and sorrow
I am bound until I die.

John sits on one of the home-made chairs playing his mouth organ. He seems as all mouth-organ players the world over: his right foot tapping out the measures and his small shoulders now round and hunched above the cupped hand instrument.

"Come now and sing with us, John," says the old man.

Obediently he takes the mouth organ from his mouth and shakes the moisture drops upon his sleeve. All three of them begin to sing, spanning easily the half century of time that touches their extremes. The old and the young singing now their songs of loss in different comprehensions. Stranded here, alien of my middle generation, I tap my leather foot self-consciously upon the linoleum. The words sweep up and swirl about my head. Fog does not touch like snow yet it is more heavy and more dense. Oh moisture comes in many forms!

All alone as I strayed by the banks of the river
Watching the moonbeams at evening of day
All alone as I wandered I spied a young stranger
Weeping and wailing with many a sigh.

Weeping for one who is now lying lonely
Weeping for one who no mortal can save
As the foaming dark waters flow silently past him
Onward they flow over young Jenny's grave.

Oh Jenny my darling come tarry here with me
Don't leave me alone, love, distracted in pain
For as death is the dagger that plied us asunder
Wide is the gulf, love, between you and I.

After the singing stops we all sit rather uncomfortably for a moment. The mood seeming to hang heavily upon our shoulders. Then with my single exception all come suddenly to action. John gets up and takes his battered school books to the kitchen table. The dog jumps up on a chair beside him and watches solemnly in a supervisory manner. The woman takes some navy yarn the colour of her husband's jersey and begins to knit. She is making another jersey and is working on the sleeve. The old man rises and beckons me to follow him into the tiny parlour. The stuffed furniture is old and worn. There is a tiny wood-burning heater in the centre of the room. It stands on a square of galvanized metal which protects the floor from falling, burning coals. The stovepipe rises and vanishes into the wall on its way to the upstairs. There is an old-fashioned mantelpiece on the wall behind the stove. It is covered with odd shapes of driftwood from the shore and a variety of exotically shaped bottles, blue and green and red, which are from the shore as well. There are pictures here too: of the couple in the other picture; and one of them with their five daughters; and one of the five daughters by themselves. In that far-off picture time all of the daughters seem roughly between the ages of ten and eighteen. The youngest has the reddest hair of all. So red that it seems to triumph over the non-photographic colours of lonely black and white. The pictures are in standard wooden frames.

From behind the ancient chesterfield the old man pulls a collapsible card table and pulls down its warped and shaky legs. Also from behind the chesterfield he takes a faded checkerboard and a large old-fashioned matchbox of rattling wooden checkers. The spine of the board is almost cracked through and is strengthened by layers of adhesive tape. The checkers are circumferences of wood sawed from a length of broom handle. They are about three quarters of an inch thick. Half of them are painted a very bright blue and the other half an equally eye-catching red. "John made these," says the old man, "all of them are not really the same thickness but they are good enough. He gave it a good try."

We begin to play checkers. He takes the blue and I the red. The house is silent with only the click-clack of the knitting needles sounding through the quiet rooms. From time to time the old man lights his pipe, digging out the old ashes with a flattened nail and tamping in the fresh tobacco with the same nail's head. The blue smoke winds lazily and haphazardly toward the low-beamed ceiling. The game is solemn as is the next and then the next. Neither of us loses all of the time.

"It is time for some of us to be in bed," says the old woman after a while. She gathers up her knitting and rises from her chair. In the kitchen John neatly stacks his school books on one corner of the table in anticipation of the morning. He goes outside for a moment and then returns. Saying good-night very formally he goes up the stairs to bed. In a short while the old woman follows, her footsteps travelling the same route.

We continue to play our checkers, wreathed in smoke and only partially aware of the muffled footfalls sounding softly above our heads.

When the old man gets up to go outside I am not really surprised, any more than I am when he returns with the brown, ostensible vinegar jug. Poking at the declining kitchen fire, he moves the kettle about seeking the warmest spot on the cooling stove. He takes two glasses from the cupboard, a sugar bowl and two spoons. The kettle begins to boil.

Even before tasting it, I know the rum to be strong and overproof. It comes at night and in fog from the French islands of St. Pierre and Miquelon. Coming over in the low-throttled fishing boats, riding in imitation gas cans. He mixes the rum and the sugar first, watching them marry and dissolve. Then to prevent the breakage of the glasses he places a teaspoon in each and adds the boiling water. The odour rises richly, its sweetness hung in steam. He brings the glasses to the table, holding them by their tops so that his fingers will not burn.

We do not say anything for some time, sitting upon the chairs, while the sweetened, heated richness moves warmly through and from our stomachs and spreads upward to our brains. Outside the wind begins to blow, moaning and faintly rattling the window's whitened shutters. He rises and brings refills. We are warm within the dark and still within the wind. A clock strikes regularly the strokes of ten.

It is difficult to talk at times with or without liquor; difficult to achieve the actual act of saying. Sitting still we listen further to the rattle of the wind; not knowing where nor how we should begin. Again the glasses are refilled.

"When she married in Toronto," he says at last, "we figured that maybe John should be with her and with her husband. That maybe he would be having more of a chance there in the city. But we would be putting it off and it weren't until nigh on two years ago that he went. Went with a woman from down the cove going to visit her daughter. Well, what was wrong was that we missed him wonderful awful. More fearful than we ever thought. Even the dog. Just pacing the floor and looking out the window and walking along the rocks of the shore. Like us had no moorings, lost in the fog or on the ice-floes in a snow squall. Nigh sick unto our hearts we was. Even the grandmother who before that was maybe thinking small to herself that he was trouble in her old age. Ourselves having never had no sons only daughters."

He pauses, then rising goes upstairs and returns with an envelope. From it he takes a picture which shows two young people standing self-consciously before a half-ton pickup with a wooden extension ladder fastened to its side. They appear to be in their middle twenties. The door of the truck has the information: "Jim Farrell, Toronto: House-painting, Eavestroughing, Aluminum Siding, Phone 535-3484," lettered on its surface.

"This was in the last letter," he says. "That Farrell I guess was a nice enough fellow, from Heartsick Bay he was.

"Anyway they could have no more peace with John than we could without him. Like I says he was here too long before his going and it all took ahold of us the way it will. They sent word that he was coming on the plane to St. John's with a woman they'd met through a Newfound-land club. I was to go to St. John's to meet him. Well, it was all wrong the night before the going. The signs all bad; the grandmother knocked off the lampshade and it broke in a hunnerd pieces—the sign of death; and the window blind fell and clattered there on the floor and then lied still. And the dog runned around like he was crazy, moanen and cryen worse than the swiles does out on the ice, and thrown hisself against the walls and jumpen on the table and at the window where the blind fell until we would have to be letten him out. But it be no better for he runned and throwed hisself in the sea and then come back and howled outside the same window and jumped against the wall, splashen the water from his coat all over it. Then he be runnen back to the sea again. All the neighbours heard him and said I should bide at home and not go to St. John's at all. We be all wonderful scared and not know what to do and the next mornen, first thing I drops me knife.

"But still I feels I has to go. It be foggy all the day and everyone be thinken the plane won't come or be able to land. And I says, small to myself, now here in the fog be the bad luck and the death but then there the plane be, almost like a ghost ship comen out the fog with all its lights shinen. I think maybe he won't be on it but soon he comen through the fog, first with the woman and then see'n me and starten to run, closer and closer till I can feel him in me arms and the tears on both our cheeks. Powerful strange how things will take one. That night they be killed."

From the envelope that contained the picture he draws forth a tattered clipping:

Jennifer Farrell of Roncesvalles Avenue was instantly killed early this morning and her husband James died later in emergency at St. Joseph's Hospital. The accident occurred about 2 A.M. when the pickup truck in which they were travelling went out of control on Queen St. W. and struck a utility pole. It is thought that bad visibility caused by a heavy fog may have contributed to the accident. The Farrells were originally from Newfoundland.

Again he moves to refill the glasses. "We be all alone," he says. "All our other daughters married and far away in Montreal, Toronto, or the States. Hard for them to come back here, even to visit; they comes only every three years or so for perhaps a week. So we be hav'n only him."

And now my head begins to reel even as I move to the filling of my own glass. Not waiting this time for the courtesy of his offer. Making myself perhaps too much at home with this man's glass and this man's rum and this man's house and all the feelings of his love. Even as I did before. Still locked again for words.

Outside we stand and urinate, turning our backs to the seeming gale so as not to splash our wind-snapped trousers. We are almost driven forward to rock upon our toes and settle on our heels, so blow the gusts. Yet in spite of all, the stars shine clearly down. It will indeed be a good day for the fishing and this wind eventually will calm. The salt hangs heavy in the air and the water booms against the rugged rocks. I take a stone and throw it against the wind into the sea.

Going up the stairs we clutch the wooden bannister unsteadily and say good-night.

The room has changed very little. The window rattles in the wind and the unfinished beams sway and creak. The room is full of sound. Like a foolish Lockwood I approach the window although I hear no voice. There is no Catherine who cries to be let in. Standing unsteadily on one foot when required I manage to undress, draping my trousers across the wooden chair. The bed is clean. It makes no sound. It is plain and wooden, its mattress stuffed with hay or kelp. I feel it with my hand and pull back the heavy patchwork quilts. Still I do not go into it. Instead I go back to the door which has no knob but only an ingenious latch formed from a twisted nail. Turning it, I go out into the hallway. All is dark and the house seems even more inclined to creak where there is no window. Feeling along the wall with my outstretched hand I find the door quite easily. It is closed with the same kind of latch and not difficult to open. But no one waits on the other side. I stand and bend my ear to hear the even sound of my one son's sleeping. He does not beckon any more than the nonexistent voice in the outside wind. I hesitate to touch the latch for fear that I may waken him and disturb his dreams. And if I did what would I say? Yet I would like to see him in his sleep this once and see the room with the quiet bed once more and the wooden chair beside it from off an old wrecked trawler. There is no boiled egg or shaker of salt or glass of water waiting on the chair within this closed room's darkness.

Once though there was a belief held in the outports, that if a girl would see her own true lover she should boil an egg and scoop out half the shell and fill it with salt. Then she should take it to bed with her and eat it, leaving a glass of water by her bedside. In the night her future husband or a vision of him would appear and offer her the glass. But she must only do it once.

It is the type of belief that bright young graduate students were collecting eleven years ago for the theses and archives of North America and also, they hoped, for their own fame. Even as they sought the near-Elizabethan songs and ballads that had sailed from County Kerry and from Devon and Cornwall. All about the wild, wide sea and the flashing silver dagger and the lost and faithless lover. Echoes to and from the lovely, lonely hills and glens of West Virginia and the standing stones of Tennessee.

Across the hall the old people are asleep. The old man's snoring rattles as do the windows; except that now and then there are catching gasps within his breath. In three or four short hours he will be awake and will go down to light his fire. I turn and walk back softly to my room.

Within the bed the warm sweetness of the rum is heavy and intense. The darkness presses down upon me but still it brings no sleep. There are no voices and no shadows that are real. There are only walls of memory touched restlessly by flickers of imagination.

Oh I would like to see my way more clearly. I, who have never understood the mystery of fog. I would perhaps like to capture it in a jar like the beautiful childhood butterflies that always die in spite of the airholes punched with nails in the covers of their captivity—leaving behind the vapours of their lives and deaths; or perhaps as the unknowing child who collects the grey moist condoms from the lovers' lanes only to have them taken from him and to be told to wash his hands. Oh I have collected many things I did not understand.

And perhaps now I should go and say, oh son of my *summa cum laude* loins, come away from the lonely gulls and the silver trout and I will take you to the land of the Tastee Freeze where you may sleep till ten of nine. And I will show you the elevator to the apartment on the sixteenth floor and introduce you to the buzzer system and the yards of the wrought-iron fences where the Doberman pinscher runs silently at night. Or may I offer you the money that is the fruit of my collecting and my most successful life? Or shall I wait to meet you in some known or unknown bitterness like Yeats's Cuchulain by the wind-whipped sea or as Sohrab and Rustum by the future flowing river?

Again I collect dreams. For I do not know enough of the fog on Toronto's Queen St. West and the grinding crash of the pickup and of lost and misplaced love.

I am up early in the morning as the man kindles the fire from the driftwood splinters. The outside light is breaking and the wind is calm. John tumbles down the stairs. Scarcely stopping to splash his face and pull on his jacket, he is gone, accompanied by the dog. The old man smokes his pipe and waits for the water to boil. When it does he pours some into the teapot then passes the kettle to me. I take it to the wash-stand and fill the small tin basin in readiness for my shaving. My face looks back from the mirrored cabinet. The woman softly descends the stairs.

"I think I will go back today," I say while looking into the mirror at my face and at those in the room behind me. I try to emphasize the "I." "I just thought I would like to make this trip—again. I think I can leave the car in St. John's and fly back directly." The woman begins to move about the table, setting out the round white plates. The man quietly tamps his pipe.

The door opens and John and the dog return. They have been down along the shore to see what has happened throughout the night. "Well, John," says the old man, "what did you find?"

He opens his hand to reveal a smooth round stone. It is of the deepest green inlaid with veins of darkest ebony. It has been worn and polished by the unrelenting restlessness of the sea and buffed and bur-nished by the gravelled sand. All of its inadequacies have been removed and it glows with the lustre of near perfection.

"It is very beautiful," I say.

"Yes," he says, "I like to collect them." Suddenly he looks up to my eyes and thrusts the stone toward me. "Here," he says, "would you like to have it?"

Even as I reach out my hand I turn my head to the others in the room. They are both looking out through the window to the sea.

"Why, thank you," I say. "Thank you very much. Yes, I would.

Thank you. Thanks." I take it from his outstretched hand and place it in my pocket.

We eat our breakfast in near silence. After it is finished the boy and dog go out once more. I prepare to leave.

"Well, I must go," I say, hesitating at the door. "It will take me a while to get to St. John's." I offer my hand to the man. He takes it in his strong fingers and shakes it firmly.

"Thank you," says the woman. "I don't know if you know what I mean but thank you."

"I think I do," I say. I stand and fiddle with the keys. "I would somehow like to help or keep in touch but . . ."

"But there is no phone," he says, "and both of us can hardly write. Perhaps that's why we never told you. John is getting to be a pretty good hand at it though."

"Good-bye," we say again, "good-bye, good-bye."

The sun is shining clearly now and the small boats are putt-putting about the harbour. I enter my unlocked car and start its engine. The gravel turns beneath the wheels. I pass the house and wave to the man and woman standing in the yard.

On a distant cliff the children are shouting. Their voices carol down through the sun-washed air and the dogs are curving and dancing about them in excited circles. They are carrying something that looks like a crippled gull. Perhaps they will make it well. I toot the horn. "Good-bye," they shout and wave, "good-bye, good-bye."

The airport terminal is strangely familiar. A symbol of impermanence, it is itself glisteningly permanent. Its formica surfaces have been designed to stay. At the counter a middle-aged man in mock exasperation is explaining to the girl that it is Newark he wishes to go to, *not* New York. There are not many of us and soon we are ticketed and lifting through and above the sun-shot fog. The meals are served in tinfoil and in plastic. We eat above the clouds looking at the tips of wings.

The man beside me is a heavy-equipment salesman who has been trying to make a sale to the developers of Labrador's resources. He has been away a week and is returning to his wife and children.

Later in the day we land in the middle of the continent. Because of the changing time zones the distance we have come seems eerily unreal. The heat shimmers in little waves upon the runway. This is the equipment salesman's final destination while for me it is but the place where I must change flights to continue even farther into the heartland. Still we go down the wheeled-up stairs together, donning our sunglasses, and stepping acoss the heated concrete and through the terminal's electronic doors. The salesman's wife stands waiting along with two small children who are the first to see him. They race toward him with their arms outstretched. "Daddy, Daddy," they cry, "what did you bring me? What did you bring me?"

It may be that there comes a time in the life of the Newfoundlander when chance flings him into the very vortex of the unleashed, swirling passions of wind, night, and the sea. That event, to be sure, never disturbs the course of the pallid days of the city men, the fellows with muscles of dough and desires all fed fat, who, as it were, wrap the fruits of toil in pink paper, tie the package with a pretty string and pass it over the colony's counter. It comes only to the brawny, dogged men of the coast, to whom cod and salmon and seal-fat are the spoils of grim battles. In that hour, it is to be said, being of a sudden torn from the marvellous contrivance of hewn wood and iron and rope and canvas, called a boat, with which the ingenuity of all past generations has equipped him, the Newfoundlander pits his naked strength against the sea: and that fight comes, to most men, at the end of life, for few survive it. Most men, too, have to face this supreme trial of brute strength in the season when they go to hunt the hair-seal which drift out of the north with the ice to whelp—but that is an empty phrase; rather, let it be said that it may be set down in significant terms, when, each with the lust of sixty dollars in his heart, they put forth into the heaving,

The Strength of Men

Norman Duncan

wind-lashed waste of ice and dusk and black, cold seas, where all the hungry forces of the north are loosed as for ravage. It came upon Saul Nash, of Ragged Harbour, this fight did, when in temperate lands mellow winds were teasing the first shy blossoms in the woods and peopled places were all yellow and a-tinkle and lazy.

At break of day—a sullen dawn which the sky's weight of waving black cloud had balked for an hour—the schooner was still fast in the grip of the floe and driving sou'west with the gale. Then the thin light, flowing through a rent at the horizon, spread itself over a sea all dull white and heaving—an expanse of ice, shattered and ground to bits, fragments of immeasurable fields, close packed, which rose and fell with the labouring waves. There was a confusion of savage noises, each proceeding from the fury and dire stress of conflict; for, aloft, where every shivering rope and spar opposed the will of the wind, the gale howled its wrath as it split and swept on, and, below decks, the timbers, though thrice braced for the voyage, cried out under the pressure and cruel grinding of the ice; but these were as a whimper to a full-lunged scream in the sum of uproar—it was the rending and crashing and crunching of the wind-driven floe, this thing of mass immense, plunging on, as under the whip of a master, which filled all the vast world with noise. The light increased; it disclosed the faces of men to men—frozen cheeks, steaming mouths, beards weighted with icicles, eyes flaring in dark pits. It disclosed the decks, where a litter of gaffs and clubs and ropes' ends lay frozen in the blood and fat of slain seal, the grimy deck-house and galley, the wrecked bowsprit, the abandoned wheel, the rigging and spars all sheathed with ice; and, beyond, as it pushed its way into the uttermost shadows, the solid shape of Deadly Rock and the Blueblack Shoal lying in the path of the wind.

"Does you see un, men?" said the skipper.

They were seven old hands who had gathered with the skipper by the windlass to wait for the morning, and they had been on the watch the night long—big, thick-chested fellows, heavy with muscles and bones—most with forbidding, leathery faces, which were not unused, however, at other times, to the play of a fine simplicity—men of knotty oak, with that look of strength, from the ground up, which some gnarled old tree has; and they were all clothed in skin boots and caps, and some coarse, home-made stuff, the last in a way so thick and bulky that it made giants of them.

"Does you see un—the Blueblack—dead ahead?" the skipper bawled, for the confusion of ice and wind had overwhelmed his voice.

They followed the direction of his arm, from the tip of his frozen mitt to the nearing shoal, dead ahead, where the sea was grinding the ice to slush. Death, to be died in that place, it might be, confronted them; but they said nothing. Yet they were not callous—every man loved his life; each had a fine regard for its duties and delights. But the schooner was in the grip of the pack, which the wind, not their will, controlled. There was nothing to be done—no call upon strength or understanding. Why talk? So they waited to see what the wind would do with the pack.

"Well, men," the skipper drawled, at last, "she'll wreck. Seems that way t' me—it do."

"Eh, b'y?" ol' Bill Anderson shouted, putting one hand to his ear and taking a new grip with the other, to keep his old hulk upright against the wind.

"She'll wreck," the skipper shouted.

"Iss," said ol' Bill, "she'll wreck." A pitch of the ship staggered him. When he had recovered his balance, he added, in a hoarse roar: "She'll strike well inside the easter' edge o' the shoal."

Thereupon there was a flash of discussion. The precise point—that was a problem having to do with the things of their calling: it was interesting.

"Noa, noa, b'y," said a young man, who had lurched up. "She'll strike handy t' the big rock west o' that by a good bit."

"Is you sure?" retorted ol' Bill, with a curl of the lip so quick that the pendant icicles rattled. "Ben't it Ezra North I hears a-talkin' agin?"

"Iss, 'tis he," North growled.

"Tell me, b'y," Anderson shouted, "has you ever been wrecked at the ice?"

"I 'low I were wrecked twice in White Bay in the fall gales, an' 'tis so bad—" A blast of wind swept the rest of the sentence out of hearing.

"At the ice, b'y, I says," ol' Bill cried. "Has you ever been wrecked *here?*"

Some fathoms off the starboard-bow a great pan of ice lifted itself out of the pack, as though seeking to relieve itself of a pressure no longer to be endured. It broke, fell with a crash, and crumbled. North's sulky negative was lost in the clap and rumble of its breaking.

"Has you ever been caught in the pack afore?" ol' Bill pursued.

"You knows I hasn't," North snapped, in a lull of the gale.

"Huh!" ol' Bill snorted. "You'll know moare about packs nex' spring, me b'y. I—*me,* b'y—I been swilin' [sealing] in these seas every spring for fifty-seven years. An' I says she'll strike inside the easter' edge o' the shoal a bit. Now, what says you?"

North said nothing, but he looked for support to Saul Nash, who was braced against the foremast—a hairy man of some forty-odd years, with great jaws, deep-set eyes, and drawn, shaggy brows; mighty in frame and brawn, true enough, but somewhat less than any there in stature.

"Maybe she will," said he, "an' maybe she woan't. 'Tis like us'll find out for sure."

" 'Twill prove me right when us do," said young North.

" 'Tis is not so sure," Nash returned. " 'Tis like she'll strike where you says she will, an' 'tis like she woan't, but 'tis moare like she woan't. But wait, b'y—bide easy. 'Twill not be long afore us knows."

"Oh, *I* knows where," said North.

But in half an hour he slunk aft, ashamed: for it was beyond dispute that she would strike where the old sealer had said. The shoal lay dead ahead in the path of the schooner's drift. In every part of it waves shook themselves free of ice and leaped high into the wind—all white and frothy against the sky, which was of the drear color of lead. Its tons were lifted and cast down—smashed—crunched: great pans were turned to finest fragments with crashing and groaning and hissing. The rocks stuck out of the sea like iron teeth. They were as nothing before the momentum of the pack—no hindrance to its slow, heavy onrush. The ice scraped over and between them, and, with the help of the waves, they ground it up in the passage. The shoal was like some gigantic machine. It was fed by the wind, which drove the pack; it was big as the wind is big. Massive chunks came through in slush. The schooner may be likened to an egg-shell thrown by chance into the feeding-chute of a crusher. The strength of the shoal was infinitely greater than her strength. Here, then, as it appeared, was a brutal tragedy—a dull, unprofitable, sickening sight, the impending denouement inevitable and all obvious. The seal hunters of Ragged Harbour, mere sentient moles, hither driven by the wind of need, were caught in the swirl of the sea's forces, which are insensate and uncontrolled. For the moment, it was past the time when sinew and courage are factors in the situation.

"Sure, men," said the skipper, " 'tis barb'rous hard t' lose the schooner —*barb'rous hard t' lose her,"* he bawled, with a glance about and a shake of the head.

He looked her over from stem to stern—along her shapely rail, and aloft, over the detail of her rigging. His glance lingered here and there—lingered wistfully. She was his life's achievement: he had build-ed her.

"Iss, skipper, sir—sure 'tis," said Saul Nash. He lurched to the skip-per's side and put a hand on his shoulder.

" 'Twere a good v'yage, skipper," ol' Bill Anderson said, lifting his voice above the noise of the pack.

" 'Twere a gran' haul off the Grey Islands—now, 'twere," said the skipper.

" 'Twere so good as ever I knowed from a schooner," said Anderson.

"I hates t' lose them pelts," said the skipper. "I do hate t' lose them pelts."

"Never yet were I wrecked with bloody decks," said Anderson, "that I didn't say 'twas a pity t' lose the cargo. Never, b'y—never! I says every time, says I, 'twas a pity t' lose the pelts."

Just then Saul's young brother John approached the group and stood to listen. He was a slight, brown-eyed boy, having the flush of health, true, and a conspicuous grace, but dark eyes instead of blue ones, and small measure of the bone and hard flesh of his mates. Saul moved under the foremast shrouds and beckoned him over.

"John, b'y," the man said, in a tender whisper, leaning over, "keep alongside o' me when—when—Come," bursting into forced heartiness, "there's a good lad, now; keep alongside o' me."

John caught his breath. "Iss, Saul," he whispered. Then he had to moisten his lips. "Iss, I will," he added, quite steadily.

"John!" in a low, inspiring cry.

"Saul!"

The swift, upward glance—the quivering glance, darting from the depths, which touched Saul's bold blue eyes for a flash and shifted to the dull sky—betrayed the boy again. He was one of those poor, dreamful folk who fear the sea. It may be that Saul loved him for that—for that strange difference.

"Come alongside, John, b'y," Saul mumbled, touching the lad on the shoulder, but not daring to look in his face. *"Close*—close alongside o' me."

"Iss, Saul."

It began to snow: not in feathery flakes, silent and soft, but the whizzing dust of flakes, which eddied and ran with the wind in blasts that stung. The snow came sweeping from the northeast in a thick, grey cloud. It engulfed the ship. The writhing ice round about and the shoal were soon covered up and hidden. Eyes were no longer of any use in the watching: but the skipper's ears told him, from moment to moment, that the shoal was nearer than it had been. Most of the crew went below to get warm while there was yet time—that they might be warm, warm and supple, in the crisis. Also they ate their fill of pork and biscuit and drank their fill of water; being wise in the ways of the ice, each stuffed his stomach, which they call, at such times with grim humour, the long-pocket. Some took off their jackets to give their arms freer play in the coming fight, some tightened their belts, some filled their pockets with the things they loved most: all made ready. Then they sat down to wait; and the waiting, in that sweltering, pitching hole, with its shadows and flickering light, was voiceless and fidgety. It was the brewing time of panic. In the words of the Newfoundlander, it would soon be every man for his life—that dread hour when, by the accepted creed of that coast, earth is in mercy curtained from heaven and the impassive angel's book is closed. At such times, escape is for the strong: the weak ask for no help; they are thrust aside; they find no hand stretched out. Compassion, and all the other kin of love, being overborne in the tumult, flee the hearts of men: there remains but the brute greed of life—*more life*. Every man for his own *life*—for his life. Each watched the other as though that other sought to wrest some advantage from him. Such was the temper of the men, then, that when the skipper roared for all hands there was a rush for the ladder and a scuffle for place at the foot of it.

"Men," the skipper bawled, when the crew had huddled amidships, cowering from the wind, "the ship'll strike the Blueblack inside o' thirty minutes. 'Tis every man for his life."

The old man was up on the port-rail with the snow curling about him. He had a grip of the mainmast shrouds to stay himself against the wind and the lunging of the ship. The thud and swish of waves falling back and the din of grinding ice broke from the depths of the snow over the bow—from some place near and hidden—and the gale was roaring past. The men crowded closer to hear him.

" 'Tis time t' take t' the ice," he cried.

"Iss, skipper!"

"Sure, sir!"

Young John Nash was in the shelter of Saul's great body: he was touching the skirt of the man's great-coat—like a child in a crowd. He looked from the skipper's face, which was hard set, and from the deck, which was known to him, to the waste of pitching ice and to the cloudy wall of snow which shut it in. Then he laid hold of a fold in the coat, which he had but touched before, and he crept a little closer.

"Is you all here?" the skipper went on. He ran his eye over them to count them. No man looked around for his friends. "Thirty-three. All right! Men, you'll follow Saul Nash. When you gets a hundred yards off the ship you'll drift clear o' the shoal. Now, over the side, all hands!" In a lull of the wind the shoal seemed suddenly very near. "Lively, men! *Lively!*"

The schooner was low with her weight of seal-fat. It was but a short leap to the pack in which she was caught—at most, but a swinging drop from the rail. That was all; even so, as the crew went over the side the shadow of the great terror fell—fell as from a cloud approaching. There was a rush to be clear of this doomed thing of wood—to be first in the way of escape, though the end of the untravelled path was a shadow: so there was a crowding at the rail, an outcry, a snarl, and the sound of a blow. The note of human frenzy was struck—a clangourous note, breaking harshly even into the mighty rage of things overhead and roundabout; and it clanged again, in a threat and a death-cry, as the men gained footing on the pack and pushed out from the schooner in the wake of Saul Nash. The ice, as I have said, was no more than a crust of incohesive fragments, which the wind kept herded close, and it rose and fell with the low, long heave of the waves: the very compactness of these separate particles depended, from moment to moment, upon the caprice of the wind and the influences at work within the body of the pack and in the waters beneath, which cannot be accounted for. Save upon the scattered pans, which had resisted the grinding of the pack, but were even then lifting themselves out of the press and falling back in pieces; save upon these few pans, there was no place where a man could rest his foot: for where he set it down there it sank. He must leap—leap—leap from one sinking fragment to another, choosing in a flash where next to alight, chancing his weight where it might be sustained for the moment of gathering to leap again—he must leap without pause; he must leap or the pack would let him through and close over his head. Moreover, the wind swept over the pack with full force and a stinging touch, and it was filled with the dust of snow: a wind which froze and choked and blinded where it could. But in the lead of Saul Nash, who was like a swaying shadow in the snow ahead, thirty men made the hundred yards and dispersed to the pans to wait—thirty of thirty-three, not counting the skipper, who had lingered far back to see the last of the work of his hands.

"Leave us—wait—here," said Saul, between convulsive pants, when, with John and ol' Bill Anderson, he had come to rest on a small pan. He turned his back to the wind to catch his breath. "Us'll clear—the shoal—here," he added.

Ol' Bill fell, exhausted. He shielded his mouth with his arm. " 'Tis so good as any place," he gasped.

" 'Tis big enough for seven men," said John.

Bill was an old hand—an old hand; and he had been in the thick of the pitiless slaughter of seals for five days. "Us'll let noa moare aboard, b'y," he cried. He started to his elbow and looked around; but he saw no one making for the pan, so he said to Saul, " 'Tis too small for three. Leave the young feller look out for hisself some other—"

"Bill," said Saul, "the lad bides here."

Bill was an old hand. He laughed in scorn. "Maybe," said he, "if the sea gets at this pan—to-morrow, or nex' day, Saul—if the sea gets at un, an' wears un down, 'tis yourself'll be the first t' push the lad off, an' not—"

"Does you hear me, Bill! I says the lad—"

John plucked Saul's sleeve. " 'Tis goain' abroad," he said, sweeping his hand over the pack.

Then a hush fell upon the ice—a hush that deepened and spread, and soon left only the swish of the gale and the muffled roar of the shoal. It came creeping from the west like a sigh of relief. The driving force of the wind had somewhere been mysteriously counteracted. The pressure was withdrawn. The pack was free. It would disperse into its separate parts. A veering of the wind—the impact of some vagrant field—a current or a tide—a far-off rock: who knows what influence? The direction of the pack was changed. It would swerve outward from the Blueblack shoal.

"Back, men! She'll goa clear o' the shoal!"

That was the skipper. They could see him standing with his back to the gale and his hands to his mouth. Beyond, in the mist of snow, the schooner lay tossing; her ropes and spars were a web and her hull was a shadow.

"Back! Back!"

There was a zigzag, plunging race for the schooner—for *more life:* for the hearth-fires of Ragged Harbour and the lips of wives and the clinging fingers of babies, which swam, as in a golden cloud, in the snow the wind was driving over the deck. The ice went abroad. The pack thinned and fell away into its fragments, which then floated free in widening gaps of sea. The way back was vanishing—even the sinking way over which they had come. Old James Moth, the father of eight, mischose the path; when he came to the end of it he teetered, for a space, on two small cakes, neither of which would bear him, and when his feet had forced them wide he fell back and was drowned. Ezra Bull—he who married pretty Mary o' Brunt Cove that winter—missed his leap and fell between two pans which swung together with crushing force in the trough of the lop; he sank without a cry when they went abroad. It was then perceived that the schooner had gathered way and was drifting faster than the pack through which she was pushing. As the ice fell away before her, her speed increased. The crew swerved to head her off. It was now a race without mercy or reproach. As the men converged upon the schooner's side their paths merged into one—a narrow, shifting way to the ice in her lee: and it was in the encounters of that place that three men lost their lives. Two tumbled to their death locked in each other's arms, and one was bested and flung down. When Saul and John, the last of all, came to that one patch of loose ice where the rail was within reach, a crowd of seven was congested there; and, with brute unreason, they were fighting for the first grip; so fast was the schooner slipping away, there was time left for but four, at most to clamber aboard. They had no firm foothold. No single bit of ice would hold a man up. It was like a fight upon quicksand. Men clawed the backs of men to save themselves from sinking; blows were struck; screams ended in coughs; throats were thick; oaths poured from mouths that were used to prayers. . . .

"Saul! Saul! She'll slip away from we."

She was drifting faster. The loosened pack divided before her prows. She was scraping through the ice, leaving it behind her, faster and faster yet. The blind crowd amidships plunged along with her, all the while losing something of their position.

"Steady, John, b'y," said Saul. "For'ard there—under the quarter."

"Iss, Saul. Oh, make haste!"

In a moment they were under the forward quarter, standing firm on a narrow pan of ice, waiting for the drift of the schooner to bring the rail within reach. When that time came, Saul caught the lad up and lifted him high. But she was dragging the men who clung to her. They were now within arm's reach of John. Even as he drew himself up a hand was raised to catch his foot. Saul struck at the arm. Then he felt a clutch on his own ankle—a grip that tightened. He looked down. His foot was released. He saw a hand stretched up, and stooped to grasp it; it was suddenly withdrawn. The face of a man wavered in the black water and disappeared. Saul knew that a touch of his hand was as near as ol' Bill Anderson had come to salvation. Then the fight was upon him. A man clambered on his back. He felt his foothold sinking—tipping—sinking. But he wriggled away, turned in a rush of terror to defend himself, and grappled with this man. They fell to the ice, each trying to free himself from the other; their weight was distributed over a wider surface of fragments, so they were borne up while they fought. The rest trampled over them. Before they could recover and make good their footing, the ship had drifted past. They were cut off from her by the open water in her wake. She slipped away like a shadow, vaguer grew, and vanished in the swirling snow. But a picture remained with Saul: that of a lad, in a cloud of snow, leaning over the rail, which was a shadow, with his mouth wide open in a cry, which was lost in the tumult of wind and hoarse voices, and with his hand stretched out; and he knew that John was aboard, and would come safe to Ragged Harbour. They would count the lost, he thought, as he leaped instinctively from cake to cake to keep himself out of the water; they would count the lost, he thought, when they had cleared the pack and were riding out the gale under bare poles.

"For'ard, there—stand by, some o' you!"

It was the skipper's voice, ringing in the white night beyond. There was an answering trample, like the sound of footfalls departing.

"Show a bit o' that jib!"

The words were now blurred by the greater distance. Saul listened for the creak and rattle of the sail running up the stays, but heard nothing.

"Sau—au—l—l!"

The long cry came as from far off, beating its way against the wind, muffled by the snow between.

That was the last.

Now, the man was stripped to his strength—to his naked strength: to his present store of vigour and heat and nutriment, plenteous or depleted, as might be; nor could he replenish it, for a mischance of the lifelong fight had at last flung him into the very swirl of the sea's forces, and he was cut off and illimitably compassed about by the five enemies. Grey shades, gathering in the snow to the east, vast and forbidding, betrayed the advance of the night. The wind, renewing its force, ran over the sea in whirling blasts; and to the wind the snow added its threefold bitterness. The open water, which widened as the pack fell away, fretted and fumed under the whip of the wind; little waves hissed viciously and flung spume to leeward, foreboding the combing swells to come. The cold pressed in, encroaching stealthfully; touching a finger here, and twining a tentacle there; sucking out warmth all the while. He was cut off, as I have said, and compassed about by the five enemies. He was stripped of rudder and sail. It was a barehanded fight—strength to strength. Escape was by endurance—by enduring the wind and the waves and the cold until such a time as the sea's passion wasted itself and she fell into that rippling, sunny mood in which she gathers strength for new assault. Even now, it was as though the fragments of ice over which he was aimlessly leaping tried to elude him—to throw him off. So he cast about for better position—for place on some pan, which would be like a wall to the back of an outnumbered man. After a time he found a pan, to which three men had already fled. He had to swim part way; but they helped him up, for the pan was thirty-feet square, and there was room for him.

"Be it you, Samuel?" said Saul.

"Iss, 'tis I—an' Matthew Weather and Andrew Butts."

Saul took off his jacket to wring it out. "Were it you, Matthew, b'y," he said, making ready to put it on again, "were it you jumped on me back—out there?"

"Sure, an' I doan't know, Saul. Maybe 'twere. I forgets. 'Twere terrible—out there."

"Iss, 'twere, b'y. I were just a-wonderin'."

They sat down—huddled in the middle of the pan; the snow eddied over and about them, and left drifts behind. Soon the pack vanished over the short circumference of sight. Then small waves began to break over the pan to windward. The water rolled to Saul's shoes and lapped them.

"How many does you leave t'hoame, Matthew?" said Saul.

"Nine, Saul."

"Sure, b'y," Matthew's brother, Samuel, cried, impatiently, "you forgets the baby. 'Tis ten, b'y, countin' the baby."

"Oh, iss—'tis true!" said Matthew. "Countin' the last baby an' little Billy Tuft, 'tis ten. I were a foster father t' little Billy. Iss—'tis ten I left. 'Tis quare I forgot the baby."

It was queer, for he loved them all, and he had had a doctor from Tilt Cove for the last baby: maybe the cold was to blame for that forgetfulness.

"You leaves moare'n me, Matthew," said Saul. "I leaves oan'y one."

The snow cloud darkened. Night had crept near. The shadow overhung the pan. More, the wind had a sweep over open water, for the pack was now widely distributed. Larger waves ran at the pan, momentarily increasing in number and height. One swept it—a thin sheet of water, curling from end to end. Then another; then three in quick succession, each rising higher.

"Iss—a lass, ben't she?" said Matthew, taking up the talk again.

"A girl, Matthew," said Saul. "A girl," he repeated, after a moment's silence, "just a wee bit of a girl. 'Tis like John 'll look after she."

"Oh, sure, b'y—sure! 'Tis like John will."

"Does you think he'll see to her schoolin', b'y?" said Saul. "She do be a bright one, that lass—that wee girlie." He smiled a tender, wistful smile—like a man who looks back, far back, upon some happiness. "'Twould be a pity," he went on, softly, "t' leave she goa without her schoolin'."

The wind was at the sea. It gathered the waves—drove them along in combing swells. It tore off their crests and swept spume with the snow. Great waves broke on every side—near at hand with a heavy swish, in the distance with a continuing roar. It was but a matter of chance, thus far, that one had not broken over the pan.

"Does you know what I thinks, Saul?" said Matthew. "Does you know what I thinks about that b'y John? He's a clever lad, that. He does well with the lobsters, now, doan't he, for a lad? Iss—"

"Iss," said Saul, "he does that, b'y. Iss he does."

"He'll have a cod trap some day, that lad. They's nothin' ol' Luke

Dart woan't do for un; an' they's noa better trader on these shores than Luke. He'll be rich, John will—rich! An' 'tis like he'll send that little maid o' yourn t' school t' Saint John's. That's what I thinks about it— 'tis."

"Does you?" said Saul. "Does you think that? May be. He've a terrible fancy for that wee girl. He brings she mussels an' lobsters, do John, an' big star-fish an' bake-apples an'—"

"Sure, he do," said Matthew. "B'y," he added, impressively, " 'twould surprise nobody if he'd give she music lessons t' Saint John's."

"That lass!" said Saul. "Does you think he'll give she music lessons —that wee thing?"

"Iss, sure! An' she'll play the organ in the church t' Ragged Harbour—when they gets one. She'll be growed up then."

"Iss, maybe," said Saul.

There was a long time in which no word was spoken. A wave broke near, and rose to the waists of the men. No one stirred.

"Does they l'arn you about—about—how t' goa about eatin', t' Saint John's?" said Saul. "All about—knives—an' forks?"

"Eh, b'y?" said Matthew, spurring himself to attend.

"I always thought I'd like she t' know about they things—when she grows up," said Saul.

Soon, he stood up: for the waves were rising higher. In the words of the Newfoundlander, he stood up to face the seas. The others had so far succumbed to cold and despair that they sat where they were, though the waves, which continuously ran over the pan, rose, from time to time, to their waists. It was night: the man's world was then no more than a frozen shadow, pitching in a space all black and writhing; and from the depths of this darkness great waves ran at him to sweep him off— increasing in might, innumerable, extending infinitely into the night. All the concerns of life—deeds done, things loved, tears, dreams, joys: these all melted into a golden, changing vision, floating far back, which glowed, and faded, and came again, and vanished. Wave came upon the heels of wave, each, as it were, with livelier hate and a harder blow—a massive shadow, rushing forth; a blow, a lifting, a tug, and a hiss behind: but none overcame him. Then a giant wave delivered its assault: it came ponderously—lifted itself high above his head, broke above him, fell, beat him down; it swept him back, rolling him over and over, but he caught a ridge of ice with his fingers, and he held his place, though the waters tugged at him mightily. He recovered his first position, and again he was beaten down; but again he rose to face the sea, and again a weight of water crushed him to his knees. Thus three more times, without pause: then a respite, in which it was made known to him that one other had survived.

"Be it you, Matthew?" said Saul.

"Noa—'tis Andrew Butts. I be fair done out, Saul."

Saul gathered his strength to continue the fight—to meet the stress and terrors of the hours to come: for it was without quarter, this fight; there is no mercy in cold, nor is there any compassion in the great Deep. Soon—it may have been two hours after the assault of the five great waves—the seas came with new venom and might; they were charged with broken ice, massed fragments of the pack, into which the wind had driven the pan, or, it may be, with the slush of pans, which the Blueblack Shoal had discharged. The ice added weight and a new terror to the waves. They bruised and dazed and sorely hurt the man when they fell upon him. No wave came but carried jagged chunks of ice—some great and some small; and these they flung at the men on the pan, needing only to strike here or there to kill them. Saul shielded his head with his arms. He was struck on the legs and on the left side; and once he was struck on the breast and knocked down. After a while—it may have been an hour after the fragments first appeared in the water—he was struck fair on the forehead; his senses wavered, but his strength continued sufficiently, and soon he forgot that he had so nearly been fordone. Again, after a time—it may now have been three hours before midnight—other greater waves came. They broke over his head. They cast their weight of ice upon him. There seemed to be no end to their number. Once, Saul, rising from where they had beaten him—rising doggedly to face them again—found that his right arm was powerless. He tried to lift it, but could not. He felt a bone grate over a bone in his shoulder—and a stab of pain. So he shielded his head from the ice in the next wave with his left arm—and from the ice in the next, and in the next, and the next. . . . The wave had broken his collarbone.

And thus in diminishing degree, for fifteen hours longer.

The folk of Neighborly Cove say that when the wind once more herded the pack and drove it inshore, Saul Nash, being alone, made his way across four miles of loose ice to the home of Abraham Coachman, in the lee of God's Warning, Sop's Arm way, where they had cornmeal for dinner; but Saul has forgotten that—this and all else that befell him after the sea struck him that brutal blow on the shoulder: the things of the whirling night, of the lagging dawn, when the snow thinned and ceased, and of the grey, frowning day, when the waves left him in peace. A crooked shoulder, which healed of itself, and a broad scar, which slants from the tip of his nose far up into his hair, tell him that the fight was hard. But what matter—all this? Notwithstanding all, when next the sea baited its trap with swarming herds, he set forth with John, his brother, to the hunt; for the world which lies hidden in the wide beyond has some strange need of seal-fat, and stands ready to pay, as of course. It pays gold to the man at the counter in Saint John's; and for what the world pays a dollar the outport warrior gets a pound of reeking pork. But what matter? What matter—all this toil and peril? What matter when the pork lies steaming on the table and the yellow duff is in plenty in the dish. What matter when, beholding it, the blue eyes of the lads and little maids flash merrily? What matter when the strength of a man provides so bounteously that his children may pass their plates for more? What matter—when there comes a night wherein a man may rest? What matter—in the end? Ease is a shame; and, for truth, old age holds nothing for any man save a seat in a corner and the sound of voices drifting in.

The doctor ticked off my symptoms on his fingers.

"Irritability of temper. Lack of appetite. Disinclination to work."

I nodded my assent to his analysis.

"What you need," he said, "is a complete rest—months of quiet in the open air. But avoid the haunts of tourists and summer boarders. Avoid excitement."

"I have been reading an interesting article about Newfoundland and Labrador," I said. "How would a trip along those coasts do?"

"The very thing," replied the doctor. "The sea-winds, the quiet nights and days, the seclusion and peace will make a new man of you."

Two weeks later I set out for those peaceful solitudes.

A Complete Rest

Theodore Goodridge Roberts

My guide was Mitchell Tobin. He was full of information. What he did not claim to know of the Labrador coast, from Belle Isle to Nain, was what did not exist. His home was in Notre Dame Bay, but his ancestors had come from a verdant island that has given gaiety and raciness of speech to many parts of the globe.

Tobin and I landed from the coastal steamer at Battle Harbour, and there purchased a staunch skiff from one George Jackson, a storekeeper. I wanted to see the country (at least, the fringe of it) in a more leisurely manner than that allowed by the steamer. We were well supplied with provisions and fly-ointment. The season was August. For a whole week we had glorious weather, sailing close along the coast and among the numerous islands during the day, and camping ashore at night. After that a fog set in, and we spent two days under canvas, in the shelter of a grove of scraggy firs, or "vars." Mitchell cheered me with tales of death and disaster due to fog. The number of ships, schooner and skiff wrecks in which he had figured as sole survivor was amazing. On the third morning we awoke to find a clear sky and a visible sun. We lost little time in folding our tent and stowing everything in the skiff. Then we ran up our tan-coloured sail and continued our journey.

"If it be divarsion ye're looking for, to clane t'at fog out o' yer heart, I kin show ye some yonder," said Tobin.

He pointed to a narrow channel between two rocks—a "tickle," in the language of the country.

I looked my enquiry.

"Troutin'," he said; "finest along t'is shore."

"Can you run through?" I enquired.

"Sure," he replied. "I knows t'is coast like t'ey smilin' skippers knows Mother Canty's sheebeen i'St. John's. T'e brook be's bilin' wid trout."

"Good!" I exclaimed, "nothing would suit me better."

He headed the skiff for the narrow channel. She scudded along like a creature of life.

"I knows it like a book," remarked Tobin, complacently, as we darted between the great lumps of rock, and sighted the still water of the little cove, and the mouth of the brook. But his complacency was ill-timed, for the words had scarcely left his lips before the bottom of the skiff smashed against a submerged ledge. I was thrown violently against the tough mast, and the skilful pilot sprawled on top of me. By the time we had scrambled to our feet the wounded craft was half full of water and settling aft, preparatory to sliding off the ledge into the unknown depths.

"Howly Sint Patrick!" cried Tobin, "now ye've did it, ye divil's own lump of a rock."

"Save your breath to swim ashore with," said I.

"Swim, be it," he cried. "Begobs, sor, ye'll have to learn me in a almighty hurry. T'e only way I kin swim be straight down."

The distance between the sinking skiff and the shore was not more than forty feet. I grabbed up my leather knapsack and hurled it toward the land-wash. It lit at the edge of the tide—the wet edge. Tobin heaved a bag of hard-bread after it. Then followed tins of meat, pots of jam, a fishing rod, and everything we could lift. Many of the articles dropped into the water not five yards from the skiff. Others landed well up the rocky beach (especially the pots of jam), and still others lit in shallow water. Then, after taking a firm grip on my guide's collar, and assuring him that I would drown him if he struggled, I slid into the water. Mitchell prayed fluently all the way, despite the fact that his face was under the water as often as above it.

Ten minutes later Mitchell Tobin sat up and looked at the spot on the placid surface of the cove where the skiff had gone down.

"Begobs," was the only appropriate sentiment he could give expression to. I did a trifle better than that; and then we gathered together the articles we had salvaged from the wreck. My companion tried to conciliate me by murmuring audible asides concerning my presence of mind in heaving the stuff ashore, and my prowess as a swimmer. But for fully a quarter of an hour I maintained a haughty and chilly demeanour.

"As you know the coast so well," I said, "please tell me how far we are from the nearest settlement?"

Mitchell seated himself on a convenient boulder and wrinkled his brows.

"T'ere be Dead Frenchman's Bight, about five mile an' twenty rod from here," he said, reflectively, "an' Nipper Drook about t'ree mile nort' o' t'at; and a mile beyand be's Penguin Rock, up Caribou Arm, where o' Skipper Denis Malloney buil' a stage t'ree year ago, an' were all but kilt entirely by t'e fairies, an'—"

"Stow all that," I cried, "and tell me the name of the nearest harbour where we can get a boat."

"Sure, an' baint I tellin' ye."

"Can I hire a boat in Frenchman's Bight?"

"Sure," said Mitchell.

It took us just a shade over four hours to reach Dead Frenchman's Bight, in spite of the fact that Tobin had named the distance so exactly as five miles and twenty rods. We found that the place consisted of about a dozen huts and drying stages clustered around a narrow anchorage. The men were all out on the fishing-grounds, but the women made us welcome. They turned glances of wonder on the mixed condition of our outfit. I told them of the loss of our skiff, and explained our predicament. They shook their heads when I enquired of the likelihood of being able to replace the skiff, and told us that they were not "livyers," but were Conception Bay people, spending the summer on the Labrador for the fishing, and that they had barely enough boats to carry on their business with.

"Does the steamer put in here?" I asked.

"Sure," said Mitchell.

"No, sir," replied one of the women, a strapping damsel with red hair and gray eyes; "she kapes miles off shore hereabouts, because o' t'ey rocks."

She pointed to a string of barren islands several miles to seaward. They were beautiful, but not conducive to safe navigation. I vented my chagrin on Tobin.

We spent three days at Dead Frenchman's Bight, and I got some good fishing in a pond on the barren above the hamlet. Every night we had a dance in the fish store, to the music of a fiddle, an accordion, and the shouts and whoops of the company. The tramp to Nipper Drook took up a whole morning.

"A long three miles," I remarked. Tobin eyed the landscape with agrieved and wondering regard.

"It do beat all," he said, as if the trail between the two harbours had played him a trick by stretching itself.

In Nipper Drook we found six families of "livyers," or permanent settlers, and a fore-and-aft schooner. The schooner proved to be on a trading cruise, and was northward bound. We boarded her, and I was so charmed with the trader and his stories that I asked him to take me along as passenger, for a consideration. He agreed readily enough. So I paid Tobin his wages and something extra to get home on.

"Home," said he. "Begobs, sir, I'se going back to Dead Frenchman's Bight, to marry t'at girl wid t'e red hair." I gave him my blessing. So long as he went I did not care what he did. I felt that his society stood for an element of excitement unauthorised by my doctor.

The name of the skipper trader was Packer. He hailed from Harbour Grace. He had been in the trade for several years and was doing well at it. His crew consisted of a boy and a man. The boy did the cooking. As Packer always stood a trick himself, and the schooner seldom sailed at night, we were not so short-handed as it sounds. His stock consisted of everything from a barrel of "salt-horse" to a trowser-button, and from a grappling-anchor to a spool of thread. The articles which seemed to be in the greatest demand were oil-skin clothing, packages of tea, tobacco, ready-made boots, and hard-bread. We worked our way northward in a leisurely manner, steadily reducing our supply of groceries and dry-goods, and filling up with cured fish. In the northern bays many of our customers were half-breed and full-blooded Esquimaux. They brought furs and carved ivory for trade.

At Seldom Seen Harbour we gave a dance aboard the *Guardian Angel* (for thus had Packer's shabby little vessel been devoutly named). It was attended by all the youth, beauty and fashion of the place. The belle of the ball was Alice Twenty-Helps, a lady of mixed Micmac and Esquimaux blood. Her hyphenated surname had come to her by way of her Micmac father who had, years before, won fame on that coast by devouring twenty helpings of plum-duff at a missionary dinner. I stepped more than one measure with the fair Alice, much to the envy of Packer and the able seaman. As a mark of my appreciation I gave her a green tin box (it had once contained fifty cigarettes), a clay pipe, a patent-medicine almanac, and five pounds of tea—the last of Packer's stock. In return she presented me with a leather tobacco-bag, cleverly worked in beads and dyed porcupine quills. Next morning, amid the mournful farewells of the Seldom Seeners, we set sail on our return trip to Harbour Grace.

The weather held clear and Packer was familiar with the coast, so for a time we sailed night and day. I took my turn at the wheel and the lookout as regularly as the others. One night I was awakened by hearing Packer going up the companion-ladder. As it was not his watch on deck I dressed and followed him, to see what the matter was. The sails were flapping in just enough wind to puff them out and let them drop. The *Guardian Angel* was rolling lazily in the slow seas. The fog was down on us like a moist snow-drift. Packer was anxious.

"It's these here currents that bothers me," he said, as I joined him on the little forecastlehead.

"Why don't you heave the lead?" I suggested.

"Heave yer grandmother," he retorted. "Man, there aint no soundin's 'round here until you get right atop the rocks—an' then you know all you want to about everything but kingdom come."

"Have you logged her?" I enquired, unabashed.

"Yes, sir," he replied more affably, "an' she's making about three knots on her course. Don't know how fast she's going off it."

"Drifting?" I queried.

He nodded. "But I'm keepin' her nose fer clear water," he said.

Half an hour later the wind freshened a bit, but the fog still clung to us. As I was not on duty I sat down with my back against the harness-cask, just aft of the foremast. I fell asleep and dreamed that Mitchell Tobin and I were aboard a wooden wash-tub, steering for a narrow channel between two frowning rocks. Tobin's face wore an expression of lofty composure. He was steering with a cricket bat. "Can you make it?" I enquired, anxiously. "Sure," he replied, "don't I know every rock along t'is coast by bote names?" Then we struck, and I awoke to find myself sprawled on the trembling deck of the *Guardian Angel*. I scrambled to my feet. Packer grabbed me by the arm. "We're sinking," he bawled. "Hump yoursel'."

I could see nothing, but the roar of surf was in my ears like unceasing thunder. The schooner bumped again, and took a sudden list to starboard. Packer and I were thrown against the rail, and nearly smothered by a great wave that dashed over us. When our heads got clear of the water we heard someone shouting that the dory had been carried away.

"We're aground, hard an' fast," exclaimed Packer. He made a line fast to a stanchion and passed it around both our waists. There we crouched, chilled to the bone and half-drowned, until morning broke gray through the fog. Peter and Mike Meehan were safe. They had tied themselves to the mainmast. The foremast was gone. Above our port bow loomed the cliff, close aboard. Spray flew above us like smoke. The seas that broke over our starboard counter had lost something of their violence. We cut our lashings and crawled forward. The roar of the surf was deafening—terrifying—the very slogan of disaster. I took a grip of Packer's belt with my left hand, not owing to physical weakness, but to a sudden feeling of terror. This passed, however, as quickly as it had come. We lay flat on the forecastlehead and looked over. The bowsprit had been carried away by the fall of the foremast. We could see that the schooner had been driven on to a submerged terrace of rock at the foot of the cliff, and that her bottom and the greater part of her starboard side had been sheered away. We looked aloft, and saw that a deep fissure zigzagged up the face of the rock.

Half an hour later we had a stout line stretched from the stump of the schooner's foremast to a jagged tooth of rock half way up the cliff. Packer had accomplished this after many throwings of the noosed rope. Now that it was securely fastened, Mike Meehan doffed his boots and oilskins and began the perilous climb. He held the rope with hands and knees, and wriggled along face up. At last he gained the rock and threw an arm about the jagged tooth. After resting thus for a minute or two, he pulled himself into the fissure. Then we cheered. He waved a hand and grinned down at us. After a good deal of work, and with the aid of more lines, we got such provisions as were undamaged safely to Meehan's resting place. They consisted of a bag of hard-bread, some tinned salmon, dried fish, and two small beakers of water. By this time the *Guardian Angel* was showing signs of breaking up that were not to be disregarded. We rushed our blankets across and quickly followed them. With two lines, one below the other, we made the passage much more quickly than Mike had done.

The ascent to the top of the cliff was accomplished safely. Seabirds wheeled about us, flashing and vanishing in the fog, their cries piercing the tumult of the waves. We explored our haven cautiously, and found it to be nothing but a bare rock of about an acre in extent. We could find no wood for a fire, no cave for a shelter. Packer was in the depths of despondency over the loss of his schooner and his season's trade. Mike Meehan seemed content that he possessed tobacco, a pipe, and matches. His young brother, Peter, was clearly in a funk. The fear and distrust of the sea was in his blood. To me it seemed a picturesque and diverting adventure. My chest swelled at the thought of the yarns I would spin on my return to civilisation. Just then I did not count the chances of not returning. The day dragged through. We talked a little, and Mike treated us to a song. Twice we ate hard-bread and drank water. At last the shadow of night fell through the gray fog. We rolled up in our blankets and went to sleep.

Two days later the fog cleared away, and the sun shone on a world of blue and white waters, blue sky and ruddy rocks. Low down on the western horizon the mainland lay pink and purple. Here and there naked rock-islands like our own rose from the intervening water. We found that the *Guardian Angel* had gone to pieces, but that several fragments of wreckage had been washed into the lower levels of the fissure. We salvaged these, and spread them out to dry in the sun. They were soon fit for fuel.

"I guess these are the Strawberry Rocks," said Packer. "The coastal boat 'ill be along in a few days. Her course lays about a mile to seaward."

"So we are sure to be picked up?" I exclaimed, with a note of relief in my voice. The fog had begun to dampen the picturesqueness of the adventure.

"Oh, *we're* safe enough, cookin' our grub an' makin' our signals with the ribs o' the old schooner," he replied, mournfully.

A month later I stepped into the doctor's consulting room. "Hullo!" he cried, "the rest *has* done you good, and no mistake. There's nothing like a few weeks' quiet when a man is run down."

"Nothing like it," I replied, heartily. "You should try it yourself, doctor."

"The other lady . . . " the ship's steward began.

"We're not together," a quiet but determined female voice explained from the corridor, one hand thrust through the doorway insisting that he take her independent tip for the bag he had just deposited on the lower bunk.

There was not room for Troy McFadden to step into the cabin until the steward had left.

"It's awfully small," Fidelity Munroe, the first occupant of the cabin, confirmed, shrinking down into her oversized duffle coat.

"It will do if we take turns," Troy McFadden decided. "I'll let you settle first, shall I?"

"I just need a place to put my bag."

The upper bunk was bolted against the cabin ceiling to leave headroom for anyone wanting to sit on the narrow upholstered bench below.

"Under my bunk," Troy McFadden suggested.

There was no other place. The single chair in the cabin was shoved in under the small, square table, and the floor of the minute closet was taken up with life jackets. The bathroom whose door Troy McFadden opened to inspect, had a coverless

Inland Passage

Jane Rule

toilet, sink and triangle of a shower. The one hook on the back of the door might make dressing there possible. When she stepped back into the cabin, she bumped into Fidelity Munroe, crouching down to stow her bag.

"I'm sorry," Fidelity said, standing up, "But I can get out now."

"Let's both get out."

They sidled along the narrow corridor, giving room to other passengers in search of their staterooms.

Glancing into one open door, Troy McFadden said, "At least we have a window."

"Deck?" Fidelity suggested.

"Oh, yes."

Neither had taken off her coat. They had to shoulder the heavy door together before they could step out into the moist sea air. Their way was blocked to the raised prow of the ship where they might otherwise have watched the cars, campers, and trucks being loaded. They turned instead and walked to the stern of the ferry to find rows of wet, white empty benches facing blankly out to sea.

"You can't even see the Gulf Islands this morning," Troy McFadden observed.

"Are you from around here?"

"Yes, from North Vancouver. We should introduce ourselves, shouldn't we?"

"I'm Fidelity Munroe. Everyone calls me Fido."

"I'm Troy McFadden, and nearly everyone calls me Mrs. McFadden."

They looked at each other uncertainly, and then both women laughed.

"Are you going all the way to Prince Rupert?" Fidelity asked.

"And back, just for the ride."

"So am I. Are we going to see a thing?"

"It doesn't look like it," Troy McFadden admitted. "I'm told you rarely do on this trip. You sail into mist and maybe get an occasional glimpse of forest or the near shore of an island. Mostly you seem to be going nowhere."

"Then why . . . ?"

"For that reason, I suppose," Troy McFadden answered, gathering her fur collar more closely around her ears.

"I was told it rarely gets rough," Fidelity Munroe offered.

"We're in open sea only two hours each way. All the rest is inland passage."

"You've been before then."

"No," Troy McFadden said. "I've heard about it for years."

"So have I, but I live in Toronto. There you hear it's beautiful."

"*Mrs.* Munroe?"

"Only technically," Fidelity answered.

"I don't think I can call you Fido."

"It's no more ridiculous than Fidelity once you get used to it."

"Does your mother call you Fido?"

"My mother hasn't spoken to me for years," Fidelity Munroe answered.

Two other passengers, a couple in their agile seventies, joined them on the deck.

"Well . . . " Troy McFadden said, in no one's direction, "I think I'll get my bearings."

She turned away, a woman who did not look as if she ever lost her bearings.

You're not really old enough to be my mother, Fidelity wanted to call after her, *Why take offense?* But it wasn't just that remark. Troy McFadden would be as daunted as Fidelity by such sudden intimacy, the risk of its smells as much as its other disclosures. She would be saying to herself, *I'm too old for this. Why on earth didn't I spend the extra thirty dollars?* Or she was on her way to the purser to see if she might be moved, if not into a single cabin then into one with someone less . . . more . . .

Fidelity looked down at Gail's much too large duffle coat, her own jeans and hiking boots. Well, there wasn't room for the boots in her suitcase, and, ridiculous as they might look for walking the few yards of deck, they might be very useful for exploring the places the ship docked.

Up yours, Mrs. McFadden, with your fur collar and your expensive, sensible shoes and matching bag. Take up the whole damned cabin!

All Fidelity needed for this mist-bound mistake of a cruise was a book out of her suitcase. She could sleep in the lounge along with the kids and the Indians, leave the staterooms (what a term!) to the geriatrics and Mrs. McFadden.

Fidelity wrenched the door open with her own strength, stomped back along the corridor like one of the invading troops, and unlocked and opened the cabin door in one gesture. There sat Troy McFadden, in surprised tears.

"I'm sorry . . . " Fidelity began, but she could not make her body retreat.

Instead she wedged herself around the door and closed it behind her. Then she sat down beside Troy McFadden, took her hand, and stared quietly at their unlikely pairs of feet. A shadow passed across the window. Fidelity looked up to meet the eyes of another passenger glancing in. She reached up with her free hand and pulled the small curtain across the window.

"I simply can't impose . . . " Troy finally brought herself to say.

"Look," Fidelity said, turning to her companion, "I may cry most of the way myself . . . it doesn't matter."

"I just can't make myself . . . walk into those public rooms . . . alone."

"How long have you been alone?" Fidelity asked.

"My husband died nearly two years ago . . . there's no excuse."

"Somebody said to me the other day, 'Shame's the last stage of grief.' 'What a rotten arrangement then,' I said. 'To be ashamed for the rest of my life.'"

"You've lost your husband?"

Fidelity shook her head, "Years ago. I divorced him."

"You hardly look old enough . . . "

"I know, but I am. I'm forty one. I've got two grown daughters."

"I have two sons," Troy said. "One offered to pay for this trip just to get me out of town for a few days. The other thought I should lend him the money instead."

"And you'd rather have?"

"It's so humiliating," Troy said.

"To be alone?"

"To be afraid."

The ship's horn sounded.

"We're about to sail," Troy said. "I didn't even have the courage to get off the ship, and here I am, making you sit in the dark . . . "

"Shall we go out and get our bearings together?"

"Let me put my face back on," Troy said.

Only then did Fidelity let go of her hand so that she could take her matching handbag into the tiny bathroom and smoothe courage back into her quite handsome and appealing face.

Fidelity pulled her bag out from under the bunk, opened it and got out her own sensible shoes. If she was going to offer this woman any sort of reassurance, she must make what gestures she could to be a bird of her feather.

The prow of the ship had been lowered and secured, and the reverse engines had ceased their vibrating by the time the two women joined the bundled passengers on deck to see, to everyone's amazement, the sun breaking through, an ache to the eyes on the shining water.

Troy McFadden reached for her sunglasses. Fidelity Munroe had forgotten hers.

"This is your captain," said an intimate male voice from a not very loud speaker just above their heads. "We are sailing into a fair day."

The shoreline they had left remained hidden in clouds crowded up against the Vancouver mountains, but the long wooded line of Galiano Island and beyond it to the west the mountains of Vancouver Island lay in a clarity of light.

"I'm hungry," Fidelity announced. "I didn't get up in time to have breakfast."

"I couldn't eat," Troy confessed.

When she hesitated at the entrance to the cafeteria, Fidelity took her arm firmly and directed her into the short line that had formed.

"Look at that!" Fidelity said with pleasure. "Sausages, ham, bacon, pancakes. How much can we have?"

"As much as you want," answered the young woman behind the counter.

"Oh, am I ever going to pig out on this trip!"

Troy took a bran muffin, apple juice and a cup of tea.

"It isn't fair," she said as they unloaded their contrasting trays at a window table. "My husband could eat like that, too, and never gain a pound."

Fidelity, having taken off her coat, revealed just how light bodied she was.

"My kids call me bird bones. They have their father to thank for being human size. People think I'm their little brother."

"Once children tower over you, being their mother is an odd business," Troy mused.

"That beautiful white hair must help," Fidelity said.

"I've had it since I was twenty-five. When the boys were little, people thought I was their grandmother."

"I suppose only famous people are mistaken for themselves in public," Fidelity said, around a mouthful of sausage; so she checked herself and chewed instead of elaborating on that observation.

"Which is horrible in its way, too, I suppose," Troy said.

Fidelity swallowed. "I don't know. I've sometimes thought I'd like it: Mighty Mouse fantasies."

She saw Troy try to smile and for a second lose the trembling control of her face. She hadn't touched her food.

"Drink your juice," Fidelity said, in the no-nonsense, cheerful voice of motherhood.

Troy's dutiful hand shook as she raised the glass to her lips, but she took a sip. She returned the glass to the table without accident and took up the much less dangerous bran muffin.

"I would like to be invisible," Troy said, a rueful apology in her voice.

"Well, we really are, aren't we?" Fidelity asked. "Except to a few people."

"Have you traveled alone a lot?"

"No," Fidelity said, "just about never. I had the girls, and they're still only semi-independent. And I had a friend, Gail. She and I took trips together. She died last year."

"I'm so sorry."

"Me, too. It's a bit like being a widow, I guess, except, nobody expects it to be. Maybe that helps."

"Did you live with Gail?"

"No, but we thought maybe we might . . . someday."

Troy sighed.

"So here we both are at someday," Fidelity said. "Day one of someday and not a bad day at that."

They both looked out at the coast, ridge after ridge of tall trees, behind which were sudden glimpses of high peaks of snow-capped mountains.

Back on the deck other people had also ventured, dressed and hatted against the wind, armed with binoculars for sighting of eagles and killer whales, for inspecting the crews of fishing boats, tugs, and pleasure craft.

"I never could use those things," Fidelity confessed. "It's not just my eyes. I feel like that woman in the Colville painting."

"Do you like his work?" Troy asked.

"I admire it," Fidelity said. "There's something a bit sinister about it: all those figures seem prisoners of normality. That woman at the shore, about to get into the car . . ."

"With the children, yes," Troy said. "They seem so vulnerable."

"Here's Jonathan Seagull!" a woman called to her binocular-blinded husband, "Right here on the rail."

"I loathed that book," Troy murmured to Fidelity.

Fidelity chuckled. "In the first place, I'm no friend to seagulls."

Finally chilled, the two women went back inside. At the door to the largest lounge, again Troy hesitated.

"Take my arm," Fidelity said, wishing it and she were more substantial.

They walked the full length of that lounge and on into the smaller space of the gift shop where Troy was distracted from her nerves by postcards, travel books, toys and souvenirs.

Fidelity quickly picked up half a dozen postcards.

"I'd get home before they would," Troy said.

"I probably will, too, but everybody likes mail."

From the gift shop, they found their way to the forward lounge where tv sets would later offer a movie, on into the children's playroom, a glassed-in area heavily padded where several toddlers tumbled and stumbled about.

"It's like an aquarium," Fidelity said.

"There aren't many children aboard."

"One of the blessings of traveling in October," Fidelity said. "Oh, I don't feel about kids the way I do about seagulls, but they aren't a holiday."

"No," Troy agreed. "I suppose I really just think I miss mine."

Beyond the playroom they found the bar with only three tables of prelunch drinkers. Troy looked in, shook her head firmly and retreated.

"Not a drinker?" Fidelity asked.

"I have a bottle of scotch in my case," Troy said. "I don't think I could ever . . . alone . . . "

"Mrs. McFadden," Fidelity said, taking her arm, "I'm going to make a hard point. You're not alone. You're with me, and we're both old enough to be grandmothers, and we're approching the turn of the 21st not the 20th century, and I think we both could use a drink."

Troy McFadden allowed herself to be steered into the bar and settled at a table, but, when the waiter came, she only looked at her hands.

"Sherry," Fidelity decided. "Two sherries," and burst out laughing.

Troy looked over at her, puzzled.

"Sherry is my idea of what you would order. I've never tasted it in my life."

"You're quite right," Troy said. "Am I such a cliché?"

"Not a cliché, an ideal. I don't know, maybe they're the same thing when it comes down to it. You have style. I really admire that. If I ever got it together enough to have shoes and matching handbag, I'd lose one of the shoes."

"Is that really your coat?" Troy asked.

Fidelity looked down at herself. "No, it belonged to Gail. It's my Linus blanket."

"I've been sleeping in my husband's old pajamas. I had to buy a nightgown to come on this trip," Troy confided. "I think it's marvelous the way you do what you want."

Fidelity bit her lip and screwed her face tight for a moment. Then she said, "But I don't want to cry any more than you do."

The waiter put their sherries before them, and Fidelity put a crumpled ten dollar bill on the table.

"Oh, you should let me," Troy said, reaching for her purse.

"Next round," Fidelity said.

Troy handled her glass more confidently than she had at breakfast, and, after her first sip, she said with relief, "Dry."

"This is your captain," the intimate male voice asserted again. "A pod of killer whales is approaching to starboard."

Fidelity and Troy looked out the window and waited. No more than a hundred yards away, a killer whale broke the water, then another, then another, their black backs arching, their bellies unbelievably white.

"They don't look real," Fidelity exclaimed.

Then one surfaced right alongside the ferry, and both women caught their breath.

"This trip is beginning to feel less like somebody else's day dream," Fidelity said. "Just look at that!"

For some moments after the whales had passed, the women continued to watch the water, newly interested in its possibilities for surprise. As if as a special reward for their attention, an enormous bird dropped out of the sky straight into the sea, then lifted off the water with a strain of great wings, a flash of fish in its talons.

"What on earth was that?" Fidelity cried.

"A bald eagle catching a salmon," Troy replied.

The ship had slowed to navigate a quite narrow passage between the mainland and a small island, its northern crescent shore fingered with docks, reached by flights of steps going back up into the trees where the glint of windows and an occasional line of roof could be seen.

"Do people live there all year long?" Fidelity asked.

"Not many. They're summer places mostly."

"How do people get there?"

"Private boats or small planes."

"Ain't the rich wealthy?" Fidelity sighed.

Troy frowned.

"Did I make a personal remark by mistake?"

"Geoff and I had a place when the boys were growing up. We didn't *have* money, but he earned a good deal . . . law. He hadn't got around to thinking about . . . retiring. I'm just awfully grateful the boys had finished their education. It scares me to think what it might have been like if it had happened earlier. You just don't think . . . we didn't anyway. Oh, now that I've sold the house, I'm perfectly comfortable. When you're just one person . . . "

"Well, on this trip with the food all paid for, I'm going to eat like an army," Fidelity said. "Let's have lunch."

Though the ship wasn't crowded, there were more people in the cafeteria than there had been for breakfast.

"Let's not sit near the Jonathan Seagulls," Fidelity said, leading the way through the tables to a quiet corner where they could do more watching than being watched. Troy had chosen a seafood salad that Fidelity considered a first course to which she added a plate of lamb chops, rice and green beans.

"I really don't believe you could eat like that all the time," Troy said.

"Would if I could."

Fidelity tried not to let greed entirely overtake her, yet she needed to eat quickly not to leave Troy with nothing to do.

"See those two over there?" Fidelity said, nodding to a nondescript pair of middle-aged women. "One's a lady cop. The other's her prisoner."

"How did you figure that out?"

"Saw the handcuffs. That's why they're sitting side by side."

"They're both right handed," Troy observed critically.

"On their ankles."

"What's she done?"

"Blown up a mortgage company," Fidelity said.

"She ought to get a medal."

"A fellow anarchist, are you?"

"Only armchair," Troy admitted modestly.

"Mrs. McFadden, you're a fun lady. I'm glad we got assigned to the same shoe box."

"Do call me Troy."

"Only if you'll call me Fido."

"Will you promise not to bark?"

"No," Fidelity said and growled convincingly at a lamb chop but quietly enough not to attract attention.

"Fido, would it be both antisocial and selfish of me to take a rest after lunch?"

"Of course not," Fidelity said. "I'll just come up and snag a book."

"Then later you could have a rest."

"I'm not good at them," Fidelity said. "I twitch and have horrible dreams if I sleep during the day. But, look, I do have to know a few intimate things about you, like do you play bridge or Scrabble or poker because I don't, but I could probably scout out some people who do . . ."

"I loathe games," Troy said. "In any case, please don't feel responsible for me. I do feel much better, thanks to you."

A tall, aging fat man nodded to Troy as they left the cafeteria and said, "Lovely day."

"Don't panic," Fidelity said out of the side of her mouth. "I bite too, that is, unless you're in the market for a shipboard romance."

"How about you?" Troy asked wryly.

"I'm not his type."

"Well, he certainly isn't mine!"

Fidelity went into the cabin first, struggled to get her case out from under the bunk and found her book, Alice Walker's collection of essays.

"Is she good?" Troy asked, looking at the cover.

"I think she's terrific, but I have odd tastes."

"Odd?"

"I'm a closet feminist."

"But isn't that perfectly respectable by now?" Troy asked.

"Nothing about me is perfectly respectable."

"You're perfectly dear," Troy said and gave Fidelity a quick, hard hug before she went into the cabin.

Fidelity paused for a moment outside the closed door to enjoy that affectionate praise before she headed off to find a window seat in the lounge where she could alternately read and watch the passing scene. An occasional deserted Indian village was now the only sign of habitation on the shores of this northern wilderness.

The book lay instead neglected in her lap, and the scenery became a transparency through which Fidelity looked at her inner landscape, a place of ruins.

A man whose wife had died of the same cancer that had killed Gail said to Fidelity, "I don't even want to take someone out to dinner without requiring her to have a thorough physical examination first."

The brutality of that remark shocked Fidelity because it located in her her own denied bitterness, that someone as lovely and funny and strong as Gail could be not only physically altered out of recognition but so horribly transformed humanly until she seemed to have nothing left but anger, guilt, and fear, burdens she tried to shift, as she couldn't her pain, onto Fidelity's shoulders, until Fidelity found herself praying for Gail's death instead of her life. Surely she had loved before she grew to dread the sight of Gail, the daily confrontations with her appalled and appalling fear. It was a face looking into a hell Fidelity knew did not exist, and yet her love had failed before it. Even now it was her love she mourned rather than Gail, for without it she could not go back to the goodness between them, believe in it and go on.

She felt herself withdraw from her daughters as if her love for them might also corrupt and then fail them. In the way of adolescents they both noticed and didn't, excused her grief and then became impatient with it. They were anyway perched at the edge of their own lives, ready to be free of her.

"Go," she encouraged them, and they did.

"I guess I only think I miss them," Troy said. Otherwise this convention of parent abandonment would be intolerable, a cruel and unusual punishment for all those years of intimate attention and care.

And here she was, temporarily paired with another woman as fragile and shamed by self-pity as she was. At least they wouldn't be bleeding all over the other passengers. If they indulged in pitying each other, well, what was the harm in it?'

Fidelity shifted uncomfortably. The possibility of harm was all around her.

"Why did you marry me then?" she had demanded of her hostile husband.

"I felt *sorry* for you," he said.

"That's a lie!"

"It's the honest truth."

So pity, even from someone else, is the seed of contempt.

Review resolutions for this trip: be cheerful, eat, indulge in Mighty Mouse fantasies, and enjoy the scenery.

An island came into focus, a large bird perched in a tree, another eagle no doubt, and she would not think of the fish except in its surprised moment of flight.

"This is your captain speaking . . . "

Fidelity plugged her ears and also shut her eyes, for even if she missed something more amazing than whales, she wanted to see or not see for herself.

"Here you are," Troy said. "What on earth are you doing?"

"Do you think he's going to do that all through the trip?" Fidelity demanded.

"Probably not after dark."

"Pray for an early sunset."

It came, as they stood watching it on deck, brilliantly red with promise, leaving the sky christened with stars.

"Tell me about these boys of yours," Fidelity said as they sat over a pre-dinner drink in the crowded bar. "We've spent a whole day together without even taking out our pictures. That's almost unnatural."

"In this den of iniquity," Troy said, glancing around, "I'm afraid people will think we're exchanging dirty postcards."

"Why oh why did I leave mine at home?"

Fidelity was surprised that Troy's sons were not better looking than they were, and she suspected Troy was surprised at how much better looking her daughters were than she had any right to expect. It's curious how really rare a handsome couple is. Beauty is either too vain for competition or indifferent to itself. Troy would have chosen a husband for his character. Fidelity had fallen for narcissistic good looks, for which her daughters were her only and lovely reward.

"Ralph's like his father," Troy said, taking back the picture of her older son, "conservative with some attractive independence of mind. So many of our friends had trouble with first children and blame it on their own inexperience. Geoff used to say, 'I guess the more we knew, the worse we did.'"

"What's the matter with Colin?" Fidelity asked.

"I've never thought there was anything the matter with him," Troy said, "except perhaps the world. Geoff didn't like his friends or his work (Colin's an actor). It was the only hard thing between Geoff and me, but it was very hard."

The face Fidelity studied was less substantial and livelier than Ralph's, though it was easy enough to tell that they were brothers.

"We ought to pair at least two of them off, don't you think?" Fidelity suggested flippantly. "Let's see. Is it better to put the conservative, responsible ones together, and let the scallywags go off and have fun, or should each kite have a tail?"

"Colin won't marry," Troy said. "He's homosexual."

Fidelity looked up from the pictures to read Troy's face. Her dark blue eyes held a question rather than a challenge.

"How lucky for him that you're his mother," Fidelity said. "Did you realize that I am, too?"

"I wondered when you spoke about your friend Gail," Troy said.

"Sometimes I envy people his age," Fidelity said. "There's so much less guilt, so much more acceptance."

"In some quarters," Troy said. "Geoff let it kill him."

"How awful!"

"That isn't true," Troy said. "It's the first time I've ever said it out loud, and it simply isn't true. But I've been so afraid Colin thought so, so angry, yes, *angry*. I always thought Geoff would finally come round. He was basically a fair-minded man. Then he had a heart attack and died. If he'd had any warning, if he'd had time . . ."

Fidelity shook her head. She did not want to say how easily that might have been worse. Why did people persist in the fantasy that facing death brought out the best in people when so often it did just the opposite?

"How does Colin feel about his father?"

"He always speaks of him very lovingly, remembering all the things he did with the boys when they were growing up. He never mentions those last, awful months when Geoff was remembering the same things but only so that he didn't have to blame himself."

"Maybe Colin's learning to let them go," Fidelity suggested.

"So why can't I?" Troy asked.

There was Fidelity's own question in Troy's mouth. *It's because they're dead,* she thought. *How do you go about forgiving the dead for dying?* Then, because she had no answer, she simply took Troy's hand.

"Is that why your mother doesn't speak to you?" Troy asked.

"That and a thousand other things," Fidelity said. "It used to get to me, but, as my girls have grown up, I think we're all better off for not trying to please someone who won't be pleased. Probably it hasn't anything to do with me, just luck, that I like my kids, and they like me pretty well most of the time."

"Did they know about you and Gail?"

"Did and didn't. We've never actually talked about it. I would have, but Gail was dead set against it. I didn't realize just how much that had to do with her own hang-ups. Once she was gone, there didn't seem to be much point, for them."

"But for you?"

"Would you like another drink?" Fidelity asked as she signaled the waiter and, at Troy's nod, ordered two. "For myself, I'd like to tell the whole damned world, but I'm still enough of my mother's child to hear her say, 'Another one of your awful self-indulgences' and to think maybe she has a point."

"It doesn't seem to me self-indulgent to be yourself," Troy said.

Fidelity laughed suddenly. "Why that's exactly what it is! Why does everything to do with the *self* have such a bad press: self-pity, self-consciousness, self-indulgence, self-satisfaction, practices of selfish people, people being themselves?"

"The way we are," Troy said.

"Yes, and I haven't felt as good about myself in months."

"Nor I," Troy said, smiling.

"Are we going to watch the movie tonight, or are we going to go on telling each other the story of our lives?"

"We have only three days," Troy said. "And this one is nearly over."

"I suppose we'd better eat before the cafeteria closes."

They lingered long over coffee after dinner until they were alone in the room, and they were still there when the movie goers came back for a late night snack. Troy yawned and looked at her watch.

"Have we put off the evil hour as long as we can?" Fidelity asked.

"You're going to try to talk me out of the lower bunk."

"I may be little, but I'm very agile," Fidelity claimed.

The top bunk had been made up, leaving only a narrow corridor in which to stand or kneel, as they had to to get at their cases. Troy took her nightgown and robe and went into the bathroom. Fidelity changed into her flannel tent and climbed from the chair to the upper bunk, too close to the ceiling for sitting. She lay on her side, her head propped up on her elbow.

It occurred to her that this cabin was the perfect setting for the horrible first night of a honeymoon and she was about to tell Troy so as she came out of the bathroom but she looked both so modest and so lovely than an easy joke seemed instead tactless.

"I didn't have the courage for a shower," Troy confessed. "Really, you know, we're too old for this."

"I think that's beginning to be part of the fun."

When they had both settled and turned out their lights, Fidelity said, "Good night, Troy."

"Good night, dear Fido."

Fidelity did not expect to sleep at once, her head full of images and revelations, but the gentle motion of the ship lulled her, and she felt herself letting go and dropping away. When she woke, it was morning, and she could hear the shower running.

"You did it!" Fidelity shouted as Troy emerged fully dressed in a plum and navy pant suit, her night things over her arm.

"I don't wholeheartedly recommend it as an experience, but I do feel better for it."

Fidelity followed Troy's example. It seemed to her the moment she turned on the water, the ship's movement became more pronounced, and she had to hang onto a bar which might have been meant for a towel rack to keep her balance, leaving only one hand for the soaping. By the time she was through, the floor was awash, and she had to sit on the coverless toilet to pull on her grey and patchily soggy trousers and fresh wool shirt.

"We're into open water," Troy said, looking out their window.

"Two hours, you said?"

"Yes."

"I think I'm going to be better off on deck," Fidelity admitted, her normally pleasurable hunger pangs suddenly unresponsive to the suggestion of sausages and eggs. "Don't let me keep you from breakfast."

"What makes you think I'm such an old sea dog myself?"

Once they were out in the sun and air of a lovely morning, the motion of the open sea was exciting. They braced themselves against the railing and plunged with the ship, crossing from the northern tip of Vancouver Island to the mainland.

A crewman informed them that the ship would be putting in at Bella Bella to drop off supplies and pick up passengers.

"Will there be time to go ashore?" Fidelity asked.

"You can see everything there is to see from here," the crewman answered.

"No stores?"

"Just the Indian store . . . for the Indians," he said, as he turned to climb to the upper deck.

"A real, lived-in Indian village!" Fidelity said. "Do you want to go ashore?"

"It doesn't sound to me as if we'd be very welcome," Troy said.

"Why not?"

"You're not aware that we're not very popular with the Indians?"

Fidelity sighed. She resented, as she always did, having to take on the sins and clichés of her race, nation, sex, and yet she was less willing to defy welcome at an Indian village than she was at the ship's bar.

They were able to see the whole of the place from the deck, irregular rows of raw wood houses climbing up a hill stripped of trees. There were more dogs than people on the dock. Several family groups, cheaply but more formally dressed than most of the other passengers, boarded.

"It's depressing," Fidelity said.

"I wish we knew how to expect something else and make it happen."

"I'm glad nobody else was living on the moon," Fidelity said, turning sadly away.

The Indian families were in the cafeteria where Troy and Fidelity went for their belated breakfast. The older members of the group were talking softly among themselves in their own language. The younger ones were chatting with the crew in a friendly enough fashion. They were all on their way to a great wedding in Prince Rupert that night and would be back on board ship when it sailed south again at midnight.

"Do you work?" Troy suddenly asked Fidelity as she put a large piece of ham in her mouth.

Fidelity nodded as she chewed.

"What do you do?"

"I'm a film editor," Fidelity said.

"Something as amazing as that, and you haven't even bothered to tell me?"

"It's nothing amazing," Fidelity said. "You sit in a dark room all by yourself, day after day, trying to make a creditable half hour or hour and a half out of hundreds of hours of film."

"You don't like it at all?"

"Oh, well enough," Fidelity said. "Sometimes it's interesting. Once I did a film on Haida carving that was shot up here in the Queen Charlottes, one of the reasons I've wanted to see this part of the country."

"How did you decide to be a film editor?"

"I didn't really. I went to art school. I was going to be a great painter. Mighty Mouse fantasy number ten. I got married instead. He didn't work; so I had to. It was a job, and after a while I got pretty good at it."

"Did he take care of the children?"

"My mother did," Fidelity said, "until they were in school. They've had to be pretty independent."

"Oh, Fido, you've done so much more with your life than I have."

"Got divorced and earned a living because I had to. Not exactly things to brag about."

"But it's ongoing, something of your own to do."

"I suppose so," Fidelity admitted," but you know, after Gail died, I looked around me and realized that, aside from my kids, I didn't really have any friends. I worked alone. I lived alone. I sometimes think now I should quit, do something entirely different. I can't risk that until the girls are really independent, not just playing house with Mother's off-stage help. Who knows? One of them might turn up on my doorstep as I did on my mother's."

"I'd love a job," Troy said, "but I'd never have the courage . . . "

"Of course you would," Fidelity said.

"Are you volunteering to take me by the hand as you did yesterday and say to the interviewer, 'This is my friend, Mrs. McFadden. She can't go into strange places by herself?'"

"Sure," Fidelity said. "I'll tell you what, let's go into business together."

"What kind of business?"

"Well, we could run a selling gallery and lose our shirts."

"Or a bookstore and lose our shirts . . . I don't really have a shirt to lose."

"Let's be more practical. How about a gay bar?"

"Oh, Fido," Troy said, laughing and shaking her head.

The ship now had entered a narrow inland passage, moving slowly and carefully past small islands. The Captain, though he still occasionally pointed out a deserted cannery, village or mine site, obviously had to pay more attention to the task of bringing his ship out of this narrow reach in a nearly silent wilderness into the noise and clutter of the town of Prince Rupert.

A bus waited to take those passengers who had signed up for a tour of the place, and Troy and Fidelity were among them. Their driver and guide was a young man fresh from Liverpool, and he looked on his duty as bizarre, for what was there really to see in Prince Rupert but one ridge of rather expensive houses overlooking the harbor and a small neighborhood of variously tasteless houses sold to fishermen in seasons when they made too much money so that they could live behind pretentious front doors on unemployment all the grey winter long. The only real stop was a small museum of Indian artifacts and old tools. The present Indian population was large and poor and hostile.

"It's like being in Greece," Fidelity said, studying a small collection of beautifully patterned baskets. "Only here it's been over for less than a hundred years."

They ate delicious seafood at an otherwise unremarkable hotel and then skipped an opportunity to shop at a mall left open in the evening for the tour's benefit, business being what it was in winter. Instead they took a taxi back to the ship.

"I think it's time to open my bottle of scotch," Troy suggested.

They got ice from a vending machine and went back to their cabin, where Fidelity turned the chair so that she could put her feet up on the bunk and Troy could sit at the far end with her feet tucked under her.

"Cozy," Troy decided.

"I wish I liked scotch," Fidelity said, making a face.

By the time the steward came to make up the bunks, returning and new passengers were boarding the ship. Troy and Fidelity out on deck watched the Indians being seen off by a large group of friends and relatives who must also have been to the wedding. Fidelity imagined them in an earlier time getting into great canoes to paddle south instead of settling down to a few hours' sleep on the lounge floor. She might as well imagine herself and Troy on a sailing ship bringing drink and disease.

A noisy group of Australians came on deck.

"You call this a ship?" they said to each other. "You call those cabins?"

They had traveled across the States and had come back across Canada, and they were not happily prepared to spend two nights in cabins even less comfortable than Fidelity's and Troy's.

"Maybe the scenery will cheer them up," Fidelity suggested as they went back to their cabin.

"They sound to me as if they've already had more scenery than they can take."

True enough. The Australians paced the decks like prisoners looking at the shore only to evaluate their means of escape, no leaping whale or plummeting eagle compensation for this coastal ferry which had been described in their brochures as a "cruise ship." How different they were from the stoically settled Indians who had quietly left the ship at Bella Bella shortly after dawn.

Fidelity and Troy stayed on deck for the open water crossing to Port Hardy on Vancouver Island, went in only long enough to get warm, then back out into the brilliant sun and sea wind to take delight in every shape of island, contour of hill, the play of light on the water, the least event of sea life until even their cloud of complaining gulls seemed part of the festival of their last day.

"Imagine preferring something like The Love Boat," Troy said.

"Gail and I were always the ferry, barge, and freighter types," Fidelity said.

Film clips moved through her mind, Gail sipping ouso in a café in Athens, Gail hailing a cab in London, Gail . . . a face she had begun to believe stricken from her memory was there in its many moods at her bidding.

"What is it?" Troy asked.

"Some much better reruns in my head," Fidelity said, smiling. "I guess it takes having fun to remember how often I have."

"What time is your plane tomorrow?" Troy asked.

The question hit Fidelity like a blow.

"Noon," she managed to say before she excused herself and left Troy for the first time since she had pledged herself to Troy's need.

Back in their cabin, sitting on the bunk that was also Troy's bed, Fidelity was saying to herself, "You're such an idiot, such an idiot, such an idiot!"

Two and a half days playing Mighty Mouse better than she ever had in her life, and suddenly she was dissolving into a maudlin fool, into tears of a sort she hadn't shed since her delayed adolescence.

"I can't want her. I just can't," Fidelity chanted.

It was worse than coming down with a toothache, breaking out in boils, this stupid, sweet desire which she simply had to hide from a woman getting better and better at reading her face unless she wanted to wreck the last hours of this lovely trip.

Troy shoved open the cabin door.

"Did I say something . . . ?"

Fidelity shook her head, "No, just my turn, I guess."

"You don't want to miss your last dinner, do you?"

"Of course not," Fidelity said, trying to summon up an appetite she could indulge in.

They were shy of each other over dinner, made conversation in a way they hadn't needed to from the first few minutes of their meeting. The strain of it made Fidelity both long for sleep and dread the intimacy of their cabin where their new polite reserve would be unbearable.

"Shall we have an early night?" Troy suggested. "We have to be up awfully early to disembark."

As they knelt together, getting out their night things, Troy said, mocking their awkward position, "I'd say a prayer of thanks if I thought there was anybody up there to pray to."

Fidelity *was* praying for whatever help there was against her every instinct.

"I'm going to find it awfully hard to say good-bye to you, Fido."

Fidelity had to turn then to Troy's lovely, vulnerable face.

"I just can't . . . " Fidelity began.

Then, unable to understand that it could happen, Fidelity was embracing Troy, and they moved into love-making as trustingly as they had talked.

At six in the morning, when Troy's travel alarm went off, she said, "I don't think I can move."

Fidelity, unable to feel the arm that lay under Troy, whispered, "We're much too old for this."

"I was afraid you thought I was," Troy said as she slowly and painfully untangled herself, "and now I'm going to prove it."

"Do you know what I almost said to you the first night?" Fidelity asked, loving the sight of Troy's naked body in the light of the desk lamp she'd just turned on. "I almost said, 'what a great setting for the first horrible night of a honeymoon.'"

"Why didn't you?"

"You were so lovely, coming out of the bathroom," Fidelity explained, knowing it wasn't an explanation.

"You were wrong," Troy said, defying her painful stiffness to lean down to kiss Fidelity.

"Young lovers would skip breakfast," Fidelity said.

"But you're starved."

Fidelity nodded, having no easy time getting out of bed herself.

It occurred to her to disturb the virgin neatness of her own upper bunk only because it would have been the first thing to occur to Gail, a bed ravager of obsessive proportions. If it didn't trouble Troy, it would not trouble Fidelity.

As they sat eating, the sun rose over the Vancouver mountains, catching the windows of the apartment blocks on the north shore.

"I live over there," Troy said.

"Troy?"

"Will you invite me to visit you in Toronto?"

"Come with me."

"I have to see Colin . . . and Ralph. I could be there in a week."

"I was wrong about those two over there," Fidelity said. "They sit side by side because they're lovers."

"And you thought so in the first place," Troy said.

Fidelity nodded.

"This is your captain speaking . . ."

Because he was giving them instructions about how to disembark, Fidelity did listen but only with one ear, for she had to keep her own set of instructions clearly in her head. She, of course, had to see her children, too.

Sophie

Emily Carr

Sophie knocked gently on my Vancouver studio door.

"Baskets. I got baskets."

They were beautiful, made by her own people, West Coast Indian baskets. She had big ones in a cloth tied at the four corners and little ones in a flour-sack.

She had a baby slung on her back in a shawl, a girl child clinging to her skirts, and a heavy-faced boy plodding behind her.

"I have no money for baskets."

"Money no matter," said Sophie. "Old clo', waum skirt—good fo' basket."

I wanted the big round one. Its price was eight dollars.

"Next month I am going to Victoria. I will bring back some clothes and get your basket."

I asked her in to rest a while and gave the youngsters bread and jam. When she tied up her baskets she left the one I coveted on the floor.

"Take it away," I said. "It will be a month before I can go to Victoria. Then I will bring clothes back with me and come to get the basket."

"You keep now. Bymby pay," said Sophie.

"Where do you live?"

"North Vancouver Mission."

"What is your name?"

"Me Sophie Frank. Everybody know me."

Sophie's house was bare but clean. It had three rooms. Later when it got cold Sophie's Frank would cut out all the partition walls. Sophie said, "Thlee loom, thlee stobe. One loom, one stobe." The floor of the house was clean scrubbed. It was chair, table and bed for the family. There was one chair; the coal-oil lamp sat on that. Sophie pushed the babies into corners, spread my old clothes on the floor to appraise them, and was satisfied. So, having tested each other's trade straightness, we began a long, long friendship—forty years. I have seen Sophie glad, sad, sick and drunk. I have asked her why she did this or that thing—Indian ways that I did not understand—her answer was invariably "Nice ladies always do." That was Sophie's ideal—being nice.

Every year Sophie had a new baby. Almost every year she buried one. Her little graves were dotted all over the cemetery. I never knew more than three of her twenty one children to be alive at one time. By the time she was in her early fifties every child was dead and Sophie had cried her eyes dry. Then she took to drink.

"I got a new baby. I got a new baby."

Sophie, seated on the floor of her house, saw me coming through the open door and waved the papoose cradle. Two little girls rolled round on the floor; the new baby was near her in a basket-cradle. Sophie took off the cloth tented over the basket and exhibited the baby, a lean poor thing.

Sophie herself was small and spare. Her black hair sprang thick and strong on each side of the clean, straight parting and hung in twin braids across her shoulders. Her eyes were sad and heavy-lidded. Between prominent, rounded cheekbones her nose lay rather flat, broadening and snubby at the tip. Her wide upper lip pouted. It was sharp edged, puckering over a row of poor teeth—the soothing pucker of lips trying to ease an aching tooth or to hush a crying child. She had a soft little body, a back straight as honesty itself, and the small hands and feet of an Indian.

Sophie's English was good enough, but when Frank, her husband, was there she became dumb as a plate.

"Why won't you talk before Frank, Sophie?"

"Frank he learn school English. Me, no. Frank laugh my English words."

When we were alone she chattered to me like a sparrow.

In May, when the village was white with cherry blossom and the blue water of Burrard Inlet crept almost to Sophie's door—just a streak of grey sand and a plank walk between—and when Vancouver city was more beautiful to look at across the water than to be in—it was then I loved to take the ferry to the North Shore and go to Sophie's.

Behind the village stood mountains topped by the grand old "Lions", twin peaks, very white and blue. The nearer mountains were every shade of young foliage, tender grey green, getting greener and greener till, when they were close, you saw that the village grass out-greened them all. Hens strutted their broods, papooses and pups and kittens rolled everywhere—it was good indeed to spend a day on the Reserve in spring.

Sophie and I went to see her babies' graves first. Sophie took her best plaid skirt, the one that had three rows of velvet ribbon round the hem, from a nail on the wall, and bound a yellow silk handkerchief round her head. No matter what the weather, she always wore her great shawl, clamping it down with her arms, the fringe trickling over her fingers. Sophie wore her shoes when she walked with me, if she remembered.

Across the water we could see the city. The Indian Reserve was a different world—no hurry, no business.

We walked over the twisty, up-and-down road to the cemetery. Casamin, Tommy, George, Rosie, Maria, Mary, Emily, and all the rest were there under a tangle of vines. We rambled, seeking out Sophie's graves. Some had little wooden crosses, some had stones. Two babies lay outside the cemetery fence: they had not faced life long enough for baptism.

"See! Me got stone for Rosie now."

"It looks very nice. It must have cost lots of money, Sophie."

"Grave man make cheap for me. He say, 'You got lots, lots stone from me, Sophie. Maybe bymby you get some more died baby, then you want more stone. So I make cheap for you.'"

Sophie's kitchen was crammed with excited women. They had come to see Sophie's brand new twins. Sophie was on a mattress beside the cook stove. The twin girls were in small basket papoose cradles, woven by Sophie herself. The babies were wrapped in cotton wool which made their dark little faces look darker; they were laced into their baskets and stuck up at the edge of Sophie's mattress beside the kitchen stove. Their brown, wrinkled faces were like potatoes baked in their jackets, their hands no bigger than brown spiders.

They were thrilling, those very, very tiny babies. Everybody was excited over them. I sat down on the floor close to Sophie.

"Sophie, if the baby was a girl it was to have my name. There are two babies and I have only one name. What are we going to do about it?"

"The biggest and the best is yours," said Sophie.

My Em'ly lived three months. Sophie's Maria lived three weeks. I bought Em'ly's tombstone. Sophie bought Maria's.

Sophie's "mad" rampaged inside her like a lion roaring in the breast of a dove.

"Look see," she said, holding a red and yellow handkerchief, caught together at the corners and chinking with broken glass and bits of plaster of Paris. "Bad boy bloke my grave flower! Cost five dollar one, and now boy all bloke fo' me. Bad, bad boy! You come talk me fo' p'liceman?"

At the City Hall she spread the handkerchief on the table and held half a plaster of Paris lily and a dove's tail up to the eyes of the law, while I talked.

"My mad fo' boy bloke my plitty grave flower," she said, forgetting, in her fury, to be shy of the "English words".

The big man of the law was kind. He said, "It's too bad, Sophie. What do you want me to do about it?"

"You make boy buy more this plitty kind for my grave."

"The boy has no money but I can make his old grandmother pay a little every week."

Sophie looked long at the broken pieces and shook her head.

"That ole, ole woman got no money." Sophie's anger was dying, soothed by sympathy like a child, the woman in her tender towards old Granny. "My bloke no matter for ole woman," said Sophie, gathering up the pieces. "You scold boy big, Policeman? No make glanny pay."

"I sure will, Sophie."

There was a black skirt spread over the top of the packing case in the centre of Sophie's room. On it stood the small white coffin. A lighted candle was at the head, another at the foot. The little dead girl in the coffin held a doll in her arms. It had hardly been out of them since I had taken it to her a week before. The glassy eyes of the doll stared out of the coffin, up past the closed eyelids of the child.

Though Sophie had been through this nineteen times before, the twentieth time was no easier. Her two friends, Susan and Sara, were there by the coffin, crying for her.

The outer door opened and a half dozen women came in, their shawls drawn low across their foreheads, their faces grim. They stepped over to the coffin and looked in. Then they sat around it on the floor and began to cry, first with baby whimpers, softly, then louder, louder still— with violence and strong howling: torrents of tears burst from their eyes and rolled down their cheeks. Sophie and Sara and Susan did it too. It sounded horrible—like tortured dogs.

Suddenly they stopped. Sophie went to the bucket and got water in a tin basin. She took a towel in her hand and went to each of the guests in turn holding the basin while they washed their faces and dried them on the towel. Then the women all went out except Sophie, Sara and Susan. This crying had gone on at intervals for three days—ever since the child had died. Sophie was worn out. There had been, too, all the long weeks of Rosie's tubercular dying to go through.

"Sophie, couldn't you lie down and rest?"

She shook her head. "Nobody sleep in Injun house till dead people go to cemet'ry."

The beds had all been taken away.

"When is the funeral?"

"I dunno. Pliest go Vancouver. He not come two more day."

She laid her hands on the corner of the little coffin.

"See! Coffin man think box fo' Injun baby no matter."

The seams of the cheap little coffin had burst.

As Sophie and I were coming down the village street we met an Indian woman whom I did not know. She nodded to Sophie, looked at me and half paused. Sophie's mouth was set, her bare feet pattered quick, hurrying me past the woman.

"Go church house now?" she asked me.

The Catholic church had twin towers. Wide steps led up to the front door which was always open. Inside it was bright, in a misty way, and still except for the wind and sea-echoes. The windows were gay coloured glass; when you knelt the wooden footstools and pews creaked. Hush lurked in every corner. Always a few candles burned. Everything but those flickers of flame was stonestill.

When we came out of the church we sat on the steps for a little. I said, "Who was that woman we met, Sophie?"

"Mrs. Chief Joe Capilano."

"Oh! I would like to know Mrs. Chief Joe Capilano. Why did you hurry by so quick? She wanted to stop."

"I don't want you know Mrs. Chief Joe."

"Why?"

"You fliend for me, not fliend for her."

"My heart has room for more than one friend, Sophie."

"You fliend for me, I not want Mrs. Chief Joe get you."

"You are always my first and best friend, Sophie." She hung her head, her mouth obstinate. We went to Sara's house.

Sara was Sophie's aunt, a wizened bit of a woman whose eyes, nose, mouth and wrinkles were all twisted to the perpetual expressing of pain. Once she had had a merry heart, but pain had trampled out the merriness. She lay on a bed draped with hangings of clean, white rags dangling from poles. The wall behind her bed, too, was padded heavily with newspaper to keep draughts off her "Lumatiz."

"Hello, Sara. How are you?"

"Em'ly! Sophie's Em'ly!"

The pain wrinkles scuttled off to make way for Sara's smile, but hurried back to twist for her pain.

"I dunno what for I got Lumatiz, Em'ly. I dunno. I dunno."

Everything perplexed poor Sara. Her merry heart and tortured body was always at odds. She drew a humped wrist across her nose and said, "I dunno, I dunno", after each remark.

"Goodbye, Sophie's Em'ly; come some more soon. I like that you come. I dunno why I got pain, lots pain. I dunno—I dunno."

I said to Sophie, "You see! the others know I am your big friend. They call me 'Sophie's Em'ly'."

She was happy.

Susan lived on one side of Sophie's house and Mrs. Johnson, the Indian widow of a white man, on the other. The widow's house was beyond words clean. The cookstove was a mirror, the floor white as a sheet from scrubbing. Mrs. Johnson's hands were clever and busy. The row of hard kitchen chairs had each its own antimacassar and cushion. The crocheted bedspread and embroidered pillowslips, all the work of Mrs. Johnson's hands, were smoothed taut. Mrs. Johnson's husband had been a sea captain. She had loved him deeply and remained a widow though she had had many offers of marriage after he died. Once the Indian agent came, and said:

"Mrs. Johnson, there is a good man who has a farm and money in the bank. He is shy, so he sent me to ask if you will marry him."

"Tell that good man, 'Thank you', Mr. Agent, but tell him, too, that Mrs. Johnson only got love for her dead Johnson."

Sophie's other neighbour, Susan, produced and buried babies almost as fast as Sophie herself. The two women laughed for each other and cried for each other. With babies on their backs and baskets on their arms they crossed over on the ferry to Vancouver and sold their baskets from door to door. When they came to my studio they rested and drank tea with me. My parrot, sheep dog, the white rats and the totem pole pictures all interested them. "An' you got Injun flower, too," said Susan.

"Indian flowers?"

She pointed to ferns and wild things I had brought in from the woods.

Sophie's house was shut up. There was a chain and padlock on the gate. I went to Susan.

"Where is Sophie?"

"Sophie in sick house. Got sick eye."

I went to the hospital. The little Indian ward had four beds. I took ice cream and the nurse divided it into four portions.

A homesick little Indian girl cried in the bed in one corner, an old woman grumbled in another. In a third there was a young mother with a baby, and in the fourth bed was Sophie.

There were flowers. The room was bright. It seemed to me that the four brown faces on the four white pillows should be happier and far more comfortable here than lying on mattresses on the hard floors in the village, with all the family muddle going on about them.

"How nice it is here, Sophie."

"Not much good of hospital, Em'ly."

"Oh! What is the matter with it?"

"Bad bed."

"What is wrong with the beds?"

"Move, move, all time shake. 'Spose me move, bed move too."

She rolled herself to show how the springs worked. "Me ole-fashion, Em'ly. Me like kitchen floor fo' sick."

Susan and Sophie were in my kitchen, rocking their sorrows back and forth and alternately wagging their heads and giggling with shut eyes at some small joke.

"You go live Victoria now, Em'ly," wailed Sophie, "and we never see those babies, never!"

Neither woman had a baby on her back these days. But each had a little new grave in the cemetery. I had told them about a friend's twin babies. I went to the telephone.

"Mrs. Dingle, you said I might bring Sophie to see the twins?"

"Surely, any time," came the ready reply.

"Come, Sophie and Susan, we can go and see the babies now."

The mothers of all those little cemetery mounds stood looking and looking at the thriving white babies, kicking and sprawling on their bed. The women said, "Oh my!—Oh my!" over and over.

Susan's hand crept from beneath her shawl to touch a baby's leg. Sophie's hand shot out and slapped Susan's.

The mother of the babies said, "It's all right, Susan; you may touch my baby."

Sophie's eyes burned Susan for daring to do what she so longed to do herself. She folded her hands resolutely under her shawl and whispered to me.

"Nice ladies don't touch, Em'ly."

About the Editor

Norman Ravvin is a writer, critic, and teacher. His
prize-winning books include a collection of stories,
Sex, Skyscrapers, and Standard Yiddish, a novel, *Café
des Westens*, and volume of essays, *A House of Words:
Jewish Writing, Identity, and Memory*. He grew up in
Calgary but has lived in Toronto, Fredericton, and
Vancouver. His short stories and journalism have
appeared in Canadian magazines and on CBC radio.
He is presently Chair of the Centre for Canadian
Jewish Studies at Concordia University, Montreal.